THE
LAST
PROMISE

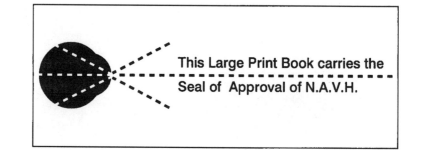

This Large Print Book carries the
Seal of Approval of N.A.V.H.

THE
LAST
PROMISE

RICHARD PAUL EVANS

Italian proverbs from *Treasury of Italian Love: Poems, Quotations & Proverbs in Italian and English* and *Dictionary of 1000 Italian Proverbs*, published by Hippocrene Books.

Published in 2003 by arrangement with Dutton, a member of Penguin Putnam Inc.

Wheeler Large Print Hardcover Series.

The text of this Large Print edition is unabridged.
Other aspects of the book may vary from the original edition.

Set in 16 pt. Plantin by Al Chase.

Printed in the United States on permanent paper.

Library of Congress Cataloging-in-Publication Data

Evans, Richard Paul.
  The last promise / Richard Paul Evans.
    p. cm.
  ISBN 1-58724-375-X (lg. print : hc : alk. paper)
  1. Americans — Italy — Fiction. 2. Mothers and sons —
Fiction. 3. Tuscany (Italy) — Fiction. 4. Women — Italy —
Fiction. 5. Domestic fiction. lcsh I. Title.
PS3555.V259 L3 2003
  813'.54—dc21   2002191026

To Carole Baron,
con affetto

ACKNOWLEDGMENTS

Tante grazie to the following: Laurie Chittenden, for your insight, enthusiasm and patience. It's nice being with you again. The whole Dutton crew: Carole, Lisa, Brian, Kim and Stephanie. Thank you for welcoming me into your family. My dear friend Laurie Liss (and Kate and Timothy), for everything, as usual. Artist Steve Smulka and Dolores Libera, for sharing your hearts. Author James McBride and Stephanie McBride, for your help in relocating. (Miracle at St. Anna's was wonderful, James.) My staff, Celeste, Krista, Lisa, Karen, Fran, Dad, Paula, Tawna and Heather. Thank you for keeping the home fires burning.

The Last Promise would not have been possible without the assistance of my new Italy friends: Vahe and Andrea Keushguerian of Rendola — may your vineyards flourish! Enrico Marelli, with admiration. Miriam DiMarco — thank you for being so good to me. Andrea Venturini (www.accademiarealty.com). Luigi Tomassi, who first brought me to the villa. Andrea, Anna and Patrizio Santurro. My dear friend Maurizio Ventura (who in no way resembles the Maurizio in this book), Alberto and Maria Teresa Sottili. Laura Mongiat and the entire AISF crew. The Ferrini famly. Diane and Ugo Punteri. Steve and Mia Harper of the American Consulate in Florence. John Pitanzo, *buon fortunata* with your book. Megan and Mark at Villa Bagnolo.

Of course my *amore*, Keri, and my children: Jenna, Allyson, Abigail, McKenna and Michael. And my Italy daughter, Cammy. Thank you for embracing a new life as well as a new country. You are my reason.

And "Eliana" — the woman by the pool.

PROLOGUE

*"Who has been in Italy can forget all other regions.
Who has been in heaven does not desire the earth."*
— Gogol

Italians think of God as a fellow countryman, and walking a gravel incline alongside a Chianti vineyard, I wonder if they might not be right. The early sun in Tuscany paints the landscape with a different palette than the rest of the world, gilding the hills and vineyard trellises in a rose-gold hue and the otherwise drab, finger-leafed olive trees in silver that glitters in the dawn wind like a school of herring.

It's early in the morning, before the first bells of the San Donato Tower, quiet, except for the occasional, distant pop of rifles echoing through the Valdarno Valley. The men are out hunting *cinghiale* — the wild boar. In my wanderings through the countryside I've encountered neither of them, hunter nor beast. But I hear the shots fired every morning, popping like corks off wine bottles, sometimes in my dreams.

I woke at four this morning, even before the hunters, and lay in bed for nearly an hour. Then I dressed and went out to walk. My wife is used to me crawling out of bed at all hours of night like an obstetrician. It's an appropriate metaphor, I think. Stories, like babies, don't often

9

wait for decent hours to be born. I've been thinking all night about a story that has come to me.

Some stories are crafted as if by blueprint, built line by line and brick by brick. There are stories born of angst, wrung painfully from an author's mind onto pages that, in the end, are more of bandage than paper. Then there are those stories that seek the writer, drifting through time and space like thistle seed, until they find fertile ground on which to land and take root. This is one such story. It found me during my second week in Italy.

I met her at the poolside of an Italian country club called Ugolino; about nine kilometers southwest of Florence. She looked thirtyish, slender, attractive. She was wearing a peach-colored bikini, luminous against her bronze skin, with a sheer, pastel wraparound skirt. Her hair was nearly black with a few strands of honey-colored highlights, though where it fell back over her shoulders the sun revealed a natural brown-gold tint. What I noticed first was her eyes. They were exotic and teardrop-shaped.

She was reclined in a lounge chair reading a paperback *romanzo* and doing her best to ignore the stream of Italian men who paraded in front of her to ogle and drop lines that could be understood even without knowing the language.

It was a sweltering hot day. *Solleone,* the Florentines call it — *lion sun*. The pool area was mobbed with children playing noisily in the water while the adults stretched out on the white plastic lounge chairs that surrounded the tiled perimeter of the pool.

I'm told that it takes three confirmed miracles to merit sainthood in the Roman Catholic Church. I believe that finding a parking space in downtown Florence or a lounge chair by a pool in summer should both qualify. Heaven smiled on me that day. As I entered the pool area, a man was gathering his things, leaving the only vacancy. It happened to be a chaise next to her.

After draping my towel across the length of the chair and covering my body with 30+ sunscreen, I took my laptop from my bag and turned it on. The image on the screen was too vague from the sun's glare, so I closed it back up and went for my standby: a mechanical pencil and a wire-bound notepad I had purchased the day before at a supermarket in Florence. On the notepad's cover was a photograph of a lemon wearing round-lensed granny glasses. The picture was titled *John Lemon*. I wondered if the Italians understood the pun.

I lifted my pencil to the page, not because I had words, but because a blank page beckoned. Perhaps I inherited this trait from my father. *A new board begs a nail,* he once told me. My father is a carpenter.

But there was too much noise and motion around me to write. After ten minutes I put the notebook away, took out a book and began to read. Suddenly a thin, bald Italian man stopped in front of me. He had skin as brown as leather and was wearing what looked like the bottom half of a woman's bikini.

"Non si puo portare le scarpe sul piano vasca, signore."

I looked up at him. *"Scusa,"* I said in my two-week-old Italian. *"No capito."*

He pointed at my feet. In truth I had no idea what he wanted. I wore only white-soled tennis shoes. The worst infraction I could conceive being guilty of was a fashion faux pas. I looked at him blankly.

Suddenly the woman next to me said in perfect English, "He's telling you that shoes are not allowed in the pool area."

I glanced over at the woman, whom I had assumed was Italian, then back at the man. *"Mi dispiace,"* I said, as I removed my shoes.

"Grazie, signorina," he said to the woman and walked away.

I sat back in my chair. "Thank you."

"It's nothing." After a moment she asked, "Where in the States are you from?"

I wondered that I was so obvious an American. "Salt Lake City."

A smile broke across her face. "Really? I'm from Vernal."

"Vernal, Utah?"

"Sì. Il mondo e piccolo." It's a small world.

Vernal is a small town in the eastern desert of Utah: a stop on the way to someplace else. Even

12

in Utah I had never met anyone from Vernal.

"I thought you were Italian."

"So do the Italians. I lived here for six years. After that much time you start looking like a local." She lay her book in her lap and leaned over, extending her hand. "I'm Eliana."

I likewise introduced myself. Just then a man, shirtless, maybe in his late fifties with a belly hanging over his swimsuit and a cigar clamped between his front teeth, stopped in front of her chair. *"Buon giorno, zuccherino."*

She flicked her hand at him as if to brush him away. *"Vai, vai, vai."*

He walked away smiling. Eliana turned back, shaking her head, though more amused than annoyed. "He called me his *little sugar.* I hope my husband gets here soon. The Italian men regard a lone woman the same way they would a bill on the sidewalk."

I smiled at her metaphor. It was true.

She took a drink of bottled water then settled back in her chair. She asked, "How did you find this place? You're a long way from the usual tourist haunts."

"My real estate agent told me about it. I'm not really a tourist. I moved here with my family two weeks ago. We have a cottage, about eight kilometers from here in San Donato in Collina."

"It's beautiful in San Donato. Do you have any children?"

"Five."

13

"Five. That's a lot of children. Especially for Italy."

"Women always congratulate us. They say *complimenti*. The men just ask *'perché?'* " *Why?*

Her mouth twisted with a smile of understanding. "Yes, they would. How are you all adapting to your new life?"

"Good. Mostly. It's not all gardenias and Bella Tuscany."

"Every sweetness has its bitter. The romance usually ends for Americans after they get pickpocketed or run over by a scooter."

"We've had our moments. When we landed in Venice our Italian guide never showed up. We took one of those unmarked taxis and ended up paying seventy dollars for what should have been a three-minute cab ride. Then, after we got to Florence, the car dealership wouldn't give us the car we paid for. They said we needed some number from a *permesso di* something. They gave me an address in downtown Florence where I could get it."

She nodded. "It's the address of the *questura* — the police headquarters. You need a *permesso di soggiorno*. But it's not that easy to get."

"What is it?"

"Basically it's permission to live in Florence."

"I thought that's what our visa was for."

"No, it's something else. With Italian bureaucracy it's always something else."

"How long does it take to get a *permesso di . . . ?*"

"*Sog-gior-no,*" she said slowly, breaking the

word into syllables for my benefit. "It takes a while. Unless you know someone high up in government, or the priest of one of the bureaucrats, it could take as long as a year. How long do you plan to stay in Italy?"

I groaned. "About a year. The car dealership won't release our car until we have one. We're still renting a car."

"Don't worry. There's always a back door. Go to the *questura* and apply, then take the receipt from your application to the dealership. If you ask nicely, they'll likely give you the car anyway."

"You think that will work?"

She tilted her head to one side. "Probably. Italy's too bureaucratic and the Italians know it, so they find ways around things. If they didn't, nothing would ever get done."

"Thanks."

"I should warn you. Don't insist that they do it for you. Entitlement is an American mind-set. Here it's a cardinal sin. They'll fight you just over principle and you'll lose. But if you ask nicely, as a favor, most Italians will walk over broken glass for you."

"Thanks again."

"Did you come here for work?"

"Indirectly. I'm an author, so I can work anywhere. But I was hoping to find inspiration."

Her face lit. "Really? I'm a voracious reader. What kind of books do you write?"

I looked at the cover of the book spread in her

lap. "Probably what you're reading."

"*Romanzo rosa?* Love stories?"

I nodded.

"Are you famous?"

"Have you heard of me?"

She thought for a moment. "No."

"If you have to tell someone you're famous — you're not."

She laughed at this. "But you are published? You're not just one of those guys who calls himself a writer to meet women?"

At this I laughed. I too had met such men. "No, I'm published. And happily married."

"How are your books doing?"

"Not bad."

"Have you ever written a best-seller?"

"A few."

"I'm sorry, I should know you. I've just been reading Italian authors for the last decade." She leaned over to get her bag. "Do you mind if I get your autograph?"

"Why would you want the autograph of someone you've never heard of?"

"Because I'll regret it later if I don't. And I want to tell my friends that I met a best-selling author." She pulled a pen from her bag and handed it to me with the paperback she had been reading. "Just sign in the book, if that's all right."

"*Certo.*" I opened the book and scribbled my name across its fore page, then handed it back to her. "So how is this book?"

16

"I've read better. But once I start a book I can't stop until I finish it. It's a compulsion."

"Do you have a favorite love story?"

She thought for a moment then a smile slowly spread across her face. "Mine."

"Yours?"

"I've yet to read a love story that compares with mine."

"Really. Tell me about it."

She did. This is Eliana's story.

CHAPTER 1

"Ogni cuore ha il suo segreto."
Every heart has its secret.

— Italian Proverb

Two years earlier. July 1999.
Tuscany, Italy.

Eliana released the clasp on the cedar shutters, then unlatched one side of the wood-framed window and pushed it open, welcoming a rush of fresh air into her second-story painting studio. In the window's thick glass she saw her own pale reflection. Her umber hair, still unwashed, was pulled back and bound with elastic. Her usually beautiful eyes were puffy from another hard night. *There are more beautiful things to see in Tuscany at six in the morning,* she thought.

From between the two large cypress trees that flanked the window, she could see the neatly lined trellises of the Chianti vineyards, faded in the distance by a morning mist. *Sembra una cartolina,* she thought. *Just like a postcard.* She had thought the same thing when she arrived in Tuscany almost six years earlier, only then her thoughts had been in English. In spite of her hardships, the country had not lost its beauty to her. She was grateful for this. It was one of the joys life had not stolen from her.

18

As difficult as the previous night had been, she was ready to start again. She had learned to live this way, discarding the past each night and starting each day anew   picking joy where she could find it — like hunting for mushrooms in the Chianti forests. Sometimes her own endurance astonished her.

The fifteenth-century villa where she lived was two-storied and horseshoe-shaped, enclosed with a front wall, forming a sizable courtyard. Her family's apartment was the largest in the villa and took the entire east wing. While she was a new bride still living in America, her groom, Maurizio, had told her that their apartment in Italy was part of the *new* section of the restored villa. It was only after she arrived in Italy, three years later, that she realized that "new" is relative in an old country: the "new wing" was only two hundred and seventy years old.

The villa's center apartment was smaller than Eliana's by half and was occupied by her sister-in-law, Anna, who had lived in the villa since her husband left her five years previous.

The western wing of the villa was used for storage and there was also a small apartment there that was rented out. An arched, wrought-iron gate in the center of that wing led to the villa's garden.

The other buildings on the property were nearly a quarter mile away, surrounded by vineyards: a small, stucco home where Luca, the winery manager, and his wife lived, next to the three-story, ochre cantina where the grapes were processed into wine, aged, bottled and shipped.

Eliana's painting studio was rectangular in shape, with white stucco walls that slanted slightly in toward the center of the house. It had a high, vaulted ceiling supported by heavy, wooden trusses that had been hewn by an axe. The room was on the second floor at the end of the hallway and the only room in the villa where one could see both the inner courtyard and the world outside the villa, depending on which side of the room one stood in. The space was larger than Eliana needed and she had only moved into one half of the room, piling the other half with blank canvases and unframed paintings.

Eliana had wondered if the room was haunted. The first few weeks after she had moved in, she came in each morning to find six of the seven paintings she had hung on the walls tipped to their sides. Each day she checked the paintings' hooks and wires then righted them, only to find them all tilted again the next morning. All of the pictures except for one.

"All villas in Italy have *fantasmi*," an old man wearing a bloodstained apron in the butcher shop had told her. Actually the phenomenon was little more than a curiosity to Eliana, and after two weeks, when it stopped, she was disappointed. *Fantasmi* or not, she liked the idea that she wasn't alone.

Against the far wall of Eliana's studio was a gray, cast-iron *stufa* that she used to heat the room in the late fall and winter months when the thick outer walls of the villa turned cold with the season. Above the stove was the only picture in the room not of her own hand, the one her ghost had left alone — a portrait of the Holy Blessed Mother, her hands lifted in adoration, her heart revealed. It hung above an icon where Eliana kept her rosary beads and a score of stout candles in shallow glass dishes. She was a devout Catholic, though it had been some while since she had attended mass. This was not by choice. Her six-year-old son, Alessio, was severely asthmatic, and the priest at the small church near the villa used copious amounts of incense in his worship, which was too much an irritant for her son's lungs, setting off an asthma attack almost immediately upon their entering the chapel. As much as she craved to worship in the company of others, it was unthinkable for her to ask the priest to desist, for it was an old church, an old priest and an old congregation, and nowhere is tradition and religion so interwoven as in the Italian countryside. She had tried other churches in the area and found them all to be the same, their chapels reeking from centuries of incense even without lighting new.

She attended church only when her husband was in town, which was rare on weekends, so Eliana mostly worshipped in solitude, pausing before the picture in her studio each morning, crossing herself, then lighting a candle to carry her petitions heavenward. She had many. The

Holy Mother was the patron saint of mothers. She would know Eliana's heart. More than anyone else, the mother of Christ would understand; for she had suffered what Eliana feared most — losing her son.

Alessio had manifested the first signs of his asthma at the age of two, just thirteen weeks after their coming to Italy. One summer evening as she was putting him to bed, he suddenly began gasping for breath. It would have been a frightening moment for any mother, but Maurizio was out of town on business when it happened, leaving Eliana alone in a foreign country where she didn't know who to call or where to go in an emergency, even if she could speak the language. It was the most terrifying moment of her life. Not knowing what else to do, she prayed for help. Almost immediately there was a knock at the door. Anna and her husband had decided to stop by for a visit. They rushed Alessio and Eliana to the hospital.

It was the beginning of a new life. Every year since, Alessio had suffered from attacks severe enough to send them running to the nearest emergency room.

After she finished her daily rite, Eliana would go to the kitchen to make herself a cup of hot ginger tea which she brought back to the small round table next to her easel. Then she would turn on her music.

On the counter behind her easel were a CD player and a wooden case that contained CDs by mostly Italian artists — Pavarotti, Bocelli, Battisti, Zucchero — her collection diversified with a few country-westerns, Garth Brooks, Reba McEntire, Clint Black, an album of Gregorian chants and a Barbra Streisand album that now seemed to her a thousand years old.

This morning she chose Pavarotti, inserted the disk and turned on her stereo. The music started too loudly and she quickly turned it down. Just two doors away from her, Alessio was still asleep. With any luck he would remain so.

The two of them were alone in the house. Maurizio was away on business. *As usual.* He had called sometime during the night, woken her, to say he'd been delayed. He'd be home Saturday or Sunday, she didn't remember. She didn't care that much anymore. She wondered why he'd bothered to call. He hadn't thought to ask how Alessio was or why her voice was so hoarse. He didn't know that she'd been up half the night as their son struggled to breathe.

After he was breathing regularly and had gone back to sleep, she lay on the couch next to him listening for each breath and quietly crying until sleep silenced her. As distant as she and Maurizio had grown in the last seven years, in spite of all his lies and infidelities, she had wanted him then. She wanted him to hold her. For just ten minutes she wanted to be weak.

She put on her painting smock, then sat down on her leather-covered stool, unscrewed the lid of a tube of white oil paint and squeezed a large

23

circle of it onto her palette. *Italian girls dream of marriage. Italian wives dream of love,* an elderly Italian woman had once told her. What, then, do American women who marry Italian men dream of? She could speak only for herself. She dreamt of home. Home in a small town no one in Italy had even heard of. Vernal, Utah. Back where they still called her Ellen and where her mother still fretted over her raspberry bushes all year long, then spent days putting up bottles of jam in wide-mouthed Kerr bottles just to give them away to her neighbors.

After six years in Italy it was sometimes hard for her to believe that such a place as Vernal still existed — a pinprick on a map in a different world. By comparison the Florence countryside made Vernal look as drab as a lunar landscape. But, be it ever so humble, it was still home. And better a warm cottage than a cold *castello*.

Eliana's friends in Vernal still spoke of her fairytale life — the hometown girl who made good, swept off her feet by an Italian lover and taken to a beautiful foreign land, where the language was spoken like poetry and the food was their daily sacrament. A land where immortals like Michelangelo, Brunelleschi and Botticelli had gilded the lily of a country God Himself had already painted. She understood their fantasies, clichés and all, as the fantasies had also once been hers.

Back in Vernal they didn't know how things had changed: how her "lover" was usually away from home six days out of seven; the lonely times she called her husband on the road only to have the phone answered by some strange woman, followed by a covered mouthpiece and muffled talking. They didn't know about the days and nights of solitude spent caring for her son, Alessio. She was the lucky one, they still said of her, the one that got out.

She cut back a line of cadmium red from the canvas with a palette knife. The painting that she worked on this morning was from a photograph she had taken outside rural Siena, a landscape of a stone farmstead, the hills behind it stitched with grape trellises like a great, rolling quilt, fading off into the distance as if already feathered with a brush.

During her first three years in Italy, Eliana and Alessio flew back to Utah to spend Christmas with her mother. But Alessio's worsening condition had made it too difficult to make the twenty-six-hour plane journey there and back. The last time they had tried to make the trip, flying from Da Vinci Airport in Rome, the airplane had been delayed by traffic and waited on the airstrip for forty minutes. The fumes of the other jets affected the cabin's air and a half hour after takeoff Alessio suffered a severe asthma attack.

Eliana, with the assistance of the flight attendants, had administered his inhalers, followed by oxygen, but he continued to struggle for breath. A doctor was found on board, and she rummaged through the jet's first aid kit, found a vial of epinephrine which she shot directly into Alessio's arm. It was only marginally effective, only enough to buy time, and the jet was forced to dump fuel and return to Rome, where an ambulance met them on the airstrip.

As traumatic as the experience had been, more frightening was the realization that had the attack come just an hour later, Alessio likely would have died before they could make it back to ground. She hadn't flown with him since.

Neither could she leave Alessio at home alone with her husband. She wouldn't dare, even if Maurizio had been willing to watch him — which he wasn't. Her husband had no idea how to take care of his own son's basic needs, let alone his medical ones. It wasn't something men in Italy did, he told her. *E' un lavoro da donne. It is woman's work.*

Maurizio hadn't always been that way. While they were courting in America, he helped out, doing dishes, vacuuming and even proving himself the better cook of the two of them. But within their first month back in Italy all that changed. None of his friends' wives expected their husbands' help in "domestic" matters, especially with children, and "neither should she," he said. More than that, she should learn to serve him as his friends' wives served their husbands.

She only blamed herself for not seeing it coming. Maurizio's mother, Antonella, had slaved over him his entire life, from ironing his underwear to laying out his clothes every morning, up to the day he was married. She clearly felt that Eliana wasn't doing her part as the dutiful wife and would demonstrate to her whenever she was in their home exactly how she should be taking care of her son and grandson — taking over like a veteran pilot pulling the wheel from a trainee.

Once, while Eliana was still fresh in Italy and newly pregnant with their second child (she miscarried in the third month), Antonella had demonstrated to her how Maurizio liked his socks ironed, emphasizing the length of time the iron should be pressed. Eliana had watched incredulously. She wanted to say *You've got to be kidding.* Antonella wasn't. Maurizio's expectations were not all his fault, Eliana decided. He had been well trained to accept servitude. Something had to give with these Italian women.

A few years earlier, at Eliana's insistence, she and Maurizio had gone to see a marriage counselor. The counselor, an older Italian man, nodded as she spoke of her frustration. Yes, he saw the problem. It was *her.*

"You are no longer in America," he said. "As difficult as it may seem, you need to accept a new life and a new culture." He even suggested that only Italian should be spoken in the home. No more English.

Eliana was stunned. "Forget that it's English, this is *my* language."

"What do you mean?"

She said, "This is *my* language. This is who I am."

"Who you *were*," he corrected. "You must quit clinging to the past in order to transcend it. You must accept a new life. You owe this to your family."

She cried as they left the session. *Accept a new life?* To what point? When she said "I do," this wasn't the deal she had bought into. Nor was this the man. The man she had married was romantic and caring. She felt like a victim of marital bait and switch.

Maurizio claimed the same of her. "You used to be much more fun," he once complained, "more *spontànea*. You've changed."

She had changed. She was a mother now. Parenthood is a fork in the road. It requires sacrifices and responsibility. Eliana didn't make it that way — it's just the way it is. It was a crucial point in their relationship. They could either grow up together or they could grow apart. For them the latter was true. Sometimes she felt as if Maurizio blamed her for the changes a child brought into their lives — especially one with special needs. She feared that on some level Maurizio resented Alessio as well and this was why he spent so little time with him. With them.

As school was out for the summer, Eliana's life revolved around Alessio even more now. Still, she never thought of him as a burden — only as her boy. A little boy with a big heart who sensed her sadness and solitude and tried to be the man in her life. She didn't know what she would do if something ever happened to him.

Nor did she allow her thoughts to linger on the possibility. It was far too real. There had been too many close calls in the past four years. Too many white-knuckle, late-night runs to the emergency room.

She was weary of being strong and stoic, and, most of all, alone. She wanted a partner in life's journey. A man to share a glass of wine and then a bed with. Someone to make her feel worthy of love again. But, as hope can be the cruelest of tormenters, she learned to avoid such thoughts. For better or worse she was married. Married and lonely and locked away in her beautiful villa in the quiet Tuscan countryside twelve kilometers from Florence.

CHAPTER 2

*"Of all the fairest Cities of the Earth
None is so fair as Florence. 'Tis a gem
Of purest ray; and what a light broke forth,
When it emerged from darkness!
Search within, Without; all is enchantment!"*
— Samuel Rogers, 1830

"I have seen pictures of Florence in books and travel guides and thought it beautiful, but now, surrounded by the sensuality of the city, I realize that it has been the difference between looking at a menu and eating."
— Ross Story's diary

JULY 1999. FLORENCE, ITALY.

The Arno River flows west from the Apennine Mountains, snaking through the Valdarno Valley until it breaks through the center of Florence, dividing the city like a broken heart. Scores of bridges had been built to span the river, but through time and war nearly all have been destroyed. Of the ancient city only Ponte Vecchio, the "old bridge," remains.

Ross Story stopped near the center of the bridge to rest against its broad metal railing and rub the beaded sweat from his face. The bridge looked more like a mall than a thoroughfare. To both sides of him were the bright, glittering shops of jewelers and goldsmiths, crowded with tourists and sidewalk merchants, as they had been for centuries.

"The climate of Florence is *brutto*," a Portuguese woman had told him. "The worst of all Italy. The hottest summers, the coldest winters." Then she warned, "The people are like the weather. Settle in Capri or Sicily, where the weather and people are kind."

In the stifling heat, Ross knew that at least half of what the woman had said was true. He slipped his backpack from his shoulder to the ground and looked east, into the warm wind, then to the river below. The river's surface reflected the ochre and mustard hues of the old city, both vague and beautiful, like an Italian dream. A slim canoe glided across the green, rippled water near a group of old men fishing from the riverbank in the shade of the bridge.

Ross had arrived in Italy six months earlier, on a rainy day with gray, stone skies. He disembarked at Rome's Da Vinci Airport, exchanged his dollars into lire and found a *pensione* in a convent at only 100,000 lire a night. He spent his first week in Rome, seeking out the city's art, dining in the splendor of the Bernini fountains in Piazza Navona and standing in the Sistine Chapel, his head craned back to look at its ceiling, tears flowing freely down his cheeks.

Then he hopped a train south to Naples. After just one day he decided the city was overly populated, crime infested and polluted, so after visiting its central museum, he moved on to Sorrento and the beautiful Amalfi coast, the Isle of Capri, then farther south, ferrying across the Strait of Messina into Sicily. He took a train into the city of Taormina, where he lived in a *pensione* along the Mediterranean Sea for the rest of the spring, eating blood oranges and writing his thoughts in a leather-bound journal he had bought at a street market.

He traveled throughout Sicily, ingesting the island by train and bus, from the Greek ruins in the Valley of the Temples near Agrigento to snowcapped Mount Etna, where he gathered a pocket of small volcanic rocks as souvenirs.

In late May, when the weather turned warmer and the rain stopped, his travels took him northwest, along the western coast of the Tyrrhenian Sea to La Spezia. He hiked the five cities of the Cinque Terre, taking refuge from a rainstorm in a concrete German World War II bunker. He spent a week in Genova and two weeks in the bustling metropolis of Milan, where he saw Leonardo's *L'Ultima Cena* (*The Last Supper*). Then he turned eastward, first to Verona, then on to Venice, wandering the labyrinth of islands for nearly three weeks. He spent two days on the island of Murano, where he watched artisans blow glass into art.

He was in no hurry, which is a virtue in all things Italian, but as summer waned he felt the desire to settle. And so in late August, his tourist visa expired, he came to Florence, where he hoped to find work at the Uffizi, Florence's world-famous art gallery.

Though he had been alone since his arrival, now, in a town famed for its bachelors, from Donatello and Michelangelo to its present-day *mammoni*, he felt the extent of his loneliness amplified by his new surroundings. Florence is a city of lovers. It seemed to him that everywhere he looked there were reminders of his solitude.

Earlier that day he had sat alone in a café, watching a young Italian couple across from him as they drank their cappuccinos and looked into each other's eyes, the two of them laughing and flirting and touching. Ross felt envy rise in his chest like an illness. It had been a long time since he had been with a woman. Still, something, a voice from some shadowed corridor of his mind, told him that it hadn't been long enough.

Ross lifted his pack, slipped into it, then walked to the end of the bridge and west to the arched *loggiato* of the Uffizi.

The Uffizi's courtyard was swollen with tourists. Though he had envisioned the inside of the museum a thousand times in his mind, Ross had never considered the transient community that thrived at its gates: the crisp-uniformed *carabinieri* with their crimson-striped pants, the gypsy beggars with frowning children carried in their arms as props, the tour guides with their frantic faces and closed umbrellas held up like lightning rods, and the sidewalk peddlers from

Nigeria and Morocco with their posters and handbags and Taiwan-made trinkets spread out on blankets. The air of the Uffizi courtyard was filled with the babble of a hundred different tongues, like a daily Pentecost descending on the gallery.

A line stretched from the admission door nearly a hundred yards to the end of the building's long corridor, to the Palazzo Vecchio and its fraudulent *David*. Ross walked to the less crowded reservation line and waited outside the nylon-roped stanchions that surrounded the entrance. A stocky, barrel-chested Italian, with pocked skin and black, wavy hair pulled back in a ponytail, stood guard at the entrance, clipboard in hand, occasionally calling out to the line the names of those with reservations. Ross stepped up to him.

"Excuse me, *signore*, I am here to apply for a job."

The man looked up from his list. "What job?"

"As a tour guide."

"They hire for all jobs inside. Past the gift shop there is a door."

The man unhooked the rope and waved Ross on through.

For more than three years he had waited and hoped for this moment, and it filled him with electricity as noticeable as the cool air that met him as he stepped inside. The lobby was crowded as a bus of Japanese tourists congregated in the room while their guide helped them gain admittance. In the room's center was a glass cubicle with the sign *"Biglietti"* where four women sat behind Plexiglas with their cash registers and ticket machines, each facing a different direction, watching the crowd with boredom. In the back of the room, under an archway, was a small gift shop where maps and guidebooks were sold.

Past it, around the corner, was a door with a small plaque that read, *"Direzione del Museo."* The door was partially open and Ross looked inside. A slender, beak-nosed woman with thick-rimmed eyeglasses sat at a cluttered desk, writing. Her hair was dark, pulled back from her forehead. She glanced up.

"May I help you?" She spoke in clear English slightly bent with a Florentine accent.

"I was sent here to see you."

"Who sent you?"

"The man outside. He said this is where you were taking applications for tour guide positions."

She looked at him quizzically. "Come in, please." Ross stepped inside, laying his pack on the floor. "I do not know why he would say that. We do not hire that way. There is an exam given once a year. It is very competitive. We usually have more than a thousand applicants for the position."

Ross frowned. He hadn't counted on this and he felt a little ridiculous for his assumption. As he contemplated this dilemma, the woman looked him over and seemed to decide he was handsome.

"You are American?"

"Yes."

She motioned to the wooden chairs in front of her desk. "Please sit down."

Ross came around and sat.

"You have been a tour guide before?"

"No. But I know the Uffizi well."

"Then you are a professor?"

"No." Ross leaned back a little from the desk. "But I know everything about the Uffizi."

"What do you mean 'everything'?"

"Ask me something."

She considered his challenge. "Tell me about the gallery."

"The Uffizi is one of the finest art galleries in the world and the first museum of modern Europe. It was officially opened in 1765, though the building and some of its art existed for nearly two hundred years before that. The building itself was constructed in 1560, when Medici duke Cosimo I commissioned Giorgio Vasari to design a grand palace along the river, with the appearance of 'floating in air.' The gallery has not been without its challenges. It has survived World War II, a major flood and even a bomb planted by the Mafia." He rested. "I know everything about the Uffizi."

"Tell me about the exhibits."

"The Uffizi houses work from Raffaello, Rem-

36

brandt, Michelangelo, Leonardo, Cimabue, Botticelli, as well as hundreds of other artists. Choose one."

"Tell me about Botticelli."

"Alessandro Filipepi, also called Sandro Botticelli, was born in Florence in 1445, where he resided until his death in 1510. *Botticelli* means 'little barrels' and was actually a nickname given to Alessandro's older brother on account of his being overweight. Unfortunately for the Filipepi family, it stuck to all of them. Botticelli has twelve paintings in the Uffizi. They are among the most popular works of the gallery, including the *Primavera*, oil tempera on wood, painted for Lorenzo Medici in 1498, acquired by the Uffizi in 1919 and recently restored in 1982, and the *Birth of Venus*, also whimsically called 'Venus on the Half Shell.' The medium is tempera on linen canvas, and its patron and origins are unknown, though many experts speculate that it was also commissioned by the Medici family. This work was acquired by the Uffizi in 1815 and restored in 1987. Like the *Primavera*, there is controversy over the actual meaning of the work. Some say Botticelli's works capture the essence of the Florentine woman, past and modern — the sad eyes, the lips bent with a hint of sardonic grin. It's an appraisal with which I happen to agree. His works may be found in rooms nine to fourteen in the first corridor."

"*Bravo.* That is impressive."

"I've memorized the entire gallery, every

37

painting, fresco, tapestry and sculpture; the artist, the patron who commissioned it, the date it was started and finished, its artistic significance and the year it was acquired by the Uffizi."

The woman looked at him in astonishment. "There are thousands of exhibits. That would take many years to learn."

"Only one and a half. But I worked at it nine hours a day."

"You studied the Uffizi nine hours a day?"

"I had a lot of time on my hands."

She gazed at him curiously. With employment an impossibility, Ross wondered why she was spending so much time with him.

"Do you speak Italian?"

"Some. *Il mio Italiano e ancora un po brutto.*"

This made her smile. "Actually, you speak well. Where did you learn?"

"Mostly from books. But I had a few Italian friends in America."

She gazed at him for a moment without word then said, "Just a moment." She left the room. She returned accompanied by an older and taller woman with honey-colored hair and blue, square-lensed Gucci sunglasses. She wore leather pants and a silk blouse, with a scarf tied around her throat.

The first woman returned to her desk, and the tall woman sat down in a chair next to her, crossed her legs and smiled at Ross, but said nothing.

"Excuse me, sir, I forgot to ask your name."

"Ross Story."

"Story?"

"*Sì*. Like a book."

She spoke to the other woman then turned her attention back to Ross. "Signor Story, this is Francesca Punteri. She is one of our guides."

She smiled at her own introduction. Ross smiled back.

"I have asked Francesca if she could employ you as an assistant. Some of the guides have more work than they can handle or cannot take English-speaking groups because their English is not good enough. For Francesca both are true."

"My English not so well," the woman interjected, proving the assertion.

". . . so they take on others as assistants and split the fee. This way they can make more money. Technically it's not legal, but there are ways around things in Italy."

"What is the fee?"

"They usually receive two hundred thousand lire a tour, so about half of that."

"So I would do the same work and she would take half?"

"*Sì*."

"What if I just found groups on my own and took them through the gallery?"

Her expression tightened. "That is prohibited. If you are caught there is a big fine."

"How big?" Ross said, as if weighing his odds. Her expression tightened more.

"The fine is three million lire."

Ross's brow furrowed. "That is a big fine. Who would catch me?"

"You must have a badge to lead a group. There is much security here, of course. And there are the other guides. Not all of them are busy. They protect each other."

"I think half is too much to give away," Ross said.

"And you would keep all tips for yourself, of course," she added. "I think it is a fair offer."

In spite of her limited English, Francesca understood the conversation. *"Sessanta per cento."* *Sixty percent.*

Ross looked over at her. Her eyes were on him, anticipating his response. He answered in Italian, *"Grazie.* When would I start?"

"Oggi pomeriggio, se vuole." *This afternoon if you want.*

He nodded. "Very good. When would you like me to meet you?"

"At three, outside the reservations entrance."

"Three it is." At this Francesca stood and Ross likewise stood and shook her hand. "I will be there. It was a pleasure meeting you."

"Piacere mio." *My pleasure.*

Francesca walked out of the room and the young woman smiled at him.

"Thank you for your help," Ross said. "I don't know your name."

"My name is Patrizia."

"Piacere, Patrizia." *It's a pleasure.*

She smiled. "Welcome to the Uffizi. If you would like, I have a little time right now. I could show you around. Then we could take a coffee at the bar."

"Thank you. I'd like that."

"You may leave your bag in here. It will be safe."

Patrizia led Ross out of her office, past the ticket counter and up four flights of stone stairs to the second-floor gallery. As he walked down the wide, high-ceilinged corridor, a sense of awe fell over him. This place, these works of art, had saved his life. Not in a figurative sense, but in reality. *Perhaps life did come full circle,* he thought. Perhaps this was recompense for the injustices of his life. Maybe. If so, the first installment had been paid.

CHAPTER 3

"L'amore e cieco, ma il matrimonio gli rida la vista."
Love is blind. Marriage restores one's vision.
— Italian Proverb

Alessio straddled the back of the living room's leather couch as he gazed out the window. He had been bouncing a rubber ball against the window as well, but he had dropped it and it had rolled out of reach beneath the couch and so now he just looked. Eliana walked down the stairs, her arms full with a laundry basket.

"Don't sit on the back of the couch, honey."

He continued to gaze outside, as if he hadn't heard his mother.

"Alessio."

He moaned and slid one leg down.

"What are you looking at, sport?"

"Nothing."

"Get down. And what *nothing* are you looking at?"

He reluctantly slid off the back of the couch, slumping back in the sofa's thick cushions, his heels on the edge, his knees higher than his head. "Is it three o'clock yet?"

"Feet off the couch. You know better than that. And it's way past three."

He dropped his feet, which barely reached the floor. "Oh," he said, sighing loudly.

"Since when do you care what time it is?"

"Dad said on the phone yesterday he'd be home at three."

Eliana groaned. Her countenance softened then she set her basket down and walked to Alessio's side, sitting on the couch next to him. She put her arms around him and pulled him close. "He must have gotten caught in some traffic."

She felt stupid offering the same worn excuses for her husband. She should be good at covering for Maurizio by now, but she wasn't. It just seemed to get harder.

Alessio's face was still bent in dejection. "I don't like traffic," he said sadly. "It's always catching Dad."

Eliana would have smiled at his observation had she not hurt for him. "Why don't you go outside and play?"

"Dad told me that we'd go to the park and kick goals. He was going to teach me how to play."

"He'll be home soon, honey," she said, hoping it was true. She honestly had no idea if he would be home or not. There was no telling with Maurizio. "Why don't I go out and kick the ball with you?"

"Moms can't do that."

"Of course they can."

"Dad says girls can't play soccer."

"He did, huh?" She didn't doubt it; it was typical Maurizio. "Well, there are women who can play soccer better than your father."

"Really?"

"Really."

"Can you play better than Dad?"

"I don't know. I've never tried."

He thought about this. "We can play if you want."

"Okay. Let me check dinner first. You go get the ball."

"It's right there." A fluorescent yellow and black soccer ball was sitting on the floor next to the couch. "Can I wear my Totti shirt Dad gave me?"

"What's a Totti shirt?"

"You know. Totti. He plays on Team Italia," he said, incredulous at his mother's ignorance of one of the country's best players.

"Yes, you may."

"Can we go to the park?"

"I would, honey, but I'm still making dinner. We'll just play in the courtyard. Now go change your shirt while I check the oven."

Alessio ran upstairs. Eliana lifted her laundry basket. *Why do you make promises you can't keep, Maurizio?* she thought.

It was dark outside. Eliana was reading in the den when she heard the gravel crunching beneath the Alfa Romeo's wheels as Maurizio drove his car up the driveway five hours later than he'd promised to be home. Alessio had been fed, bathed and had gone to bed. Their

44

dinner had gone cold.

The front door opened and he announced his return, dropped his suit coat on the sofa, loosened his tie and then, with a loud sigh of exhaustion, collapsed in front of the television. Eliana put down her book, and went to the kitchen to reheat their dinner. She did not greet him, certain that anything she said would come out more as a rebuke than a welcome. He had been gone for two weeks this time. She didn't want to start fighting the second he got home.

With the exception of a load of wash and forty-five minutes of soccer with Alessio, she had spent the entire afternoon in the kitchen preparing a special meal for Maurizio's return: spinach-pear ravioli in walnut cream sauce, bresaola with rucola, mushroom crostini and broiled Chianina steak. There was a bottle of their own best wine, L'incanto, in the center of the table, next to a sterling silver candelabra.

The food wasn't all Eliana had paid special attention to. She had painted her nails, taken a long bath with scented oils and carefully shaved her legs so they'd be smooth for him. She had also spent extra time on her hair, but she was now regretting all of it. With each minute he'd been late, her mood had deteriorated still more. By the time dinner was served, she did not even bother to light the candles at the table.

She called him to dinner. A minute later he walked in, looked over the spread. "You shouldn't have gone to this much trouble," he said, acting magnanimous.

Eliana looked up at him, bridling her temper. She picked her words carefully. "I wanted to do something special for you."

"You shouldn't have troubled," he repeated as he sat down.

She watched him for a moment as he picked at his food. "Did you already eat?" she asked.

"No. Well, just a snack. I had to get gas and I picked up a hamburger at the Autogrill."

She wanted to scream. Instead she just quietly sighed.

"Where's Alessio?"

"He's in bed."

Without comment, Maurizio cut a thin strip from his steak, raised it to his mouth.

"He waited for you. You promised him you'd play soccer with him."

"I didn't promise him. I told him if I was home in time."

"It's the same thing to a child."

"They are not the same things. Someone should teach him that."

"I think you are."

For the rest of dinner the only sound coming from the table was the conflict of silverware against porcelain. Maurizio, not oblivious to her anger, complimented her cooking. His gesture was met with silence and he resigned himself to her sullen companionship.

American women are crazy, he thought. *She*

works all day to make me a meal then sulks through it.

Eliana finished eating before him, put her dishes in the sink and then went upstairs to her studio. She picked up Maurizio's coat from the back of the sofa as she passed by.

As soon as she was out of the room, Maurizio pushed back from the table, took the bottle of wine and went into the living room to watch the soccer game. He shut the door and lit a cigarette. Because of Alessio's asthma, Eliana had forbidden him to smoke in the house, a regulation he regularly flouted, as much on principle as desire. "A single man has no master," his unmarried colleagues derided him. *A woman shouldn't be telling a man what to do in his own house.* Still he limited his smoking to two rooms, the living room and the bedroom.

In spite of Eliana's silent treatment, he was content. He had eaten well. Twice, in fact. Drank well. His team, Fiorentina, was playing well for a change. Eliana was sulking about something, but that was predictable, he thought. The reentry ritual was one they had been through a hundred times before. He had it down to a science. Eliana would sulk for a while then she'd blow, inevitably launching into a tirade about how little time he spent at home or why he hadn't bothered to call her. He would let her blow off steam then he would remind her of how fortunate she was to be so well provided for and the sacrifices and loneliness his life on the road

47

required. He might even throw in anecdotes of his business associates who made him look like husband of the year by comparison.

Either way, Eliana didn't have the stomach for conflict that he had. She would go off for a while then come back and be civil — *be a good wife*.

Always the same foolishness, he thought. *If she wants me home so much, why does she make it so damn miserable to come home?*

Still, the situation was manageable. And there was the upside. His wife was a good cook, she kept a good home and she was a good mother. There was a price for those things. Even Eden had snakes.

At around midnight Maurizio shut off the television and went into their bedroom. Eliana had finished painting and come back downstairs to do the dishes more than an hour before and had still not spoken to him. *Not a good omen*, he thought. She was like a pressure cooker. The more time that went by, the more steam built up.

He dropped his clothes on the floor at the side of the bed and climbed naked under the sheets. He lit another cigarette, stretched back in bed then called out for her.

"Eliana. Come to bed, *amore*. It's late."

No response. A moment later he tried again.

"I've been away from my woman too long," he said playfully. "Don't make your man wait any longer."

A few minutes later Eliana walked into the room. She stopped at the foot of the bed, eyeing

48

him fiercely. Her voice was low, simmering. "So tell me, Maurizio, was it lonely on the road?"

"It is always lonely, *amore.*"

"So you were all alone?"

He looked at her carefully, trying to guess the intent of her question. *"Certo."* *Of course.*

"Then who do these belong to?" She dangled two diamond earrings in front of him. "They were in your coat pocket."

His eyes darted from the earrings to her. He laughed nervously. *"Per te, amore.* They're for you. I thought they would look nice with your green dress. You know the one I gave you last summer from Venice. I was running late, I didn't have time to have them wrapped."

"Really?" Eliana's eyes flashed. She raised her other hand. "And the lipstick I found with them — that too was a gift for me, Maurizio? Maybe next time you should buy some that isn't already used."

For a moment the two stared at each other, then Maurizio surrendered with a loud sigh. "Eliana, *e così.*"

Eliana exploded. "No, it's not just the way it is! It's the way *you* are." She flung the earrings and lipstick case against the wall. "I won't do this anymore. I won't. It's over, Maurizio. It's over between us."

"Amore, no," he said calmly.

"Don't you dare call me that. Don't you ever call me that again."

"We have a good life here, *amore. Una dolce vita.*"

"What do you know of the life I have here? You are never here. You are always someplace else with some other woman while I stay and keep your house clean and your son alive. You know nothing of my life, Maurizio. *Niente!*"

He looked away from her, yet his demeanor didn't change. He was strong that way. "Where will you go?"

"Home. I'm taking Alessio and going back to America."

Maurizio took a long drag from his cigarette, then looked up at her coolly. "No, you will not be taking my son to America."

"Yes, I will."

"No, I will not permit it. You are not in America, Eliana. You cannot take Alessio without my consent. And without my consent you would have to prove to a judge that you could give your son a better life in America. Unless you have some buried treasure I do not know about, I do not think that is possible. What will you do? Be a waitress? Maybe a secretary? You have no skills. You have no money. You have no insurance. How will you pay for Alessio's health care? Be reasonable, Eliana. A judge in Italy will decide for Alessio, not you. A judge will never allow you to take him."

Eliana just stared at him.

"You know I am right, Eliana. You know there are many foreign women living in Italy because they cannot take their children back to America. You have told me about them yourself. So you make your choice. You divorce me and live in Italy alone and try to find a job, while someone else watches your son, or you go back to America alone. Or you stay with me and have a nice home in the countryside and take care of our son. But these are the only choices you have, because I will not allow you to take him from Italy. It is not in his best interest."

Eliana stood staring at him, as breathless as if she had just been slugged in the stomach. She could not answer him. He had her and they both knew it. Maurizio smiled at her sympathetically. "It's not so bad, Eliana. I'm just doing what all men do. The problem is only with how you see things." He ground his cigarette out in a glass dish near the bed. "You'll get used to it, *amore*. Then you'll be happy. Now be a good wife and come to bed."

CHAPTER 4

"Amor, che al cor gentil ratto s'apprende."
Love is quickly caught in the gentle heart.

— Dante

Ross's commute to work was less than fifteen minutes and could have been pulled from a travel book's walking tour of Florence. He crossed the Arno at Ponte Vecchio, against the backdrop of the central landmark of Florence: the cathedral of Santa Maria del Fiore, the Duomo, its roan dome rising above the city like a great matron. The Duomo was enigmatic to Ross, both majestic and peculiar in her green, rose and white marble, as unlikely as a gingerbread house built for God.

The Uffizi was just on the other side of the bridge.

The first tour Ross conducted concluded about two hours after it began. Francesca had followed along on his tour without interference, and afterward the two of them took coffee together to evaluate his presentation. She was pleased. She had only a few suggestions, minor ones, and pointed out his one mistake, attributing Fiorentino's *Musician Angel* to Raffaello, which no one noticed but Francesca. "Don't worry about it," she said with a grin, adding in Italian, "these bus monkeys didn't know their Donatello from their Bernini. You could have told them that Titian's *Venus of Urbino* was a paint by numbers and they would have believed you."

In spite of Ross's knowledge and love for the art, it was his interaction with the group that she was most pleased with. Twelve years in the business had taught her a peculiar truism: most tourists spend more time looking at the guide than the art.

She gave him a hundred and twenty thousand lire in cash along with her cellular and home phone numbers and the time of his next tour. She had already booked him a tour for the next morning. Francesca was a shrewd marketer and had arrangements with most of the large hotels. She led more tours than any other guide in the city and still turned down nearly half her offers.

They parted and Ross set out for his next task. After six months of sleeping in hotels and hostels, he was ready to settle down. He remembered passing a real estate office near the train station, and he headed off to find it, wandering slowly through the back streets toward the station. He stopped briefly at the open market at San Lorenzo, where he looked at leather-bound books and a sweater, but purchased nothing. Forty minutes later he found the agency.

The office was small with two wooden desks. A young man was speaking on the phone behind one of them. A cigarette burned in his hand, its smoke rising in wisps, occasionally dissipated by an oscillating desk fan. His other hand held a pen, which he tapped rhythmically on the desk. Despite the summer heat, he wore a tweed jacket with a collared shirt beneath.

As the door shut behind Ross, the man looked up and acknowledged him with a curt nod. Ross glanced around then walked to the side of the room, where handwritten apartment information was posted on the wall.

Five minutes later the young man hung up the phone. *"Buona sera.* May I help you, sir?" He spoke in clear English.

Ross turned around. "I'm looking for an apartment."

"Yes. Please sit down."

Ross sat in one of the small metal chairs in front of the desk.

"You are looking for something in Florence?"

"Outside the city a little. Perhaps in Chianti."

He took a short puff of the cigarette. "Yes, in Chianti. You are quite fortunate as there are now many places free." He reached for a black binder on the desktop and opened it. "Chiocchio, Strada in Chianti, Impruneta. Greve. There are many. How many rooms will you require?"

"It's just for me. I would like something with a fireplace and a good view. Someplace interesting. Perhaps an old farmhouse or in a villa near a vineyard."

"In Chianti they are all near vineyards." He stood from behind the desk. He was in actuality much taller than he had looked sitting down. He extinguished his cigarette in a glass ashtray, then extended his hand. "My name is Luigi Tommassi."

"My name is Ross. You speak good English."

"Yes, well, I went to school in San Diego for three semesters. Do you speak Italian?"

"A little," Ross said, though more as a matter of courtesy than truth. His Italian was as good as the man's English.

"How long of a lease do you wish to make?"

"I plan to live here indefinitely, but I might decide to change apartments after I know the city better. A one-year lease would be good."

"That is not a problem. When would you be available to see something?"

"I'm living in a hotel right now, so the sooner the better. I could go today."

"Yes, well, I only have my scooter today and I will need to make some arrangement. But I am free tomorrow. If you like, I could get my car and we could see a few places."

"Tomorrow would be fine."

"I must talk to the people with the apartments, of course, but early afternoon would probably be the best time."

"How about three o'clock?"

Luigi looked at a calendar on the wall. "*Alle tre,* yes, three o'clock would be good. Do you have a phone number where you can be called?"

"Yes." Ross wrote down the number and handed it to him. "That's my cellular." The agent looked at the number then slipped it into his front pocket.

"I will only call if something comes up. Otherwise we can plan to meet here at three tomorrow. I will have a car to drive. *Va bene?*"

Ross stood, *"Va bene. Grazie."*

"A domani." See you tomorrow.

The next morning Francesca was nearly twenty minutes late for the tour, and Ross, sensing the group's growing impatience, started without her, which simultaneously pleased and concerned her. When she caught up with him, she took him aside. "Don't forget you are an *abussive,*" she warned. "Some of the other guides will want to turn you in to the commune. If you are stopped, you must tell them you are only helping me and I am in the toilet or getting a coffee."

"That's how it works, huh?"

"Yes. Many are very jealous of me."

Even before he finished the tour, Francesca had arranged for another — an American group from an active Dayton retirement center. He thought that he could fit the group in before his afternoon appointment, but found that they moved from exhibit to exhibit almost as if in slow motion. By the time they reached the second corridor, they were spending more time looking for places to rest than art, so he abbreviated the last half of the tour.

Still, it was past three when Ross ran from the

Uffizi, hailed a cab and arrived at the real estate office. It was another sweltering day and the front of his shirt was stained with perspiration. He wiped his forehead with a Kleenex as he walked in.

"I'm sorry I'm late."

Luigi appeared relieved to see him. "It is no problem. I was only afraid you might not come. I have made us four appointments for today. Our first appointment is one in the country with a beautiful view, about twelve kilometers from downtown. It is a very small community near Greve in Chianti. There are many vineyards, you said you like vineyards."

Ross nodded.

"There is an apartment a little closer to town in Grassina. It would be maybe a fifteen-minute ride by *motorino* to the center of town. There is also a villa near Impruneta that I have not seen but it sounds interesting. Afterwards, if you are not too tired, there is another place we might go and see. It's on the other side of Florence in Fiesole. It is a little bit further drive but it is very beautiful in Fiesole. I haven't seen the apartment myself but my partner says it is magnificent." He took his jacket from the back of his chair. "Shall we go?"

Ross followed Luigi out to his car: a small, navy-blue Punto double-parked in front of the agency, with its hazard lights flashing.

Their first stop was in Chiocchio, a Chianti township about a half-hour drive from Florence.

The road to the community was nicknamed *la strada del vino* (*the street of wine*), as for many kilometers both sides of the road were flanked by large, well-cared-for vineyards.

The rental property was a hundred-year-old summer cottage up a gravel drive lined with cypress trees and terra-cotta figurines. It had a large front porch that looked out onto a valley of vineyards and farmhouses and a small fishing lake, *Lago Chiocchio*. Next to the home was a *limonaia*, where lemon trees grew in terra-cotta pots for the winter.

There were no homes nearby and this bothered Ross. He wanted his privacy but not solitary confinement. In addition, the home was larger than he needed, with an expansive family room and three bedrooms. The owner was a barrel-chested man with a thick Florentine accent, who offered them Chianti wine until they relented and took a glass.

After touring the house, they walked around the side patio and Luigi pulled Ross aside. "I asked the owner if they had ever rented it for winter. He said they have not. The house is heated with *gasolio* — how do you say in English?"

"Diesel fuel."

"Yes, diesel fuel is not efficient. This was built for a summerhouse, I think. I think it would be very expensive to heat in winter. And you would still be cold."

Ross looked across the yard. The place was

beautiful but not right for him. "Let's keep looking," he said.

Their second stop was closer to Florence, in a compact, busy township called Grassina. The rental property was new and clean but its decor was modern European and lacked the rustic Italian feel Ross was looking for.

Their third stop was a villa near the Chianti township of Impruneta. It was in the country-side, away from the main thoroughfare and diffi-cult to find. Luigi kept a hand-drawn map on his lap which he frequently consulted as he plied the wooded back roads, stopping, backtracking, then launching out again, each time asserting with certainty that he knew exactly where it was. He made several wrong turns before the road emerged from a forest into a large orchard of dusty olive trees. A posted, hand-lettered sign read *"Villa Rendola, 1000 metri."* Luigi said, "That is the name of the place."

"What does Rendola mean?"

"I don't know. It is only a name, maybe."

A few meters past the first sign was another: *"Olio di Oliva e Vino. Vendita diretta"* (*Olive oil and wine sold direct*).

As the Punto rose over a small knoll, Ross got his first glimpse of the villa. He liked the place immediately. It was as if they had passed through a portal and emerged five centuries ear-lier. The villa was a majestic structure sur-rounded by high, amber-colored stucco walls. A small tower rose above it. It was set back on a working *fattorìa* at the end of a long, cypress-lined driveway. On the distant hill overlooking the villa was a castle.

Luigi parked the car on a small gravel incline and they both climbed out. The landscape of the *fattorìa* was lush with foliage. There were neatly trimmed hedges of pliable, tab-leafed bosso and sturdier, rougher hedges of laurel, dark in places and bright green where new branches grew. Luigi snapped a dark leaf off a laurel bush as they walked and crumbled it in his hand before holding it out for Ross to smell. It was sweetly fragrant. "You can cook with this," he said. "And, of course, you can crown emperors."

Three massive cedars of Lebanon grew around the house — symbols of a villa's age and power. There were other trees: oak; cypress, fat-bodied and spear-shaped; a single walnut tree next to the villa. "A walnut tree is a companion for the house," Luigi added, as if the villa was in danger of loneliness.

Scattered around were myriad flowers: poppies, yellow broom, irises and a dozen others Ross couldn't put a name to.

"This is a villa that has been divided up into three apartments," Luigi said. "The sheet on it says that there is a one-bedroom apartment available and it is furnished."

The villa was surrounded by an eight-foot stucco wall, with a large spray of jasmine spilling over its top like a white-crested wave.

Ross pushed the gate — a large, wooden door

shackled with iron hardware, nearly black with rust and age — which opened to an enclosed courtyard. They stepped inside. The ground was paved in large black and gray blocks of pietra serena cobblestone, which had been worn and grooved through centuries of weathering. Moss grew from the porous stone in green and white splatters resembling a painter's drop cloth. To his immediate right was the back door of the villa's stone chapel, next to a wall shrouded by a large hedge of white oleander and hyacinth. In the center of the courtyard was a stone well with a wrought iron canopy from which an oak bucket hung by a rope and a large, round pulley.

There were terra-cotta pots and grow boxes around the perimeter of the courtyard filled with red and pink geraniums. And on the west wall was a climbing rose near a stone archway that led to the garden.

"How old is this place?" Ross asked.

"It was built more than five hundred years ago. The landlord said on the phone that this used to be the country home of Machiavelli."

"*The* Machiavelli?"

"Yes, the writer," Luigi said. "If you are interested, I will ask her about it."

Ross nodded. "*Sì*. I am."

The woman who managed the villa was in the courtyard. She was softly singing as she held a tin watering can over one of the potted plants. When she saw them, she greeted them loudly with *"Benvenuti, signori,"* then she walked over to shake hands. She introduced herself as Anna Ferrini. She was a short, stout woman with dark, clear skin and reddish hair. Ross guessed her to be a decade older than himself. She lived in the villa as well as managed it.

Luigi asked, *"Signora,* is it true that Machiavelli once lived here?"

"Sì." She launched into a partial explanation of the villa's history, which coincided with what Ross already knew of Machiavelli's life. After his fall from grace, the Medicis banished Machiavelli to this country villa, away from the tongue and muscle of the politics he loved. Here, in the very section of the villa Ross was looking to rent, he wrote the essays and tomes that made him famous. He had died in the villa, though no one knew exactly where.

Anna spoke of the former tenant casually, but to Ross this fact held intrigue even beyond the obvious historical significance of the place itself. He saw it as an omen. He too was an exile of sorts.

The villa had been in the Ferrini family for many generations. They had only started renting out the apartment in the last three years. With the explanation completed, Anna waved them forward. *"Venite, signori."* Come, gentlemen. "It is too hot outside."

As they followed her toward the apartment, Ross asked Luigi, "Has it been available long?"

"No. And I think it will rent fast. This is a nice

place. A German couple lived here for more than a year. It has been vacant only a few weeks. They only rent to foreigners."

Ross thought that peculiar. "Why is that?"

"Because of the laws in Italy it is almost impossible to make someone leave once they have moved in. Sometimes the landlord has to pay a lot of money to get them out. If you tell foreigners to leave, they will."

Anna directed them into the kitchen. Though the apartment had no air-conditioning — few homes in Italy did — it was significantly cooler inside the apartment, as the villa's thick stone walls kept out the heat. The kitchen was small, with a gas stove, an oven and a sink that looked like a trough cut from unglazed stone. Ross ran his hand across the basin and was pleased.

In the center of the room there was a small table with painted tiles and two oak chairs. The refrigerator was typical Italian, small, with rounded corners like an appliance nostalgic of mid-century America. To the side of the refrigerator was a door, no higher than five feet, which led downstairs to a wine and prosciutto cellar. Anna flipped on a light switch and they descended the narrow stairwell single file. The air was musty and pungent. The space was bigger than Ross expected, easily as big as the kitchen above it. It was illuminated by a single bare light bulb dangling from a cord. A large slab of red, cured prosciutto still hung from a hook toward the back of the room. The meat was flat on one end where a knife had shaved off strips. "The Germans left it," Anna said. "It comes with the apartment." It was clear from her tone that she considered this a benefit.

There were also several large bottles of clouded green olive oil and a woven wine demijohn in the corner of the room with a missing cap, indicating its emptiness. They climbed back up to the kitchen.

Beyond the kitchen, through a door leading outside the villa, was a newly bricked terrace with a pizza oven for summer cooking. The wall behind the oven was already blackened with use.

"This will be useful during the summer months when it is too hot to cook in the house," Luigi observed.

They went back inside. A small hallway led to the bathroom and the apartment's only bedroom. The tiny room was floored in rose-colored tile and there was a small rug at the end of the bed. The bed itself was queen-sized with an ornate wrought iron headboard bent in an intricate floral pattern. A wood carving of the Madonna and child was mounted to the wall above the headboard.

Aside from the bed the only furniture in the room was an antique wood armoire with four drawers and a closet for hanging clothes. There was one window, obscured by sheer curtains that draped from a metal rod clear to the floor. Ross pulled back the curtains then pushed open the shutters, exposing the thick foliage that grew a little taller than the windowsill, and in the distance he saw a vast landscape of hills spotted with trellises and orchards. The room had one bathroom with a tile shower bored into the wall like a cave. There were new bathroom fixtures, shiny chrome and porcelain. "The bathroom is modern," Anna said. "We updated it for the Germans."

While Anna turned off lights in the back of the apartment, Ross and Luigi stepped aside.

"It is nice, no?"

Ross nodded his approval. "How much is she asking?"

"She wants three million lire a month with at least a six-month lease. I told her that the lease is not a problem for you. If it is longer than six months, she is willing to negotiate a lower price."

"The only problem is transportation. This place is pretty remote."

"Yes, it is far. You should purchase a scooter, I think. I told the lady that you work in the city and she says that there is a bus into Florence every hour.

"They also heat with *gasolio,* like the place in the country, but I think it is not so bad here because these old villas have thick walls. There is also a swimming pool to the side of the villa. She wants to show us."

Anna had already left the apartment, and while Luigi followed her out into the courtyard, Ross lingered in the kitchen absorbing the vibrations of the old place. He felt as if he had been there a thousand times before. While the particulars were different, it was precisely where he had fled in his mind to escape his previous life. He had never imagined that he would be here this soon. If at all. He felt as if he was finally home. He glanced about once more, then followed after Anna and Luigi.

Anna led them back out through the courtyard, then outside the villa walls to a narrow dirt path that led to the swimming pool.

"Parking is here if you buy a car or scooter," said Luigi, pointing to a flat, gravel area with a simple, yet ingenious canopy that Ross stopped to examine. It was a wood-beam frame with chain-link fence thrown over the top, now rendered solid by a heavy grapevine that had snaked in and around the fencing until it was thick as a thatch roof.

Ross hadn't seen the pool when they entered as it was around the west side of the villa, built on a terrace overlooking the vineyards. There was a lattice archway leading into it with grapevines growing around it, the seasoned vines overtaking the structure and appearing to support the aged wood rather than the opposite.

The pool was large and its cool aqua-blue water shimmered. Not far from the pool there was a child's slide and swing set.

As Ross looked around he saw that they weren't alone. On the far side of the pool, lying on a blanket, was a young woman wearing a light, beige sundress, the straps down over her shoulders. She had sleek, well-proportioned features, a slender waist, full breasts and long, thin legs. She had high, narrow cheeks, and her hair was pulled back, falling over one shoulder. She was lying on her side next to a small boy, her eyes fixed on the novel she held. The child lay on his stomach, crashing his toys together in combat.

Just then the woman looked up. Ross could not look away. Though she was as beautiful in form as any woman he had ever seen, it was her eyes that struck him most profoundly. She had beautiful, hazel eyes — the sad, fawnlike eyes of the *fiorentina*. Like a Botticelli painting.

Anna waved. *"Ciao, Eliana, buona giornata."*

"Ciao, Anna," the young woman returned in a friendly voice.

The woman looked from Anna to Ross, and they shared eye contact, but she quickly turned her attention back to her book. Ross turned away, though out of politeness, not desire. He wanted to stare at her as he might a painting, and perhaps just as intensely. Beauty took time to properly digest.

Anna whispered something to Luigi, which, after a few moments, he shared with Ross as well.

"She says that besides herself, this woman will be your only neighbor. She has only the one boy and he is very quiet. So you need not be concerned about the noise." Then Luigi added, "I think there is something wrong with the child.

He has some sickness, I believe."

Ross looked back toward the child but found himself staring at the woman again.

"She is a pretty woman, no?" Luigi asked.

Ross turned away, slightly embarrassed at being caught staring. *"Sì,"* he said.

Anna began talking again, pointing out the distant boundaries of the property. Luigi translated, though unnecessarily. "This is a working *fattorìa*. The Ferrini family is well known in Chianti for their olive oil. They also have good wine. A premium wine. I have tried it. But they are not famous for it. You can try some and decide for yourself if it is good. She says that if you decide to rent you are invited to join them at the *Vendemmia* — the grape harvest in October." Then he added, "It is really a great thing. They have a big feast afterwards."

"Great," Ross said, not fully digesting what had been offered. He was still distracted by the woman by the pool.

"So what do you think?" Luigi asked.

Ross stirred. "About?"

Luigi grinned. "About the apartment."

"Of course. When will it be available?"

"You are decided?"

"Sì."

Luigi looked surprised. "I think soon. I will ask. When would you like to move in?"

"Immediately."

"Adesso," Luigi said to himself. He spoke to Anna, then told Ross, "She says it is ready, but

she still needs the cleaning lady to go through it. Also she needs to get some new sheets for the bed."

"Is that everything?"

"There is a lease that needs to be signed. Along with the matter of the deposit."

Ross looked out over the landscape. Here was every seduction the countryside offered. "Go ahead and prepare the paperwork. How much of a deposit does she need?"

"She was asking for the first month's rent and an additional five million lire, but I think that it is too much. I think four is better."

"Four will be okay," Ross said though he didn't really care. He had already made up his mind.

"I will ask her."

There was an animated exchange between Luigi and Anna, with escalating voices and broad hand gestures. All he could hear of it was Luigi's calm voice, *Signora . . . Signora.* " For a moment Ross thought it might turn bad and he considered intervening, but then the voices stopped and Luigi returned, smiling as if nothing had happened. "She says that four will be fine."

Ross laughed to himself. *If only business in America had been so straightforward,* he thought.

"We can come back tomorrow and sign the papers."

Ross nodded his approval. "I'll need to wire some money. Do you have a bank account number for her?"

"It will be on the contract. I will call you with it."

Ross looked around the grounds but again found his gaze drawn to the woman. "I would like to move in tomorrow afternoon. Ask her if that will be possible."

"You can move all your things in by then?"

"I don't own much," Ross said.

Luigi spoke with Anna then returned with the news that tomorrow would be satisfactory, even preferable. Anna would soon be leaving on holiday, and after Thursday all would be delayed as they would have to wait till sometime next week for her brother to return from a business trip to sign the lease agreement. But she could not guarantee that the house would be cleaned by tomorrow until she talked to her cleaning lady. Ross shrugged. *"Non e importante."* It was already clean enough for him.

As they walked back toward the villa, Ross glanced back once more at the woman by the pool. She was looking up at him and for a brief moment they again shared eye contact. This time he was the first to turn away. He walked back to the car in silence. He had just made a decision on where he would live for the next year, and all he could think about was some woman he didn't know. He did not believe in love at first sight or any such foolishness. She had barely even acknowledged his presence. Yet there was something that drew him to her.

He couldn't say what it was. For all he knew

it was the pull of the moon on the Italian countryside. All he was certain of was that he hoped to see her again soon.

CHAPTER 5

"Una donna, la sua sorte
e fatta dell'amore ch'ella acetta."
A woman's fate is determined by the love she accepts.
— Italian Proverb

Anna stood in the gravel driveway and watched the Punto vanish down the drive beneath a line of swaying cypress. On its way out of Rendola the car passed a postal scooter driving to the villa. Anna heard the thin, familiar whine of the scooter's engine and waited. The postal worker stopped her scooter just an arm's length away from Anna, turned and took from her mail pouch a small stack of mail, which she handed to Anna. It was a familiar ritual and the whole of their conversation consisted of three words:

"Prego."

"Grazie."

"Prego."

Anna sorted through the mail as she walked back to the pool. She set the stack of envelopes on the ground next to Eliana. "It's all for you," she said. Then she sat down on a reclining chair, took off her glasses and wiped the sweat from the bridge of her nose.

"Come stai?" Anna asked. *How are you?*

"Abbastanza bene," Eliana replied. *Good enough.*

Though Eliana had been teaching English to Anna for more than three years, she was an unmotivated student and the women only spoke Italian in conversation. Anna scratched the back of her head. "We have a new tenant. He will move in tomorrow."

"Good." She turned to Alessio. "Why don't you get in the pool, honey?"

"You come too, Mommy."

"Not today. I'll just watch. Take your towel with you."

Alessio stood up and walked to the shallow end of the pool, where he sat on its edge, dangling his legs in the pool, deciding whether or not to get in.

"We need some art for the new tenant," Anna said, watching Alessio. "The Germans purchased all of the pictures you put in last time. They wanted all of them. I have money for you."

"That's good."

"You are very good, Eliana. Better than you know. You should charge more for your paintings. They didn't haggle over the cost. I think they would have paid *il doppio*."

"You know I don't paint for the money," she said. She rolled to her back. "I have some landscapes that will look nice in the apartment."

"He's *Americano*," Anna said.

"Who's *Americano?*"

"The new tenant."

"He didn't look American."

"*Sì*. He's *Americano.*" Her voice held a trace of

73

excitement. "And he's single."

Eliana grinned. Anna talked to her as if she were single rather than a married woman. Even more peculiar was that Eliana was Anna's *cognata*, her sister-in-law. Anna sat back in the chair, her eyes closed, the sun in her face. "He was *bello*, no?"

"I didn't notice."

"Trust me. He was *bello*."

Eliana let Anna's remark dissipate with the breeze that swept over them. Then she said, "I think Alessio's coming down with something."

"In the summer?"

"Penso di si." I think so.

"Where's Manuela? Isn't she supposed to be watching Alessio today?"

"She's still sick. She's had the influenza."

"She probably gave it to Alessio."

"I hope he doesn't have it." She looked over at her son. He still hadn't climbed into the water, which in itself she found peculiar. She looked back at Anna. "Are you still leaving for the sea Friday?"

"Yes. Are you still decided not to join me?"

"I'm sorry."

"Not as sorry as I am. It means I'll be alone with my boring cousin Claudia." She sighed. "Can I do anything for you before I go? I could shop for groceries for you."

"No, *grazie*. I have enough food for the week. When Manuela comes I will go shopping. Besides I need to get out of the house. I've been

74

looking forward to it."

"*Sì*, you need to get out more. I will watch Alessio this afternoon and you can go out. Go into Florence and buy yourself something pretty. I will give you the money from your paintings."

"No, Anna. You keep the money for your vacation. Besides, you have much to do before you leave. You have a new tenant coming."

Anna sighed. *"Vero, vero."* True. Anna would be gone on holiday for three weeks and she still hadn't finished packing. Now she also needed to see the apartment cleaned and purchase new linens for the bed.

"I will hang the paintings after Alessio naps," Eliana said. "Just leave the door unlocked."

"Grazie. When does *il cretino* return?"

"You shouldn't call him that. I don't know. He said tomorrow, but I doubt it."

Anna shook her head. *"Che cretino."*

The women seldom spoke of Maurizio. His neglect of his family and his numerous infidelities were too unpleasant a subject. Even though he was her brother, Maurizio was an embarrassment to Anna, and the two of them had argued on more occasions than Eliana could number. Now they spoke only as necessitated by the family business. Though Anna managed the villa, as the oldest son Maurizio ultimately controlled the estate.

Anna sided with Eliana not just because they were best friends, but because she understood, in part, what Eliana was going through. Anna's own husband had left her for a young Swiss woman she discovered he had been having an affair with for more than seven years. Eliana had been her support during the time of their divorce.

Anna sighed. *"Devo andare."* *I must go.* "I've still much to do." She pushed herself up from the chair.

"Anna, do not leave for the sea without saying goodbye."

"You know Idon't say goodbye." She smiled. "We'll take coffee tomorrow morning."

"Ciao, Anna."

Anna leaned over and kissed Eliana's cheeks. *"Ciao, bella."* Then she waved to Alessio.

"Ciao, bello."

"Ciao, Zia," he replied.

She walked to the end of the pool, stopped and picked a handful of sage leaves, then disappeared into the villa.

Eliana lay back and sifted through the mail. Mostly bills. One of the letters was postmarked USA. She immediately recognized the careful handwriting of her mother. She opened the letter.

Dear Ellen,

It's been a hot and dry summer. They're talking about drought again. Seems they always are. Maybe they shouldn't build cities in deserts.

Thank you for the pictures you sent of Alessio. I have them up on the refrigerator. He's getting so big. I showed them to Marge next door. Did I tell you her son has asthma too? Anyway, she mentioned what a handsome boy he is. He'll be a real heartbreaker, that's for sure. Handsome like his father. We just made it through another 24th of July Rodeo. Mark Jennings' boy, Jed, got thrown from a horse. He's okay, but he'll be in a cast for a while. Doctor says he broke his collarbone. They have the roundup for the little ones where they let loose the greased pig, then a bunch of chickens. (I don't know where they found the chickens this year, they looked pretty diseased to me.) Anyway I couldn't help but think of Alessio and wish he were out there with the others. I miss you both. Have you decided on whether or not you will be coming home for Christmas this year? Of course I understand if you can't come. Write soon. Someday I'll get Bert to show me how to send an email. They have those computers you can use down at the library. I know it costs a lot less and it's faster, but it just seems so impersonal. I like the feel of paper and ink. There's something honest about it. I know, I'm just old-fashioned. I hope you are well, sweetheart. I pray for you every night and morning.

Love,
Mom

Eliana set the letter down. It was like a broadcast from an alien planet. She missed her mother. Her mother hadn't seen Alessio since he was four years old, and Eliana knew it hurt her more than she would ever let on. Even though she often spoke to Alessio of his *Grandma in America* she wondered how much he actually remembered of her. The thought made her sad. These were years neither of them could reclaim.

Her mother had offered to fly to Italy, but Eliana wouldn't let her. Her mother's first airplane ride was at the age of fifty-seven, and even though it was a short flight of only an hour, it had terrified her so much that the flight attendants gave her a sedative. It took her nearly a week to calm down, and she took a bus back home. There was no way she could make a four-hour flight to New York followed by a ten-hour flight to Italy, at night, over the ocean.

Eliana looked over at Alessio still kicking his feet in the water without getting in. She walked over and sat down on the tile next to him, her slender, bare legs perpendicular to the edge of the pool. The sun refracted off the water in long, weblike streaks.

"Are you going to get in, little man?"

"I don't know."

"Why not?"

"I don't know."

"I could push you in," she teased.

Alessio turned to her with a grin. "I'll push you in."

She smiled. "I better not then." She rubbed

his head. "Hey, guess what? I got a letter from Grandma."

"Oh."

"She says she misses you. They just had the big Pioneer Days rodeo. Everyone in town was there. She said that she wished you were there too."

Alessio kicked at a leaf that floated near him on the water's surface.

"You know, the rodeo was always my favorite time of the year. Right up there with Christmas. We'd all dress up in our jeans and boots and cowboys hats. Some of the guys had belt buckles this big." She brought her hands together at her waist to form an oval only slightly exaggerated to the size of a football. "We'd play games and eat. We'd have barbecue beef sandwiches and apple pie and drink root beer until we were sick. Then after the sun would go down we'd all go to the arena for the rodeo. Maybe in a few years we'll be able to go back for the summer and do that. Does that sound like fun?"

Alessio nodded halfheartedly. His feet moved slowly in the water, barely turning a wake. After a moment he looked up at his mother. "Mom, what's a rodeo?"

CHAPTER 6

"There are places our spirits feel at ease,
no matter how austere, just as there are
places we cannot call home, no matter how
opulent. I have made a home in a
country villa named Rendola."
— Ross Story's diary

The next morning Ross led a Catholic choir group from Boston through the Uffizi. The group had just come up from Rome the night before and was still excited from their trip to the Vatican and their audience with the Pope.

After the tour, Ross reported to Francesca, then walked back across the Ponte Vecchio to his hotel. He had already checked out of his room, and his backpack, which had only grown slightly in weight since his arrival in Florence, and a small cardboard box waited on the floor next to the front counter.

He sat down on the steps of the hotel to read a copy of the paper while he waited for Luigi. When he arrived, they stowed Ross's things on the back seat of Luigi's car and drove off to Rendola.

On their way they stopped at the co-op in Bagno a Ripoli for groceries. Ross purchased six liters of bottled water and four plastic sacks full of food: two large rounds of hard-crusted Tuscan bread, a half kilo of prosciutto *cotto,* parmesan cheese, coffee, sugar, bread, spaghetti, crackers, penne, a bottle of Tabasco sauce, eggs, salt, Kellogg's Frosted Flakes cereal, six frozen margherita pizzas and two one-liter cartons of milk. At Luigi's suggestion he purchased three plug-in mosquito repellents. "You'll need them in the country," Luigi warned. "It is not America. They don't have screens on the windows."

They completed one more errand on the way, stopping briefly at the bus stop at the end of the long drive into the villa. Ross hopped out and checked the schedule, scribbling it into a small notepad.

Rendola's outer yard was vacant when they arrived. They crossed the courtyard and Luigi rang Anna's doorbell. She greeted them from an upper window.

"Buona sera, signori."

A moment later she emerged from her apartment carrying a large plastic envelope tucked under one arm and a bottle of red wine clutched in the other.

She led them to the apartment, unlocked the door and they went inside. They sat around the kitchen table while Anna spread the contracts out in front of them. After she had explained in meticulous detail the troubles of her morning, they signed the lease papers. Then she opened the wine, poured their glasses full and they consummated the deal with a toast.

Anna handed Ross a set of keys then walked

him and Luigi around the apartment, explaining how things worked and what to do if and when the power went out, which Ross could expect a couple times a month. She showed him how to check the radiator and bleed it of excess air when it wasn't working properly and how to restart the water heater. She gave him a *rubrica:* a phone book filled with the numbers of local restaurants and shops. They went outside, and Luigi recorded the gas levels on a meter built into the courtyard wall.

On their way driving up to the villa, Ross had noticed an older couple filling water bottles at a brass spigot at the end of the property. He asked Anna about it.

"Oh yes," she said. "It is good springwater. We all fill our bottles there. There is sign that says *'Non Potabile,'* but do not believe it. Half of Chianti would be dead if it were true. Someone put it there a couple years ago to keep outsiders away. It is better than the bottled water in stores. And it's free."

Ross thanked her and she left them. Then Luigi left as well, leaving Ross to settle into his new place. He hung his clothes, put his toiletries in the bathroom and then walked around the apartment. There were four new paintings that hadn't been there when he first came — two landscapes, one of the Chianti hills, the other of a field of sunflowers. There was one still life — a wooden platter with grapes and cheese — and one framed portrait of Saint Francis of Assisi, the patron saint of Italy. Ross had noticed the new artwork the moment he stepped foot in the apartment. Unlike the cheap reproductions passed off as art in most rentals, this art pleased him. For one they were originals. More important than that, they were good.

He examined the paintings in greater detail. He especially liked the painting of sunflowers. He heard a noise in the courtyard and pulled back the kitchen curtain. The boy he had seen by the pool was kicking a soccer ball against the inner wall. He looked around for the boy's mother, but the child was alone.

He went into his bedroom, stretched out across the bed and read.

Later that afternoon Anna came by with a housewarming gift: a bag of *biscotti,* a large bottle of olive oil and some spinach torte, hot from her oven. Though she had always wanted to learn English, for which she occasionally solicited Eliana's help, it was in the same spirit in which she wanted to lose weight, and neither had happened. Ross sensed that she was nervous to be alone with him. She spoke halting, monosyllabic English and was as relieved as she was surprised when Ross replied in Italian.

"But you speak Italian!" she exclaimed.

"Poco," he said, gesturing with his thumb and forefinger slightly apart.

"You speak better Italian than my last husband," she said, then added beneath her breath, *"Cretino."*

As she went to leave, she said, "I will be leaving tomorrow on *vacanza*. I am going to the sea. If you have an emergency, Eliana will know where to reach me."

"Eliana?"

She pointed to the green door on the opposite side of the courtyard. "She lives in the next apartment. She was the woman sitting by the pool yesterday. She was with her boy. Do you remember?"

"*Sì.*"

The villa had a satellite dish and Ross found CNN. He watched for a while, then surfed the channels until he found a soccer game. The Fiorentina were playing Juventus, their rival, and he watched the match until ten then went to bed early. He had an early tour in the morning, and as he had not yet mastered the bus system, he would have to leave at sunup.

He set his alarm clock for five-thirty, then undressed to his briefs. He opened the outer window and lay down on top of the bed.

The sounds of the country seeped into the room like the cool night air. The noises he had grown accustomed to, the horns and brakes of the city, were replaced by the alien warbling of frogs and the shrill songs of the crickets and cicadas.

For more than three years, he had wanted to be any place other than where he was. But mostly he had wanted to be here, in his own place — here, where he felt like a man. The realization that he had arrived filled him with joy.

His thoughts returned to the woman by the pool. Eliana, Anna had called her. Though he had only seen her for a few minutes, he could still see her clearly in his mind. He could see those eyes. Could she have really been that beautiful? He doubted it. It was more likely that his loneliness had painted her in the exaggerated strokes of a dream. Then again maybe she was a dream, along with every other good thing that had come to him this last week. If so, he welcomed her and hoped she stayed awhile.

As he began to drift off, there came from the open window a new sound. He opened his eyes and strained to hear. He wondered what animal could make such a noise. A wild boar, perhaps. Or was it a bird? He couldn't quite place it. It almost sounded like a woman crying.

CHAPTER 7

"La vita è breve e l'arte è lunga."
Art is long. Life is short.
— Italian Proverb

"Great art is a hymn that does not dissipate in the immediacy of time and space. I believe that there are greater sermons in the ceiling of the Sistine Chapel than in all the texts preached below it — that the brush of Michelangelo was far more articulate than the smooth tongues of the religious orators of his day, and, without a doubt, truer and far more lasting."
— Ross Story's diary

Ross woke in the same bed he had gone to sleep in, his alarm chirping a few feet from his head. *Dream or not, I'm still here,* he thought and smiled. He left his apartment before dawn, walking a quarter mile to the SITA bus stop.

He arrived in downtown Florence with more than an hour to spare, so he got off the bus at *Piazza Beccaria,* where he stopped at a *pasticcerìa* for a cappuccino and pastry before catching a compact inner-city bus. In spite of the early hour, the bus was already crowded. He moved to the back and grabbed a ceiling strap.

At the next stop a couple boarded who reminded Ross of a Duane Hanson piece he had once seen on display at an art gallery in Minnesota: *Tourists*. *They might as well wear a sign,* Ross thought, looking at the camera hanging from the man's neck. A bent tourist guidebook stuck out of the back pocket of his shorts. The woman wore a sleeveless shirt and pink-lens sunglasses, and a large bag hung over her arm.

The doors shut behind them and the couple hovered near the bus's stamp machine. When they spoke, Ross recognized the accent immediately. They were from Minnesota or Fargo, close to where Ross once called home.

"Judy, will ya just put the darn ticket in the machine?"

"What for?"

"It's what the man in the tobacco shop said to do. It stamps it or something."

"Which machine? There's two of them."

"How would I know?"

"What if I put it in the wrong one?"

"Try them both."

Ross didn't speak, but he pointed to the orange box mounted to the wall.

"Did you see that?" the woman said. "That man just pointed to the orange one. Grazee, signora."

"You just called him missus."

"I can't ever remember which one it is. He's a good-looking Italian man. Grazee, signori," she said, speaking loudly, with a large, deliberate stretch of her lips. "Th-ank y-ou."

She looked so comical Ross tightened his

mouth so as not to laugh. *"Prego, signora."*

"That means *you're welcome*," her husband said.

Just then a young man slid past Ross. Ross had noticed him as he boarded the bus and watched him as he moved closer to the couple, who were all but oblivious to what was happening around them. At a corner all the passengers leaned with the bus and the young man brushed against the tourists, easily lifting the man's wallet from his back pocket. Ross was waiting for it and caught the thief's wrist, lifting it with the black leather wallet he held. *"Ha trovato qualcosa?"* *Find something?*

Fear flashed across the thief's face. The woman screamed, "Martin, that man has your wallet!"

The tourist spun around. "Hey!"

The pickpocket, his wrist still in Ross's grasp, dropped the wallet. As the bus slowed for the next stop, the thief yanked his hand from Ross and jumped off the bus, knocking an elderly woman over as he did so. He quickly disappeared down a side street.

The man stooped down and picked up his wallet. "That was close," he said to Ross. "Thank you."

"Give him a reward, Martin," the woman said.

He fished a couple of ten-thousand-lire bills from his wallet and offered them to Ross.

Ross waved them off. *"No, grazie."*

"I insist."

"Say, insist-a. Just add an 'a' to it, sometimes they understand that."

Ross just waved. *"Veramente, no."*

"I don't think he wants it," Martin said to his wife. He turned to Ross. "Well, I sure as heck appreciate it," he said, shoving the thick wallet into the same back pocket it had just been lifted from. "Grand-ay gra-zee."

"Prego," Ross said again. They stood in silence as the bus jogged along, until a few minutes later, when the woman pointed ahead. "There's the big dome up ahead. I think the next one's our stop."

A moment later the couple stepped from the bus, and turned back before the doors closed. "Grazee, again."

Ross smiled. "There are a lot of pickpockets in Florence, sir. It's best to leave a wallet that big in your hotel."

The couple just stared at him in wonder as the door closed.

At the next stop Ross stepped off the bus and walked a half block to the Uffizi.

Even before he entered the gallery's courtyard he could feel his mood begin to change.

The Uffizi was more than a gallery to Ross, it was a temple, and standing before its art was a religious experience.

During his darkest hours, when faith deserted him, art had been his closest link to divinity and it still sustained him. He felt his work a calling in the same way some feel a calling to preach the

89

Word. That is what he was, he decided — a preacher, expounding the divinity of art. Though more times than not his pearls were cast before swine, before those too jet-lagged and culture-shocked to hear, but sometimes his sermons fell on willing ears, and he saw the light come into their eyes, and sometimes tears, and that was when he was happiest.

By nine o'clock Ross had completed his first tour of the day. His second group canceled. Their tour bus had broken down in Siena, and Ross had waited in the courtyard for nearly an hour before Francesca found him and gave him the news. He took coffee at a bar in Piazza della Signoria then went out to the city to purchase a scooter.

His first week in Italy he had decided that riding a scooter on the Italian roads was akin to a death wish, but he had since repented of the thought. A scooter was the only practical way around Florence. After a little while he found one he liked, a Piaggio Vespa, black and yellow like a wasp. He bought a helmet and lock and drove out of the dealership feeling more like a native. He drove to the northeast perimeter of Florence, upward to the hills of San Domenico and Fiesole. He stayed awhile in Fiesole, toured the Etruscan amphitheater and tombs. The town square, Piazza Mino, was as beautiful as he had been told it was, but there were too many tourists, so he drove back down from the hills, across the Arno toward Rendola.

Earlier that morning, while Ross commuted to work, Eliana had taken coffee with Anna. The sky was a brilliant blue, and Eliana had opened an upstairs window near the parlor overlooking the courtyard.

Anna spooned her third teaspoon of sugar into her coffee.

"The American moved in yesterday."

"I saw him."

"He leaves for work early. He left at six this morning."

"Are you spying on him?"

"Every chance I get. He's very *bello*. And he speaks *un buon Italiano*."

"Really?"

"He speaks better Italian than my ex. I told him so."

"Gorbachev speaks better Italian than your ex. I could never understand his accent."

"Maybe you should go welcome him to the villa."

Eliana looked up over her cup at Anna. "By welcome him do you really mean seduce him?"

"*Certo.*"

Eliana laughed. "I'm married, Anna. For worse maybe, but until death do us part."

"We could only be so fortunate."

Eliana ignored the comment. "Why don't you make a go of it? You definitely could use a man."

"Perhaps when I return. I may not have my

looks anymore, but I'm definitely available. Isn't that half the battle?"

Eliana smiled, looked at Anna's cup. "More coffee?"

"Just half a cup, *per favore.*"

Eliana took the cup to the counter and poured the coffee. "What's his name?"

"Ross," she said, though the way she said it sounded more like Roz.

"Is he here for work?"

"I don't know. I didn't ask. He wired his rent from Switzerland."

Eliana finished her coffee, looking out over the courtyard at Ross's apartment door.

"Is Alessio still asleep?"

"Penso di si." I think so.

"It's a shame. I wanted to say goodbye."

"I'd wake him but he needs to sleep. I'm pretty sure he's sick. His cheeks are flushed."

"You'll say goodbye for me?"

"*Certo.* He'll be sorry he missed you. You won't be back until September?"

"If I can stand being with Claudia for that long."

Eliana smiled. "If she's such miserable company, why do you go on holiday with her?"

Anna raised her hands. "Who else is there? You won't come with me."

"Maybe if Maurizio was around."

"If Maurizio was around, I would not invite you." She glanced over Eliana's shoulder at the wall clock. "Is that the correct time?"

"*Sì.*"

92

"Claudia will be crazed if I'm late. I better go." She downed her coffee, then the women walked to Anna's apartment. Eliana helped her carry the last of her luggage out to her car and they kissed farewell.

"Goodbye," Eliana said.

"I don't say goodbye," Anna replied. "I'll see you soon."

Eliana leaned against the villa wall as she watched Anna drive off, her small red car disappearing at the end of the drive in a haze of dust. *The world is flat,* she thought. *It drops off just a few kilometers from the grounds of Rendola.* Maybe she should have gone to the sea. She already felt lonely.

She looked out over the valley. The olive trees bristled from a summer breeze, dusty and blanched as the soil beneath them. As she crossed the courtyard, she glanced over at Ross's door. Even though Anna had said he was gone, a part of her wished he would walk out at that moment. She wanted to meet him. And though she hadn't admitted to noticing, what Anna had said was true. He was *bello.* From her window she had watched him move into his apartment with little more than a backpack — as free as the foreigners she often passed on the Chianti roads backpacking through Tuscany. There was something about his appearance that intrigued her. He had a rugged, yet boyish look.

She buried the thought. She was starting to think like Anna. She didn't want to notice. She was married. *Married but not dead,* Anna would have countered. Sometimes she felt even that was debatable.

Still, for the next three weeks, he was her only neighbor. Was she to pretend he didn't exist? Maybe she would make him a housewarming offering as Anna had suggested. It would be the right thing to do. It would be worth it just for the conversation in English.

With the exception of her brief encounters with the American tourists who came to the wine tasting parties in the nearby *frazione* of Greve, it had been a while since she had spoken with an American.

She went into her apartment and up to Alessio's room. She quietly opened his door. Alessio was awake but still lying quietly in his bed.

"How are you feeling, munchkin?"

"Mommy, my head hurts. It feels like somebody sat on it."

She smiled. "I don't think anyone did. But let me feel it." She lay her cheek against his forehead, and as she had suspected, it was warm. And he was congested. This worried her more than the fever. The last time he had had a cold, he had suffered a serious asthma attack. She kissed his forehead. "You have a fever, little man. I'm going to get you a little medicine."

"No."

"It's okay, it's the grape chewy kind you like.

And also a little something for your cough that tastes like cherry."

"Okay."

"Would you like a gelato to go with it?"

"*Sì.*"

"Chocolate or *limone?*"

"Chocolate."

She kissed his forehead. "I'll be right back."

A few minutes later Eliana returned with her hands full of health care: a damp washcloth, cough medicine, a plastic Mickey Mouse bowl filled with gelato and a couple children's Tylenol. She gave him the medicine, then folded the washcloth and laid it across his forehead.

"Want me to read a book to you?"

"I want to play Nintendo."

"Later. Books are better." She went to a cabinet and brought out a stack of books. The first was one of his favorites: *Prosciutto e Uova Verdi. Green Eggs and Ham.* A thought crossed her mind. If someone had told her that someday she'd be reading Dr. Seuss to her child in Italian, she'd have thought them *pazzo.* She read several other books as well, in both English and Italian — it didn't matter to Alessio — including his absolute favorite, an Italian pop-up book she had bought him for Halloween: *Paura ed Orrore in via del Terrore. Fear and Horror on Terror Road.*

Alessio ate his gelato as she read. She paused once as he had a coughing fit and she set down the book to hold him. Alessio often coughed, as is common with asthma, but it was never without Eliana's concern. She set up a small nest of sofa cushions and blankets in her painting studio then wheeled the television into the room, so she could keep an eye on him as she painted. She could not risk leaving his side.

There was a new blank space on the wall in her studio. She had taken her favorite landscape to the new apartment — *I Girasole di Arezzo*, she called it. It was a picture of sunflowers she had painted last summer just outside the Tuscan township of Arezzo. She already missed it. She wondered why she had given that one to the new tenant.

Why does a man come alone to live in Italy? she wondered. She had lived in Italy long enough, had met enough expatriates, to know that whether anyone knows it or not, no one lands in Italy by accident. And if you listen to their excuses long enough and care enough to ask questions, you will eventually discover the real reason they are there, and it usually turns out to be only a shadow of the reason first proffered.

She thought of her own reason for being there and of the man who had brought her. Where was Maurizio now? Where would he be tonight? Or with whom? A darkness rose up in her thoughts. If she didn't love him, why did his philandering still make her crazy with jealousy? Was jealousy a sign of love? She wasn't sure, but if so, maybe there was hope for her marriage yet, as Maurizio was wildly jealous of her. *As jealous as a Sicilian,* Anna had said.

During their second year in Italy, as they prepared to rent out part of the villa, they had had some electrical work done. One of the electricians, a young, handsome apprentice maybe three years younger than Eliana, had paid more attention to Eliana than Maurizio thought necessary. Maurizio threatened him so fiercely that the young man dared not even look at her, would not speak to her again — not even to request payment.

But if Maurizio loved her, how could he cheat on her? What part of his love for her allowed him to rendezvous with a different woman in every city? Or was it a different woman? She honestly didn't know if he had just one mistress or many. If she had to choose, it would be many. Dozens. Hundreds. That way they could remain faceless. That way it wouldn't be about how she compared to another woman. It would be more about him. But his dalliances were not the only hardship in their relationship. She was equally jealous of his most demanding mistress — his work. *I do it for you,* he said, *You and Alessio.* But that is not what she or Alessio needed. What they needed most was his attention and companionship.

The reality was that Maurizio would live his life this way whether she and Alessio existed or not. Even when he was home, which was less than one week out of the month, his distance had become increasingly obvious.

He rarely left the house while he was in town,

as he was always too tired for going out to dinner or to the cinema. *I eat out every night,* he said. *I'm tired of eating out. I want your cooking.* He intended it as a compliment and never understood why it didn't please her.

Four years earlier, fearful of the rut their relationship was falling into, she began looking for something that they might do together. She had loved to dance, once. So had he. They had met dancing. So she spent a week looking into dance classes. She found an adult class taught weekly at the community center in Grassina. She arranged with Manuela to watch Alessio one night a week, and she put a small deposit down to hold their place.

When she told Maurizio what she had done, he laughed out loud. Only after he saw how angry it had made her did he take her seriously. He told her to go without him. *Take Anna; she needs something to do. Surely there are other women you could dance with.*

She forfeited the deposit.

When they were together, there was little more than polite conversation. No discussions about life or death or God or health or schooling or cooking. No more discussions of art, hers or others. Nothing of beauty was ever talked about. No theology, or poetry, or philosophy. At this point she'd welcome a travelogue, but he no longer even spoke of business, where he'd been or what he'd seen. For the most part their talk had become pragmatic.

But perhaps most painful of all was that Maurizio seemed to have lost interest in her physically. He had once raved over her beauty. *Tesoro mio,* he called her when they first dated. *My treasure.* Now he did not even seem to notice her. She had no doubt that she could dress in her sexiest lingerie and parade in front of the television set during a soccer match and he would only ask her to move. She wondered if her looks had changed that much in the last six years, or if she only failed by comparison to other women younger and without blemish. Women with firmer breasts untouched by babies, with hips unbroadened and skin unstretched by childbirth.

This rejection hurt less when he was gone, and as lonesome as she was, she would take the loneliness to his rejection — a dull ache compared to a sharp sting. She could handle ache. Handling ache was simply a matter of distraction, and there was always something else to occupy her mind.

Alessio fell asleep in front of the television set. His fever had not yet broken, but his breathing seemed calm. She put away her paints and, without waking him, brought him out to the living room sofa so she could watch him while she cleaned.

Eliana kept an immaculate house. It was one part of her life where she felt in control, and as a result she had become compulsive about it. Afterward she pulled the clothes from the washer and carried them outside to hang on the line, thinking for the millionth time how much she wished she had a dryer.

Then she went into the kitchen and made two trays of chocolate chip cookies, one for them and one for their new neighbor.

As the cookies baked, she called Manuela, her nanny, on the telephone to see how she was doing. Her husband answered the phone.

"*Ciao,* Vittorio. How is Manuela?"

"She's still in bed."

"Is she feeling any better than she was yesterday?"

"No, I don't think so. She is still very sick."

"I'm sorry. Please give her my best." She hung up the phone. *It's going to be a long weekend,* she thought.

A half hour later she heard the whine of a scooter outside the courtyard walls. She went to the window and slightly parted the sheer, embroidered curtain. She saw the front gate open and Ross cross the courtyard, removing his helmet as he walked. He must have bought a *motorino,* she thought. Ross unlocked his door and disappeared inside. She looked at the plate of cookies and suddenly felt apprehensive. Why would he want to talk to her? Maybe she'd wait until Alessio was feeling better and have him take the cookies over.

Around eight, Maurizio called. His voice, typically low and calm, was difficult to hear beneath the sound of the restaurant.

"*Amore,* how's your day?"

"It's okay. Alessio is sick."

"Is he okay?"

"Yes. Where are you?"

"I'm still in Genoa. *Ascolta,* I'm not going to be home tomorrow. I need to go back to Milano. One of my clients had a problem with an order. Seems half the shipment was corked."

"Can it wait? I really need your help. Manuela's still sick. I don't have anyone to watch Alessio so I can go out."

"Why do you need to go out?"

Seven years ago the question would have astonished her. "To buy groceries, for one thing."

"Have Anna watch him for you."

"Anna left on holiday."

"Oh, that is a problem." There was a long pause. "Well, what can I do, Eliana? I need to see the client. You have food in the house."

Eliana sighed. She had no fight left in her. "When will you be home?"

"Next Wednesday. I am certain."

She ran her hand back through her hair. "All right. I'll see you then."

She hung up the phone. Then she pounded the wall with the heel of her palm. "Damn, damn, damn, damn."

When she went back to Alessio, he was still asleep. She carried him up to his bed, pulled the

101

blanket up to his chin, kissed his forehead, then walked out of the room. She went to the bathroom and turned on the water in the tub. She took off her clothes, looking at herself in the mirror as she did so. She had not put on any makeup or done her hair that day. She was barely thirty and she already looked worn-out, she thought. She felt like she had been run over by life. *No wonder Maurizio doesn't find me attractive,* she thought. Compared to the fresh young girls he met at business lunches, why would he? How could she compete with them? But why should she have to? Was she still pretty?

She had been, hadn't she? She had been the first runner up in the Miss Vernal Pioneer Days beauty pageant. The thought made her grin. Even then she had hated the idea of the thing: women being judged like cattle (in fact they were paraded before the judges on the same reinforced plywood stage the cattle were brought up on an hour later; same judges too). But at the time it was what all girls did. She didn't know which was more pathetic: that she had participated in the pageant or that she now looked to it for validation.

She took a sip of her tea, then set the cup to the side of the tub and stepped into the water. It was too hot, but bearable. She turned off the faucet then let herself slowly slip into the porcelain tub until it covered all of her body up to her neck. Then she bent her knees and slid deeper into the water until it was on her chin. She closed her eyes and let the water soothe her. She just wanted to dissolve into the hot water, like sugar. Into something else. Something that didn't hurt or tire or bruise. *Another day in paradise,* she thought. And then, a few minutes later, as her thoughts began to calm, she heard Alessio's cry.

CHAPTER 8

"Amore la spinge e tira, non per elezion
ma per destino."
Love drives on not by choice but by destiny.
— Italian Proverb

Ross had only taken three bites of his dinner when there was forceful pounding on his front door. He got up from his dinner and opened the door to find Eliana standing there. Her hair was stringy and wet and she was wearing a light jacket over a nightshirt. Her face was bent with desperation.

"Can you help me? I need to get my son to the hospital." She sounded panicked.

"I only have a scooter."

"My car's already out front. My son's inside."

Ross followed her out. A forest green BMW was idling outside the villa's walls, its headlamps illuminated. She slid into the back of the car, lifting Alessio's head onto her lap. Ross climbed into the driver's seat and quickly oriented himself to the controls.

"Hurry, please. He can't breathe."

Ross grabbed the gearshift then looked back over his shoulder to turn the car around and saw the little boy. He reminded Ross of a fish fallen out of its tank. The wheezing of his strained lungs was harrowing.

"Breathe, Alessio. Come on, son. Breathe

easy, not too fast." She took an inhaler from a small plastic sack. "You'll be okay," she said as she inserted the device into his mouth. "This will help. This will help."

Ross spun the car around. He pulled out a little too quickly, and the back wheels spewed gravel as the car lurched forward, bouncing over the rough drive.

Ross said, "I'm sorry, I don't know the way to the hospital."

Her voice was controlled. "Turn right up ahead. Follow the road to Grassina. You know where Grassina is?"

"Yes."

"You'll take the first right turn at the round-about. Please drive fast."

Ross pressed further on the accelerator as she turned her attention back to her son. The cabin light was on and she could see that his lips were beginning to turn blue. She was losing him and she knew it. She was staring into her son's eyes. "Come on, Alessio. Stay with me."

Ross slowed where the dirt road met the asphalt of the main drive, then he pulled up onto the road. On the narrow but deserted country roads, he pushed the speedometer past a hundred kilometers per hour. Ross converted it in his mind: sixty-two miles per hour and change. Eliana was suddenly quiet, and on a straightaway he stole a glance in the mirror. Her eyes were closed. *She's praying,* he thought.

They passed through two townships, where he

slowed only slightly for the vacant intersections, then ran the red lights. At the Grassina round-about he veered right and came around a slight bend. The hospital, a great, gray concrete structure, suddenly loomed ahead. A road sign read, *"Ospedale Santa Maria." Saint Mary's Hospital.*

"The emergency room is up front. The first turnoff." She pointed. "Right there." Her voice was now trembling.

He raced the car up to where an orange and white ambulance was idling, then he screeched to a stop. Eliana flung her door open and began lifting her son out. Ross ran around the car, taking the child in his own arms. "I've got him. Just show me where to go."

Eliana ran to the emergency doors with Ross after her. She yelled to the women in the lobby, *"Mio figlio ha un attacco d'asma, non respira."*

A nurse came running out and waved them forward. Just then Alessio went limp.

"He's passed out," Ross shouted. *"E svenuto!"*

A doctor wearing hospital greens appeared at Ross's side. He asked Ross in Italian, "Are you his father?"

"No."

"I'm his mother," Eliana said.

"How have you been treating him?"

"I've given him two doses of albuterol in the last fifteen minutes."

"Get him into ICU. Nurse, get me an oxygen mask and a nebulizer. I need an IV of SoluMedrol. Get an oximeter on him, *subito.*"

A nurse placed an oxygen mask over Alessio's face as they wheeled him into the ICU. Only Ross waited behind, standing outside the door as they all went inside. He stood for a moment wondering what to do before he walked out to the car and moved it from the emergency lane, parking it across the street in a lot. Then he came back in to wait for news.

CHAPTER 9

"Il linguaggio dell'amore e negli occhi."
The language of love is in the eyes.
— Italian Proverb

Ross checked his watch. It was nearly a quarter of one. He sat alone on the vinyl sofa in the front lobby. He had been up since four-thirty and was fighting sleep. He had been at the hospital for nearly two hours and still hadn't received word on the boy's condition. It must mean good news, he thought. Hoped.

He had already read every magazine that held any interest for him, and now the lobby was deserted except for a gaunt, weary-looking man in custodial coveralls who dragged a mop across the marble floor. Ross would give it another hour, then he'd find someone with whom to leave her keys. He closed his eyes and lay back on the sofa.

Forty-five minutes later Eliana walked out of the ICU. She found Ross lying on the couch, his eyes closed. He was lightly snoring. She stood by him for a moment hoping he would wake at her presence. When he didn't, she crouched down next to him. She realized that she had never really seen him up close. Even earlier that evening, standing in the doorway, she had not really seen him, as she had been too worried about Alessio.

His skin was clear but not without flaws and

108

his face was rough with the shadow of beard growth. His hair, slightly curled, fell over his forehead. He had well-formed lips, full for a man, she thought, yet still masculine. *Bello.*

She reached over and gently touched his arm. His eyes fluttered open. It took him a moment to remember where he was.

"Hi," she said softly.

Ross rubbed a hand across his face then sat up. "Hi. How is he?"

"He's fine. He's sleeping now."

"That's good," Ross said, his voice hoarse.

"I'm sorry to leave you out here."

"I have your keys." He sat forward in the chair then extended his hand, smiling slightly. "I'm Ross."

She smiled back as she took his hand. "This is a rather odd introduction. I'm Eliana."

"Eliana. It's a pleasure. Here, sit down." Ross slid over on the sofa. Then he yawned again.

"I was up pretty early."

"I'm so sorry. Thank you for helping me."

"You're welcome. What happened?"

"My son has asthma. He's been congested the last few days and it triggered a severe attack. Usually the inhalers work, but tonight . . ."

She couldn't speak and Ross saw that she was completely exhausted. "Are you okay?"

"I'm fine." Then tears began to well up in her eyes. Ross put one arm around her. "It's okay. It's your son."

She lay her head against his shoulder and

began to cry. Now that the emergency was over, all of her fear released and bubbled forth and she sobbed for several minutes. Ross put his other arm around her, pulling her into himself. When she could finally speak, she said, "It was just so close this time."

"It was," Ross said softly. "But he's okay now. He's okay."

It was a few more minutes before she regained her composure and wiped her eyes with her hands. Ross grabbed a Kleenex from a nearby dispenser and handed it to her.

"Thank you." She dabbed her eyes. "I'm sorry, I don't even know you."

Ross smiled at her and she thought he had a gentle smile. "It's okay, we're neighbors. We *Americani* need to stick together."

"Thank you."

"You know, I thought you were Italian."

"Most people do. My husband is. I'm American. We've lived here for six years."

Something inside of Ross stiffened at the word *husband.* Up to this point he hadn't really known if she was married. There had been no sign of another man. Even the landlady had only spoken of the woman and child. *Of course she is,* he thought, and he didn't know why it should even matter to him.

She wiped her eyes again, then folded the Kleenex. "I need to stay here with Alessio tonight. If you'd like to take the car back, we'll take a taxi home."

"No, I'll take a cab. There's a stand out front."

"It might be hard finding a taxi this time of night. Or morning. What time is it?"

Ross looked down at his watch. "It's almost two. But I have my cell phone; I can call a taxi. Besides I'd probably just get lost on the way back anyway."

She looked at him gratefully. "Can I at least give you some cab money?"

"No."

She sighed. "You're a real saint. Thank you."

"I'm no saint. But you're welcome all the same." He put his hand in his pocket and brought out the keys. "You'll need these. Your car's parked in the lot across the street, near the bus stop on the end of the row, you can't miss it."

She took the keys from him, touching his hand as she did, and for a moment she looked at him, as if she wanted, or needed, to say something, but realized that she just didn't want him to go. She brushed the hair back from her face.

"I better get back to my son."

"You have a place to sleep here?" Ross asked.

"They brought in a cot." Her eyebrows lowered in concern. "You're sure you'll be all right?"

He smiled. "It's no problem. I'll see you back at the ranch."

"Okay. *Ciao, ciao.* Good night, Ross." She turned and walked back to the ICU. Ross watched her disappear behind the emergency room doors then went out to find a cab.

111

CHAPTER 10

"L'amore e un erba spontanea,
non una pianta da giardino."
Love is a spontaneous grass,
not a plant cultivated in the garden.

— Nievo

There were no tours for Ross the next day, which, in light of the night's events, he was glad for. He slept in until ten then drove to the Uffizi. Francesca was leading a tour, and he accompanied her from the room of the Flemish Renaissance painters to the second corridor, then wandered off alone.

His thoughts were on the previous night and his meeting of Eliana. A voice had been added to the woman he had admired from afar. In the throes of crisis we see either the best or the worst in each other, and he liked what he'd seen. There was something honest about her personality that made her even more beautiful to him.

It was late afternoon when he returned to Rendola. When he got home, Eliana's BMW was parked next to the shed. He was surprised that she was back from the hospital so soon. He thought to check on her but then decided she probably had her hands full without him, so he instead went into his apartment, dropped his helmet on the ground near the door and exchanged his slacks and sport shirt for gym shorts and a loose-fitting tank top.

He did push-ups until he couldn't do any more, seventy-seven straight, then he went out to jog. It was a warm evening and he completed his run in a little under an hour, past rolling hills of orchards and vineyards and dense forests.

When he got home, he turned on the shower and had just taken off his clothes when there was a light knock on his front door. He put on his robe, tied the sash around his waist, then went out front. Eliana stood in the corridor holding a plate wrapped in foil. She glanced down at his robe. *"Buona sera."*

"Buona sera. You came home sooner than I thought you would."

"The hospital discharged us around noon."

"Everything's okay?"

"Yes, thank you. Alessio just needs to take it easy for the next week."

"Would you like to come in?"

"Thank you, but I better not. I need to listen for Alessio." Ross saw that her door was wide open. "Did I get you out of the shower?"

"Almost. You knocked just in time."

"I came over a little earlier but you weren't home."

"I was out running."

She lifted her offering. "Well, Alessio and I made you some chocolate chip cookies." She handed the plate to him. "I'm sorry they're not still warm. We made them yesterday before everything got crazy."

Ross lifted a corner of the foil. "Real chocolate chip cookies?"

"It's hard to find chocolate chips here so I cut up chocolate bars. We wanted to welcome you to Rendola."

"Thank you. Are you sure you won't come in and have a coffee or a glass of wine?"

This time she hesitated. "I better not. I just want you to know how much I appreciate what you did for us last night." Her expression turned serious. "It's a good thing for us that you were here. You saved my son's life."

Ross felt uncomfortable accepting such praise. "No, you and the doctors saved his life. But I'm glad I was able to help. If you ever need me again, just holler. Any time. I know the route now. I'm betting I could shave another minute off my time."

She smiled. "You drove like a crazy man. How many red lights did you run?"

"Only four. But in Italy they don't count after midnight."

Eliana laughed. "No, they don't." The moment turned into a pleasant silence for both of them. She twisted a strand of her hair.

"We'd like to do something to thank you. Alessio and I were wondering if you would have dinner with us tomorrow night. I know it's short notice, so I'll understand if you have other plans."

"No plans. Just frozen pizza. It can wait."

She smiled. "Then how about seven?"

"Seven will be great."

"Well then, Alessio and I will be looking forward to it. Good night."

"Good night, Eliana."

As she walked back to her apartment, a smile bent her lips. She liked the way he said her name. Or maybe she just liked that he knew it.

CHAPTER 11

"Chiusa fiamma e piu ardente e se pur cresce."
A silent passion increases more ardently.
— Italian Proverb

The next day was Ross's busiest yet at the Uffizi. He led four large tours — three groups from the UK and one American. Between his tours, and sometimes during them, he thought about Eliana. On the way home from the Uffizi, he drove his scooter past the villa to the nearby hamlet of Impruneta, where he stopped at a restaurant and purchased a bottle of red wine, then, realizing that he didn't know the night's menu, returned and bought a bottle of white as well. He went home, took a quick shower and put on fresh clothes as the Tuscan heat tended to wilt everything before sunset. Even though he usually didn't give his attire more than a few moments' thought, tonight he had trouble deciding what to wear. He finally selected a black shirt and jeans. *You can't ever go wrong with black,* the woman who sold him the shirt had told him. *Black is confident. Black is slimming,* she said like a daily affirmation, then added, *Not that you need it.*

He knocked on Eliana's door at the top of the hour. As she opened the door, his first thought was how remarkably different she looked than she had the night before. She was wearing light

116

makeup and her hair was styled, carefully pulled back to accent the curvature of her face. She wore a satin blouse buttoned only halfway up like the young Italian women did and a dark skirt. For a woman naturally beautiful, she was stunning with a little work.

"You look nice."

"Thank you." She had been thinking the same about him but the words wouldn't come. "I must have been a fright the other evening."

"No, you weren't. You looked pretty then, too."

It had been a while since anyone other than strangers had told her that, and she blushed. "You brought wine."

Ross glanced down at the bottles. "*Sì*. I didn't know what you were planning, so I brought red and white."

"You're very thoughtful. Here, come in."

Ross stepped inside. The house smelled of sage, oregano, basil and other enticing odors, rich and sweet, that he could not identify.

"It smells *buono*," he said.

"It's not frozen pizza, but you might find something you like," she said. "I'm sorry I'm running a little behind."

"You're right on time for Italy."

"*Vero.*" *True.* "I'm making spaghetti carbonara, and it's best if you wait to finish it just when you're ready to eat. I'll only be a minute. Look around the house, if you like."

"Thank you."

As she walked back to the kitchen, Ross surveyed the apartment. It was many times larger than his own and far more luxurious. The foyer opened to a large *sala* with a vaulted ceiling, a massive, stone-lined fireplace and an ivory-colored piano in the far corner. There were four windows, tall and arched, and they were covered with exquisite drapery, the outer layers in thick velvet fabric with burgundy and golden fringe, the inner curtains of sheer silk, glowing amber with the setting sun.

With the exception of a Murano glass chandelier in the center of the room, all lighting was indirect, behind brass sconces that feathered the walls from mustard-gold to deep umber in the shadows. The home was immaculately kept and expensively decorated with antique furniture, both Italian and foreign. Some of it looked as if it had originally belonged to the home.

Most impressive to Ross was the amount of art that filled the house. There were paintings or intricate wall tapestries mounted on every wall: landscapes, portraits and still lifes.

A stereo in the main hallway softly played Mozart. After a while he walked into the kitchen. A pot of pasta was boiling on the stove, the steam rising into the black collector above it. On the back burner a smaller pot simmered with a dark, pungent sauce. Eliana was standing at a wooden cutting board, dicing pancetta with a large cleaver. When she finished chopping the meat, she walked to the stove, lifted the boiling pot of spaghetti and poured it into a stainless steel colander in the sink, tilting her head to one side to avoid the rising cloud of steam. Then she poured the spaghetti back into the pot with a chunk of unsalted butter.

He looked around the kitchen. It was a blend of old style decor complemented by modern accessories. Then he noticed, on an oiled wood beam above a shelf of copper pots, a neat row of empty wine bottles. He looked carefully at the labels. They were all identical, though labeled with different years. L'incanto. The same wine he had brought for their dinner.

"Is that the wine you make?"

She bit her lower lip. She had hoped he wouldn't notice. "Yes."

"I brought you your own wine."

She smiled. "Yes. But that's very flattering."

"It's what the shop recommended," he said. He put his hands in his pockets, looking slightly embarrassed. "Where's your son?"

"He's watching television upstairs. His name is Alessio."

"How is he?"

"He finally seems to be over his sickness, thank goodness." She reached over and put a frying pan on the stove. "A cold takes on a whole new meaning with asthma."

"How long has he had asthma?"

"His whole life, probably. But our first real episode was when he was two." She slid the pancetta across the cutting board with her knife, pushing the meat into the pan. It started to sizzle and the smell of the meat added to the room's bouquet. She let it fry until it was browned on both sides.

"You don't have to wait in here. There's a soccer game on tonight. The television is in the room next to the dining room."

"If it's the same to you, I'd rather just hang out. If you don't mind me in your kitchen, that is."

She smiled. *Right answer,* she thought. "Of course not. Want to help?"

"*Certo.* What would you like me to do?"

"To start you can hand me the eggs. They're behind me, on the counter."

Ross found a small, woven straw basket with brown eggs in it. "Do you need them opened or scrambled or something?"

She smiled at *opened.* He really was a bachelor. "I need three of them mixed in that glass bowl. Just use that fork there."

Ross cracked all of the eggs.

"What should I do with the shell that I didn't get in with the yolk?"

Eliana laughed. "The garbage is under the sink."

He discarded the shells then came back and picked the rest out of the bowl. "Sorry. I'm an amateur."

"If you want, I'll teach you how to make carbonara."

"I'd like that."

She lifted the pan, poured the pancetta into the saucepan and stirred it around. "I hope you're not watching your fat intake. It tastes better with some of the grease." She handed him a small cup with clear yellow liquid. "Here, you pour this in while I stir."

"What am I adding?"

"Chicken broth."

He moved next to her, lightly pressing against her. She could feel the warmth of his body beneath his shirt and she didn't move back. She liked the feel of him close to her. He slowly poured the broth in then tapped the cup against the rim of the pan. Eliana began stirring again. "We'll let this heat up a little and then we add the egg and parmesan." She looked up at him while she stirred. "This is really easy to make. Do you cook much?"

"No. I'm still in the spaghetti-with-store-bought-sauce phase."

"I've been there." She looked up at him. She adjusted the heat on the stove. "Did you wonder why I didn't just call an ambulance the other night?"

"It crossed my mind."

"A year ago Alessio had a major attack. We almost lost him while we waited for the ambulance. Rendola is hard to find."

"My real estate agent and I got lost the first time we came."

She nodded. "When I moved here from the States, the FedEx and DHL people were always calling for directions."

"I've been meaning to ask you, does Rendola mean something? It's not in my Italian dictionary."

"For most Italians it's just a name. Rendola actually comes from Latin. It means where God meets the earth. That's how Maurizio explained it to me when I first came."

"It matches the villa. It's a beautiful place."

She smiled. "I love Toscana, but especially Chianti."

Ross took a step back and looked toward the kitchen door. "It must be difficult for you, never knowing when your son might have an attack."

"It's just the hand we were dealt, I guess. God doesn't give us anything we can't handle."

"You believe that?"

"Yes. You don't?"

He shook his head slowly. "No, I don't. But I don't think God's doing all the giving either." Ross looked toward the kitchen door. "He's a brave little boy, isn't he?"

She looked up. "Yes, he is. He's a great little boy." She set her spoon to the side of the range then went to the refrigerator and brought out a package of buffalo mozzarella and a bowl of tomatoes.

"I'm making Caprese salad. I hope you like tomatoes."

"I do. Here, I'll help."

Ross took a knife and began slicing tomatoes while she opened the package of mozzarella over the sink, letting the white milk drain from it.

"Does buffalo mozzarella really come from buffaloes?" Ross asked.

"That's what they say."

"Have you ever seen a buffalo in Italy?"

"No. But I've never seen one in the U.S. either."

"I'd like to see someone milk a buffalo."

Eliana laughed, then took a knife from a drawer. "Here, the blade on that one's dull. Use this one."

"Thank you."

"Prego."

Ross cut the last of the tomatoes, leaving them on the cutting board. "Anything else?"

"No, I'm just about done."

Ross went to the sink and washed his hands. "You have a really nice place here."

"Thank you."

"I approve of your choice of art. Especially the oil paintings. I have some by the same artist in my place. She's really gifted."

Eliana hid her pleasure at his comment. "How do you know the artist is a *she?*"

"I don't really know. It just feels like it."

"What do you mean?"

"You know how you can usually tell if a book was written by a man or a woman? It's the same thing. I guess it's a little like handwriting analysis. I tried to make out the signature but couldn't. Whoever the artist is, *he or she* has a remarkable touch. I mean to ask Anna about the pictures when she returns from holiday."

"I know the artist," Eliana said.

"You do?"

"Quite well, actually. And yes, she's female."

"At least I'm right half the time. What is she like?"

"You tell me. Analyze the handwriting."

"All right." Ross walked over to one of Eliana's paintings. "First, I think she's older. Definitely older, maybe in her late sixties, seventies."

Eliana looked up with an amused smile. "Why is that?"

"The depth of feeling. Sometimes someone young has that, but it's rare. It usually takes a lifetime to acquire. Either that or a hard life." He looked back at her. "Am I right?"

She went back to slicing the mozzarella. "I'll tell you when you're done. Continue."

"Okay. This is between us, right?"

"I won't tell a soul."

"I think she's a little repressed. She's afraid to say all that she feels, so she limits her palette."

Eliana cocked her head. "Interesting."

Ross looked back at her. "And, wherever she is, I think she's lonely."

At this Eliana stopped cutting. "Why do you say that?"

"Because that's how I feel when I look at her pictures. There's a sort of quiet, beautiful desolation to them. If that makes sense."

Eliana was silent.

Ross walked back to the counter. "So how'd I do?"

She arranged the tomatoes with the cheese on the plate. "I think you've pretty much got her figured out. She's not old — though she would tell you that she feels it."

"I'd like to meet her someday."

Eliana drizzled a thin layer of olive oil over the salad then sprinkled it with basil. "I can arrange it."

"I'd like to ask her something. There's a picture in my place of a field of sunflowers. It's my favorite of the four in my apartment. But if you look carefully, one of the flowers isn't following the sun. I wanted to ask her about it."

You noticed, she thought. She turned the stove off, then opened the oven and looked inside, then shut it again. "What do you do, Ross? Where do you work?"

"I work as a tour guide at the Uffizi."

His answer surprised her. "Really. So you're not just an armchair art critic."

"No, art is my life."

"The Uffizi. That's impressive. You must have some pretty major credentials. That's not an easy job to get."

"No credentials, just dumb luck. I got in through the back door."

She stepped back from the pan. "Would you watch this for a minute? I need to check on Alessio. He already ate, but he wanted to say hello."

"Sure. Should I stir it?"

"Yes. But gently."

She left the room and returned a few minutes later.

"Darn, he fell asleep. He's been asking about you all day."

"Really?"

"Yes. He's pretty hungry for male companionship." She looked into the pot then took the spoon from him. "This is ready for the rest of the ingredients. You can help me here. I mixed them together in that bowl. Go ahead and pour them in while I stir."

"Got it."

He poured the mixture while she continued stirring everything together for a minute longer. Then she poured the steaming pasta into a glazed ceramic bowl that was on the counter next to the stove. "Would you mind grabbing that bowl of spinach from the counter?"

"Sure. And where are your wineglasses?"

"In the cupboard next to the stove. The far side."

They brought everything over to the table. "Why don't you sit there," she said, motioning to the seat across from her. "The Batman glass is Alessio's. You don't have to use it. Unless you want to."

She untied her apron, then folded it and laid it on the counter. She took Ross's plate and ladled a large serving of pasta onto it, then did her own. "*Prima piatti.* The second course is in the oven.

You do eat meat, don't you?"

"Yes."

"I baked cinghiale in umido. It's wild boar meat marinated in red wine and garlic."

"Sounds delicious."

"I hope so. It's my first time making it. But there's a good restaurant near here that serves it and they gave me the recipe. It's traditional Tuscan cuisine." She straightened out her napkin. "Do you mind if I say grace?"

"Of course not."

She bowed her head. He watched her, then bowed his as well. She said the prayer then crossed herself, looked up at Ross and smiled. "Okay, I think we're finally ready. *Buon appetito.*"

"*Buon appetito.*"

Ross rolled the noodles on his fork and took a bite. He smiled with pleasure.

"Is it all right?"

"It's delicious."

"Thank you." She took a bite herself. "So, where are you from?"

"I was born near St. Louis, a suburb called Charlestown. But I call Minnesota home. Or I did."

"What brings you to Italy?"

Ross hesitated. To her surprise he looked slightly uncomfortable with the question. "I guess I just needed a change."

She smiled reassuringly. "We could all use a little change."

"How about you? Where in the States are you from?"

"You've never heard of it."

"I get around. Try me."

"It's a little town in eastern Utah called Vernal."

Ross's brows came together in thought. "I'm pretty sure I've heard of Utah. What state is that in?"

"Stop it."

"You're right, I've never heard of Vernal. What is Vernal famous for?"

"Famous?"

"Every town in America has something they're famous for. It might just be chocolate pecan pie or big potatoes or Bruce Willis slept there or something."

She smiled. "Vernal is famous for dinosaur bones. We have a big excavation site. It's where they found the Utah Raptor."

"Dinosaur bones," he repeated. He lifted the bottle of wine. "Wine?"

"Yes, please."

He poured the red wine into her glass.

"How long are you planning to stay in Italy?" she asked.

"Forever."

She gazed at him in surprise. "Forever? So you really meant a change."

Ross nodded. "How about you?"

"I'd go back to America tomorrow if I could."

"You don't like Italy?"

"I love Italy. I love Tuscany. But after six years it still doesn't feel like home."

"Why don't you go back then?"

"My husband doesn't want to go back. He doesn't really like America. He thinks we're a cultureless society. What we call a melting pot he calls mongrelization. Anyway, his job and property are all here. Besides it's all I can do to take care of Alessio most of the time." She forced a smile. "But it's not so bad. If you're going to get stuck somewhere on the planet, it might as well be here. The people, the scenery and the food are all great."

Ross put his fork back into his pasta. "*This* food is certainly great."

"The secret to carbonara is making sure the noodles are hot enough when you pour on the raw egg. Do you usually eat at home?"

"No, I eat in cafés or trattorias most of the time. But I'm teaching myself to cook. I bought myself a pasta machine a couple days ago."

"There's nothing like fresh pasta."

"I'll bring some over as soon as I figure out how to make it."

"I'll look forward to it. It's not that hard to make."

"You're talking to a man who considers TV dinners a challenge."

"That will change here."

"It's already started. I didn't realize how serious the Italians take their cooking. My first week in Italy I was in a *ristorante* and I committed a major faux pas."

"What happened?"

"I ordered fettuccine noodles with shrimp, then I asked for Parmesan cheese. The waiter asked what I needed the cheese for. I said, *For my pasta.* His eyes got really big then he shouted out to the entire restaurant that I was putting Parmesan on my shrimp fettuccine. Then he handed me the cheese and a grater, looking the other way as he did, so he wouldn't be an accessory. After he left my table, the couple next to me told me that I should never put cheese on seafood. I realized then that food in Italy is a religious rite and I had committed sacrilege."

She laughed. "I have also defiled many a dinner." She looked at his plate. "I'll get the next dish."

She cleared their plates then brought back two plates of carefully sliced meat, garnished with rucola leaves.

Ross speared the meat with his fork and lifted it to his mouth. Eliana watched expectantly as he chewed. When he swallowed, she raised one eyebrow. "Well?"

"You are as fluent in the kitchen as you are in the language."

"I'll take that as a compliment."

"How about a toast?"

"Oh, yes. What shall we toast? We could toast your new life in Italy. Or the wild boar."

"How about your son's health."

Her mouth rose in a gentle smile. "Thank

130

you." She raised her glass. *"Alla salute di Alessio."*

"Salute."

They touched glasses then drank.

"It's good wine." He held up his glass, turning it to the light. "L'incanto?"

She nodded.

"What's it like being in the wine business?"

"For me it's one of the good things about being in Italy. If you're here in October you can join us for the *Vendemmia,* the harvest. Then, after it's all done we have a big feast in the winery. All of the workers dress up in their Sunday best and come by with their wives or lovers," she stopped herself, "not both of them, of course . . ."

Ross grinned. "Of course."

". . . and then we have a big Tuscan feast."

"Anna was telling me about it. How long does the harvest last?"

"It depends on the weather, but usually a couple weeks."

They ate a moment in silence. Ross finished his meat then lay down his fork. "How long have you lived here?"

"In Italy?"

"The villa."

"The same. We've lived here since we came to Italy."

"You seem to have plenty of room. How big is your apartment?"

"I don't know how big in meters or feet. It's

big. We have six bedrooms and four bathrooms."

"For just the three of you?"

"It's far more than we need." She looked down at his plate. "What else can I get for you?"

"Nothing. Everything was perfect."

"Thank you. There's dessert, but if you'd like to wait I'll give you the nickel tour of the place."

"I'd like that."

He stood up and went for her chair, but she had stood up before he could help her. She only noticed afterward and smiled apologetically. "I'm sorry. It's been a while."

She led him upstairs through the arched stairwell door. She grasped the handle on the first door they came to. She said softly, "This is Alessio's room."

"If he's sleeping, we don't need to go inside."

"I need to check on him anyway."

She opened the door slowly. Alessio was asleep. The room was lit by a small night-light. Ross could see that the walls were covered with posters of soccer players from Team Italy and the Fiorentina. In the corner of the room was a net with several soccer balls, and even the wooden bed knobs were painted to look like soccer balls. Eliana listened to Alessio for a moment then closed the door behind them.

"I take it he likes soccer?"

"All Italian boys like soccer. But it's his father's thing, really. He gave him the posters. In America every father wants his son to be a baseball or football hero — same thing here, just a different sport. Alessio wants to be good. He wants his father to be proud of him."

Two doors down she stopped at the doorway. "I probably shouldn't show you this."

"Ah, skeletons."

She looked at him then opened the door to her art studio and stepped inside the darkened room. He followed her in. She flipped on the light switch. There were pictures and canvases scattered around the room and an unfinished landscape on the easel. After a moment he said, "Well, you're not seventy."

"That's about the only thing you got wrong."

"So you are repressed?"

"Definitely."

"And lonely?"

She looked at him and smiled sadly but didn't answer. Ross wondered how anyone so beautiful could be alone.

"I have some dessert wine. Vin santo. Or perhaps you would like some coffee?" she said, changing the subject.

"I'd love some coffee."

They went downstairs. While Eliana went to the kitchen, Ross sat on a leather sofa in front of a glass-topped table. Eliana came in with the coffee and two small porcelain plates on which was pastry cake, white with confectioner's sugar. She set the plates on the table and sat down on the floor across from him, her legs crossed.

"I almost forgot the dessert."

Ross cut the cake with his fork. "I love millefoglie. That's what this is, isn't it?"

She nodded. "*Sì*. You know a lot about Italy for only being here a couple weeks."

"I've been here for six months. I just train-hopped for a while." He tasted the dessert. "You made this?"

"No. The cake I bought. There's a *pasticcerìa* near Piazza Gavinana that makes great pastries. I always buy our birthday cakes there."

"I'll have to remember that." He looked up from the cake. "So you did the portrait in my place as well. The monk?"

She grinned. "That's Saint Francis of Assisi. But you can call him 'the monk' if you like."

"Sorry. Do you often paint portraits?"

"Not many. I like doing them, I just don't like working from magazine pictures. If I could work with models, I'd do more. It's hard to capture the right mood painting from a picture."

"When did you start painting?"

"When I was twelve. I used to paint desert landscapes in Vernal."

"Do you sell them?"

"Not often."

"Really, why not?"

"I'm afraid that if I started painting for money it would lose its value for me. So I just let them pile up. I give them away as presents. Who knows, if you're a good tenant you might end up with one."

"I could only hope."

She smiled then took a bite of her cake. "You know, it's nice to have company. Sometimes I get cabin fever. Or maybe I should say villa fever."

"Don't you have many friends here?"

"I have a few. But Rendola's a bit off the beaten path. Not that that's an excuse. I should make more of an effort. It's just hard with Alessio. Anna's my best friend. Ever since her husband left her."

"Anna's been really helpful."

"I love Anna. She looks out for me. She's very maternal."

Ross asked, "So how did you end up at Rendola?"

"This is one of the homes Maurizio grew up in. His family owns another villa in Siena. That's where his mother lives."

"Where did the two of you meet?"

"We met in Florence, at a discotheque. Just about every American girl here has the same story. We come to study and end up with a husband. I came for only a two-month university extension program. I was studying art history at the University of Utah. My father had just died, when this opportunity came up. I was taking my father's death pretty hard. I guess I needed to get away. I met Maurizio on my third night here. He was gorgeous. He swept me off my feet. He was also seven years older than me. I was still too young to get married and he was planning to come to America to get his MBA, so he arranged to attend the University of Utah to be near me. We dated a little more than three years and he finished schooling and was about to go back. I still felt too young to marry, but rather than lose him I said yes."

"Where does he work?"

"You're awfully interested in my husband."

"Sorry. It's a guy thing. If you'd rather not . . ."

"No, it's fine. He runs the family's wine business. He makes all the sales and business decisions. It takes him all around the world, meeting with importers and distributors, sometimes restaurateurs. America, Italy, Portugal, Bangkok, Australia, Taiwan, Japan, you name it. He speaks six languages. He's very smart."

"Sounds interesting."

"It does, doesn't it?" she said, though the tone of her voice was flat. "He's on the road more than two hundred and fifty days out of the year. I think it was in '97, in one six-month period, he was only home for three weekends. You'll meet him next week. You'll like him. Everyone likes him. He's very charming. Just not real . . . ," she paused, "available."

"How is that, taking care of a child with your husband gone so often?"

"Well, I have help. Manuela comes three days a week. She's good to Alessio. And there's Anna. As far as the husband part, you get used to being alone."

"Do you?"

She didn't answer for a moment. "You don't play games when you speak."

"Not if I can help it."

Her voice changed; it became soft and open. "No, you don't get used to it. In fact it gets harder." She ran her fingers through her hair. "Yes, I'm lonely and I feel like I want to scream and run a million miles away from Rendola." She looked up at him. "And then I see my sweet son and this beautiful country and all the nice things around me and I think, *Get a grip. There are people out there with real problems.*" She laughed at herself. "That's where I live, somewhere between loneliness and guilt." She shook her head as she looked up at him. "You probably think I'm crazy. It's okay if you do. I do."

"No, I don't."

She sighed. Her voice softened more. "About the other night. At the hospital . . . I wanted to thank you for . . . ," she hesitated, feeling suddenly awkward, "for holding me. I needed that."

"I was afraid that I was being too forward."

"No. You were being sweet. The world needs more gentlemen."

There was a moment of quiet as neither knew how to respond to the course of their conversation. Ross suddenly smiled. "That just reminded me of a joke I overheard at the Uffizi yesterday. Want to hear?"

She nodded. *"Certo."*

"A man and a woman were traveling to Sicily on a sleeping train. The train was completely full

137

and they found that they had accidentally been placed together in the same sleeping cabin, just the two of them. They were a little nervous at first but they soon just turned off the lights and went to bed, the man on the top bunk, the woman on the bottom. Sometime in the night the man said to the woman, 'Excuse me, but could you please hand me a blanket? I'm a little cold up here.'

"The woman said, 'I have a better idea. Why don't we, just for tonight, pretend that we're married.'

" 'Really?' said the man, very excited. 'Great!'

" 'Good,' said the woman. Then she rolled over and said, 'Get your own damn blanket.' "

Eliana laughed hard enough that she covered her mouth. Ross also began to laugh, though not at the joke but at the effect the joke had on her. When he started telling it, he hadn't considered its possible relevance. Now it was obvious.

As her laughter softened Ross looked up at the clock on the mantelpiece. It was nearly one.

"I can't believe it's so late. *Il tempo vola.* Can you say that in Italian?"

"Yes, *time flies.*"

"I better get out before you throw me out." Ross climbed to his feet then offered her his hand. Then he grabbed the glasses from the table. "Let me help you clean up the kitchen."

"No, it's too late. I'll clean up in the morning."

"It's okay, really. I can help."

138

"I forget that you American men are well trained. But thank you, no. This was my treat."

"Whatever you say."

He left their glasses in the kitchen and they walked to the front of the house and stood just outside the threshold. The courtyard was luminous blue, lit by the crescent moon that peeked over the western wall of the villa like a voyeur. There was a curious, powerful energy between them. Ross felt awkward, like a boy on the doorstep of his first date.

"Thank you for dinner. It was the best meal I've had since I came to Italy."

"You're just being kind."

"I think it was. Of course good company makes a meal better."

Her eyes shone.

"And thank you for showing me your artwork. I'm obviously very impressed." As he looked at her, Ross suddenly thought she had the most perfect lips he had ever seen. "And for the cookies the other night. They're just about gone already."

"Thank you again for helping us." She began fondling a single strand of hair over her forehead.

He looked into her face, their eyes locked and an unspoken conversation played back and forth in the moonlight. Then Ross put out his hand. "Well, good night."

His hand was soft, she thought, strong, but soft. "Good night, Ross. Sleep well."

Then he turned and walked from her. She stepped back inside her own apartment then turned to watch him. As he began to vanish in the darkness of the corridor, something in her could not let him leave without knowing when she'd see him again. She called after him, "Ross."

He turned, his face split by shadow. "Yes?"

"Could I paint you?"

"Paint me?"

She pulled again at the strand. "I mean a portrait of you."

"I've never modeled before."

"That doesn't matter. If a bowl of fruit can do it, how hard could it be?"

He smiled. "When would you like to start?"

She didn't want to seem too eager. "I'm just finishing up the painting I'm working on. Maybe we could start Thursday evening."

"Thursday's fine."

"What time do you get off work?"

"I have a late tour Thursday afternoon. I should be home around seven."

"Would eight be too soon?"

"No, eight works."

"Thank you."

"Good night, Eliana."

"*Buona notte,* Ross."

Ross walked slowly back to his apartment. Her door closed softly behind him. The evening had turned out perfectly. She was different than he had expected. More vulnerable, perhaps. He felt as if he had finally found a friend.

CHAPTER 12

"Il tempo di sòlito e bello quando si fa l'amore."
The weather is always fair when people are in love.
— Italian Proverb

It rained the next day: a summer storm that turned the skies above Florence gray and dampened the Tuscan countryside. Eliana gazed out her studio window lost in her thoughts, watching the water trickle down the pane, the rain splash and pool in the corners of the stone courtyard, the geraniums dance from the fall of the drops. She did not mind the sudden cloudburst. Even if it meant that Alessio was stuck inside all day and the customary whining from boredom would soon begin. There were only blue skies where she was — replaying the tape of the previous night in her mind. She felt a lightness of being that she hadn't felt in some time. Whether something had been taken from her or added, she wasn't sure. But she felt different.

The evening had been almost like a confessional. For she had bared her soul and he had listened. He seemed genuinely interested in her thoughts. But, like a confessional, there was a screen there, if only his eyes, and she knew nothing about the man behind it.

Still, she liked what she knew. He was kind. He was good-looking; not like the posters of semi-

141

nude male models plastered around the city —
he was attractive in a different way. He seemed
confident, yet still somehow vulnerable — if that
were possible — and, at the least, he clearly
wasn't arrogant. He was masculine without
being "macho."

She worked quickly to finish the painting that
occupied her easel. It had now lost importance
to her, as she was anticipating her next project
with her new model. Alessio slept in and she
painted for more than two hours, until he walked
into her studio rubbing his eyes. He was wearing
briefs and socks and a Batman cape.

"I'm hungry, mom."

"Hi, sweetie. Go in the pantry and get yourself
a plum cake. I'll be down in a few minutes and
I'll make you some oatmeal."

"Okay."

He stumbled off. She put the last touches on
the section she was painting then put her brushes
away and went downstairs to make breakfast.

Around noon Eliana was sorting laundry, sitting on the floor next to the washing machine,
when she heard the front door open. Manuela
walked in, singing to herself. She shook her
umbrella off outside then stowed it in the
corner.

"*Ciao,* Eliana. It's me."

"*Ciao,* Manuela. How are you feeling?"

"*Meglio.* " Better. "But I don't like rain."

"Neither does Alessio. He's up in his room
playing Nintendo."

Manuela hung up her coat and went off to find him. A few minutes later the front door opened again.

"*Ciao, amore.*"

Eliana jumped a little. Maurizio stood above her.

"You startled me. I didn't hear you come in. What are you doing home?"

"I had to come back to Florence."

"Will you be home for a while?"

"No. There's a wine show in Vienna this Friday; I need to be there by tomorrow afternoon."

"Vienna. I wish you had told me sooner. We would have loved to go with you."

"I'll just be working the whole time, then off again."

She continued sorting clothes. "Alessio's upstairs in his room with Manuela if you want to see him."

"I won't disturb them. I'm going to take a nap. Then you can make me lunch."

She looked at the laundry around her then dropped what was in her hands back on the floor. "All right." She stood up and stepped from the laundry, picking her way around the little piles like she was navigating a stream. "I wasn't going grocery shopping until later this afternoon. I can make you a sandwich. I have some prosciutto crudo."

"*Va bene.* And some penne with Bolognese sauce."

143

"We don't have any beef. There's some pesto sauce."

He frowned. "Okay."

Eliana went to the kitchen. Maurizio went into the front room, turned on the television and lay down on the couch.

A few minutes later Alessio entered the front room, his hands cupped before him. He stopped near the doorway.

"Ciao, Babbo."

Maurizio turned from the television and smiled. *"Ciao, Alessio."*

"I want to show you something." He opened his hands.

Maurizio strained to see what he held. *"Che cosa?* A rock?"

Alessio stepped toward his father. "It's a *real* volcano rock from a *real* volcano."

Maurizio took the porous stone from Alessio's outstretched hand, looked it over then gave it back to him.

"Where did you get it?"

"Luca gave it to me."

"Ganzo." Cool. He turned back to the television.

After a moment Alessio asked, "Do you want to play soccer with me?"

Maurizio looked back over. "Of course. But it is raining outside."

"The rain stopped."

"Yes, but everything is still all wet. You do not want to get all wet, do you?"

"I don't mind."

"Yes, but your mother will." Maurizio smiled reassuringly. "We will do it another time when it is not so wet." Alessio's countenance fell. Maurizio, sensing his disappointment, said, "When I come back from my next trip I will bring you a new ball."

"We haven't even used the last ball you gave me."

"But we will. I promise. When everything is not so wet." He patted Alessio on the arm then turned back to the television. After a few more moments Alessio took his rock back upstairs.

Ross was surrounded by a tour group from Boise, Idaho. They had been an amiable crowd, and though he'd never been to Idaho, judging from this group he thought he'd like the people.

Ross preferred leading the groups from the smaller towns. They seemed more filled with awe at what they saw.

"There is a reason for every painting," Ross said. "Sometimes we can see it within the expression of the art itself; sometimes we find it in historical perspective. There were a lot of things said in art that couldn't be said aloud. Painted between the lines, so to speak. For instance . . . " He looked over the group. "You've already been to see the Sistine Chapel, no?"

Most of group nodded in the affirmative.

"In the painting of the last judgment in the Sistine Chapel, Michelangelo put many of his rivals' faces on those unfortunate souls being pulled by demons down to hell. Contrarily he put many of his patrons' faces on those being saved and blessed by angels.

"Many of these symbols we see in paintings were very familiar and understood by the people of that era, but are not familiar to many of us today. For instance, a few rooms down is one of my favorite paintings in the Uffizi, the *Venus of Urbino* by Titian. It is a portrait of a beautiful young woman lying nude on a lounge. Though it would hardly turn a head today, at the time it was considered one of the most erotic pieces ever painted. Titian, not wishing to be misunderstood, added an important symbol to his painting. A small dog is curled up near the girl, on the foot of the bed. The dog was considered the symbol of fidelity, and it was placed there to reassure the viewer that this was a good girl. I'll point it out when we reach room twenty-eight. Remember, there is a reason for every painting." He started walking, throwing both hands in the air ahead of him as if he were directing aircraft. "*Andiamo, ragazzi.* Let's go, children."

Ross was done with the tour before noon, but he and his scooter were stuck downtown by the rain. He sat outside the Uffizi, beneath the courtyard's overhang, reading a book as he waited for the rain to stop. Around three o'clock there was a break in the weather, and he put on his helmet and started home just a few minutes before the rain started again in earnest.

By the time he reached Rendola he was drenched. At the end of the long driveway he saw a car he'd never seen before, a navy-blue Alfa Romeo with gold trim. It was parked next to Eliana's BMW. Ross rocked his scooter back onto its stand, stowed his helmet beneath the seat, then opened the front gate.

The courtyard stone was uneven, and where he entered, the rain had pooled into a small puddle four inches deep. He stepped around it.

An Italian man leaned against the wall next to Eliana's front door, smoking a cigar and watching Ross's entrance. He was lean, a hand shorter than Ross, almost feminine in form, with curled hair and bronze skin, the lower part of his face shaded with stubble, his heavy-lidded eyes fixed on Ross coolly. He bit down on his cigar, blowing out a blue-gray cloud of smoke from the gaps in his mouth where his clenched teeth bit into the leaf.

Ross nodded. *"Buona sera."*

"Buona sera." The man removed the cigar. "You are Mr. Story?"

Ross approached him. "Yes. Ross Story."

He put out his hand. "I am Maurizio Ferrini. I own the villa. You have met my sister Anna. She has told me about you. Welcome to Rendola."

"Thank you."

"So what brings you to *our neck of the woods?*"

Ross sensed that he was showing off his English.

"La dolce vita."

Maurizio laughed. "The sweet life. That is rich. You look a little too wet for that."

"I got caught in the rain."

"Where in the States are you from?"

"Minnesota."

"Minnesota," he said knowingly. "Minneapolis or St. Paul?"

"Just outside Minneapolis."

"I have been there. Once in the winter. It was too cold for my blood. Below zero Fahrenheit, I think." He stopped and examined his cigar as if it had suddenly interrupted their conversation. He looked back up at Ross. "My wife told me that you drove her and my son to the hospital the other evening. Thank you."

"You're welcome."

"You plan to live in Italy for a while?"

"For a while."

"Well, good luck. See you around."

"Likewise." Ross turned and Maurizio brought the cigar back to his mouth as he watched Ross cross the courtyard to his apartment. He wondered what the American was really doing in his country.

CHAPTER 13

"Vita privata, vita beata."
Hidden life, happy life.
— Italian Proverb

Ross woke early the next morning and went running. He ran to the end of the Rendola vineyards, then down to Impruneta's Grande Piazza, once around the square and then back, covering almost five and a half miles in all.

The clouds had vanished with the night winds, and the morning was bright and fresh and already warm enough to make him sweat. He had stopped during his run to visit with an old man with two canes, one in each hand, who was slowly walking down the street and had hailed him with "Today's my sixtieth wedding anniversary."

"Auguri," Ross said. *Best wishes. "Congratulazioni."*

"Seems like only yesterday we were married," the man said thoughtfully, wiping his forehead with his arm, then added, "and you know how awful yesterday was."

Ross laughed, wished him well and started off again.

On the way back he removed his shirt. He was wearing only his shorts and shoes when he returned to the villa. Eliana watched him cross the courtyard from her studio. She opened her window.

"Hey."

He stopped, looked up at her, shielding his eyes with his hand from the morning sun. She was wearing a terry-cloth robe and leaning partially from the window. He smiled. "Good morning."

"*Buon giorno, signore.* Are we still on for to-night?"

"If it's still good for you. I don't want to steal you from your husband."

"Maurizio's already gone. He left early this morning. I saw you talking to him."

"He was friendly."

"I told you you'd like him."

Ross didn't comment. "Eight o'clock, then?"

"Yes. Eight." She waved. *"Ciao."* She disappeared back inside the window.

The bells of Arnolfo's Tower rang the noon hour. Ross had just left the Uffizi with a small group and was standing in the *cortile* when Francesca caught up with him. She was out of breath and rested her hand on his arm.

"Ciao, Ross."

"Ciao, Francesca." They kissed cheeks.

"Can you fit in another group this afternoon?"

"No problem. I'm free until my five o'clock tour."

"Benissimo. I'll call the hotel." She took out her cell phone. "You'll be pleased with this group."

"Why is that?"

"You might know some of the people." ·
Ross looked at her. "What do you mean?"
"The hotel concierge said it's an advertising incentive trip from one of the television stations in Minneapolis. Didn't you say you were in advertising in Minneapolis?"

For a moment he was speechless, as if he'd just been delivered tragic news. "I'm sorry, I can't do it, Francesca."

"Perché?"

"I'm sorry, I just can't. You'll have to find somebody else. I've got to go. I'll be back at five for my tour."

Without further explanation he walked briskly down the corridor, disappearing around the corner into the Piazza della Signoria. Baffled, Francesca watched him go then put her cell phone back in her bag.

It was a few minutes before eight o'clock when Ross pressed Eliana's doorbell, igniting a small commotion. The electronic buzz of the doorbell was followed by a short, high-pitched scream then the sound of running feet across the tile floor. The door flung open to Alessio, looking up at him, panting from his sprint across the house. "Hi," he said breathlessly. He was dressed for bed, in baggy sky-blue shorts with a brown stripe down the side and a matching top. He was small and wiry, his hair curly with a tint of amber. His eyes, hazel like his mother's, were wide with excitement. The last time Ross had seen Alessio was as he carried him into the emergency room. He didn't look like the same boy.

"You must be Alessio."

"Yes, sir."

"Do you remember me?"

"Yes, sir."

"Is your mother here?"

"Yes, sir."

He stood staring up at Ross, his hands clenched, his mouth partially open, as if he was about to say something.

After a moment Ross said, "May I come in?"

"Yes, sir."

"Thank you." Ross stepped across the threshold.

"Guess what," Alessio said.

Ross crouched down to Alessio's height. "What?"

"I found a scorpion today. It was in my closet."

"Really?"

He nodded. "He was black. They have a stinger. The really big ones can kill you, you know."

"Was it big?"

He held his fingers about an inch apart. "This big."

"Did you put it in a bottle?"

"My mom hit it with a shoe."

Ross tried not to smile. "I'm just glad you found it before it got both of you."

Alessio nodded seriously. "Me too."

Just then Eliana called out. "I'm in the kitchen, Ross. Come on in."

Ross put his hand on Alessio's shoulder. "I'll keep my eyes open for any more. Maybe we can find one sometime and put it in a bottle to look at."

"Okay."

Ross found Eliana finishing up the dinner dishes. She smiled when she saw him. *"Ciao."*

"Ciao."

"I just need to finish these up, if you don't mind."

"Not at all. Want me to dry?"

She smiled at the offer. "No, I'm almost done. Make yourself at home." She looked down at Alessio. "All right, you saw him. Now run on up to bed."

Alessio frowned. *"Devo?"* *Do I have to?*

"Yes, you do. Give me a kiss." Eliana crouched down and Alessio kissed her on the lips then turned to Ross. "Bye, Ross."

"Mr. Story," she corrected.

Ross winked. "See you later, Alessio."

"Ciao." He walked slowly up the stairs.

When he was gone Ross said, "He's a well-mannered little boy."

"He wasn't twenty minutes ago. He wouldn't go to bed because he knew you were coming." She put the last plate in the cupboard. "He was so upset that he missed you the last time. I had to promise him that he could stay up until you came."

"He told me about the scorpion."

Eliana rolled her eyes. "I hate those things. It's one of those things you want a man around the house for."

"To kill scorpions?"

She dried her hands with a towel. "They're good for other things too," she said with a smile. "Would you like some dessert wine?"

"Please."

She stowed the towel under the sink then took a bottle of Vinsanto from the counter, took two glasses and poured them half-full. She handed a glass to Ross then leaned back against the counter with her own. "You should have just come for dinner. I always make too much."

"I should have. It smells good."

"Tonight was simple."

He sipped his wine. "How good is Alessio's Italian?"

"Perfect for a seven-year-old. Probably better than mine. He doesn't have an accent. He's grown up here, so his Italian is as good as his English. Maybe better." She took a drink and held it in her mouth before swallowing. "Maurizio won't speak to him in English of course." She set her glass down on the counter. "Well, are you ready?"

"*Sì.*"

As they climbed the stairs to her studio, Ross asked, "How many portraits have you done?"

"Maybe a dozen or so. I've done a couple portraits of Alessio. But he lasts about two minutes in a chair, if that. So I just worked from photographs of him. A couple years ago I did a portrait of Maurizio. I knew he'd never find the time to sit for one, so I found some pictures and painted it from those. I gave it to him for his birthday."

"What did he think of it?"

"He said he liked it. In fact he praised it." Eliana frowned. "Then I found it in the back of his closet a month later. He doesn't really care for my painting." She turned on the light in the studio. "Here we are."

Ross glanced around the room. Though he had seen the room before, he had not paid much attention to it then. It was cluttered with art supplies, charcoal sketches and paintings.

"You have such nice art in the house. Even besides yours. Did you choose it all?"

"Not all of it. Maurizio has good taste in art, but he only values it as an investment." She sharpened a pencil then touched the point of it with her finger. "Anyway I guess it hurt my feelings enough that it was the last time I painted someone I knew. Last year I went on an Italian *antico* kick and I painted some historical figures like Marcus Aurelius, St. Francis, Caesar, people like that. I just did them in acrylics. My models were pictures from *GQ*, so they're pretty sexy for historical figures. They're stacked over in the corner if you want to see what you're in for."

"*GQ*, huh?" Ross looked to the shadowed section of the room. "Back there?"

"I'll get the light." She flipped another switch, turning on the lights on the other side of the studio. Ross walked over to a stack of canvases leaning against the wall. He squatted down and one by one lifted them forward, examining each in turn. He stopped halfway through the pile at a picture of a young woman in a dark scarlet robe tied at one shoulder then secured at her waist with a golden sash. In one hand she held an oil lamp. In the other hand she held a loaf of bread.

He stood, lifting the portrait from the others. "This is interesting."

Eliana had just put on her painting smock and looked up. "That's my Vestal."

Ross looked back. "Vestal?"

"One of the Vestal Virgins."

"I don't know much about them, but this fall there's an exhibit coming to the Uffizi called *The Vestals*." His eyes traversed the picture. "Mostly sculptures though, I think."

"Well, then you should know something about them," she said. She walked over to his side. "In ancient Rome, the Vestals were the keepers of the temple of Vesta — the goddess of home and family. The ancient Romans believed that their empire was founded on the family, so these women were very powerful. They were given large dowries, saluted in public places, even given the best seats at the Colosseum, all the nice perks." She looked at Ross. "They were the only women in Rome allowed to own property."

"The Old World's first liberated women."

"Not exactly." She glanced from Ross to the painting. "They had three requirements, each with serious consequences should they fail them. First, they were to commit themselves completely to the goddess Vesta. Second, they were to keep the flame of the temple burning at all times. The last promise was that they were to forswear love for themselves by taking sacred vows of chastity."

She paused. "The last vow carried the most serious punishment if broken. It was horrible. Their lovers would be whipped to death before their eyes. Then they would be taken to the field of the damned, where they were placed in a small stone room beneath the ground. They would be given a loaf of bread and an oil lamp, then they would be buried alive." As she gazed at the picture, she spoke with a faraway look, as if she had witnessed it herself. "Their own families weren't even allowed to mourn them. They died alone, forsaken by everyone."

Ross looked at the painting. "Why did you choose a fallen Vestal?"

"I don't know. It just intrigued me that someone wanted, or needed, love so badly that they would risk everything, even their lives."

"So it did happen — one of them *was* buried alive."

"Eighteen of them."

Ross was surprised. "Eighteen?"

She looked up at him, as if suddenly woken from the trance. "Though one of them was raped

157

by the emperor and punished for it. Hardly fair."

"No, I think not."

"The world has always been full of double standards."

Ross felt as if she were talking about something else.

She turned back. "Shall we start?"

Ross returned the portrait to the others then came over by a chair in front of the easel.

"You want me here?"

"Yes. Just sit down, make yourself comfortable. I'll do my best to make you uncomfortable in just a moment."

Ross sat back in the chair.

"Have you ever sat for a portrait?"

"No."

"Like I said, it's easy." She was suddenly quiet as she stared at him. "Move a little forward. Okay, now put your hands here. No, like this." She came around the canvas, took his hand, moved it to his thigh, but still didn't like the pose. "Maybe you should be holding a closed book in your lap, just something to give the picture some balance. Let's try this." She handed him a book; its leather cover was dyed dark maroon, with the Florentine lily embossed on it. "Nice. That works. I was thinking of doing something a little more dramatic, so I want to try using a spotlight on you and dimming the lights."

She moved the light until it surrounded him with a small halo. Then she stepped back to her easel and studied him. Ross sat quietly and his eyes darted around the studio. It was like peeking into her mind. Not just what she painted, but what she surrounded herself with while she painted.

On the counter behind her there was a stack of books, mostly religious, intermingled with Italian love stories. There were photographs. Dozens of pictures, mostly of Alessio, chronicling his age. There was one picture of the entire family, shot at a photo studio, though it was obvious that it had been shot a while back. Alessio looked scarcely two years old in the picture. There was another of an older American woman with silver hair leaning against a fence post in front of a horse. It was pinned to the wall next to a picture of a man. The man was dressed in corduroy jeans and his hairstyle dated the picture. Ross guessed it was Eliana's father. There were several other pictures of horses, and also an actual horseshoe with writing on it that looked like a signature next to *Happy trails*.

She cocked her head to one side. "Okay, we're almost there."

She switched on a desk lamp directed toward her canvas then she turned off the room lights. She studied him again then sat down on a leather-capped stool.

"So what's the routine?" Ross asked.

"I start with a pencil sketch. Then, sometime after you're gone, I'll paint in the background, for balance. Then I start painting."

"Are you using acrylics?"

"No, I only use those to practice because they dry fast. This is special so I'm using oils."

Ross scratched his forehead, careful not to move. "That reminds me of something. Francesca, she's the woman I work for at the Uffizi, told me this story about one of the paintings. A newly wealthy merchant asked Leonardo for a portrait. They agreed on a price then the merchant asked what medium Leonardo would be painting in. 'Oils,' Leonardo said. His patron was incensed. 'Where do you think you are, Naples? In Florence we do everything in butter.' "

Eliana smiled slightly. "I would believe that's true."

"Oils. Linen canvas. So what makes this portrait special?"

"You. You're my first real model in Italy. Not counting Alessio."

"So after you paint the background, then what?"

"Over the next several sittings I'll paint a black-and-white picture of you. Then I'll start applying the paints. I'll start with your hair, just because it's higher on the picture and I can still rest my hand against the canvas, then on to your nose and work out from there."

"How long will it take?"

"That depends on how many questions the subject asks."

"At this rate?"

She grinned. "About ten years." She sat down at the easel. "All right, I'm ready."

She lifted her pencil and began to sketch, sometimes hidden behind the canvas, sometimes peering around it at Ross. Her pencil made a smooth, comforting sound against the linen. After about twenty minutes she said, "All right, let's take a break."

Ross took a deep breath and exhaled. Eliana rolled her stool out from behind the easel.

"You doing okay?"

"Yes."

He stood, walked over near her. "May I see?"

She held up her hand. "No. It's bad luck."

"You artists are all mad."

"*E vero.*" *It's true.* Her eyes darted away from him as if she was suddenly embarrassed. "Speaking of crazy, I want to apologize for the other night."

"For what?"

"My tongue was too loose. I'm sorry for dumping all of that on you."

"For the record, I really enjoyed myself the other night. A little honesty is refreshing."

"I think you're just being polite. My husband says that American women talk too much. In this case he's right. But it just felt so good to talk to an adult in English."

"It was fine. Really."

She took a sip from her glass, emptying it. "Thank you. Let me know when you're ready to start again."

"Just a minute." He stretched again. Then he sat back down. "Okay. Is this right?"

"Scoot back a little . . . to your right a little more . . . no, your other right. *Perfetto.*"

She looked at him for a moment then raised her pencil to the canvas. "So I realized that every time I asked you about yourself you changed the subject."

"Not much to tell."

"Right. You move to a foreign country — alone — plan to stay forever and you don't have a story?"

Ross grinned. "Maybe a little one. What do you want to know?"

"To begin with, what did you do in the States?"

"I was . . ." He started to turn toward her as he spoke.

"No, don't move."

"Sorry. Is this where I was?"

"Your shoulder was back a little more. There."

"Okay. I was the art director for an advertising agency in Minneapolis."

"You left that position to be a tour guide?"

"You make that sound so stupid."

"I'm sorry."

"No, that's not why I left. I had a . . . ," he stumbled on the sentence, "a falling out with my partners. Besides I was getting burned out on the caffeine-buzz lifestyle of the advertising world. The other night when you were telling me why

162

you didn't sell your paintings, I kept thinking that I wish I had had that kind of integrity. I got into art design because I loved art and I thought I could make a good living from it. I was successful, I made a lot of money, won a few awards, but after five years in the business I felt like a prostitute, selling myself to deadlines, the latest graphic fad or the client's whim. Art by committee. I felt like I was losing my soul. And your theory's right. It lost its joy. So I understand how you feel and I respect you for that. That's also why your work is so brilliant. It's honest. It's an irony you're going to have to deal with someday, because people will want to buy your pictures for the very reason you don't want to sell them. It's because they want to have back that part of themselves that they sold."

At that moment she was glad to have the canvas to hide behind. His understanding meant more to her than he could have ever imagined. Maurizio just thought that she was a fool for not making more money from her work.

"Thank you."

"You're welcome," he said softly. "So what else do you want to know?"

She returned to her drawing. "Do you have family? Any brothers or sisters?"

"I have a brother."

"He lives in Minneapolis?"

"I'm not sure."

"You're not close?"

"We're very close, actually." Ross frowned.

163

"At least we were. I haven't heard from him in more than three years. I tried to find him just before I came to Italy, but I couldn't."

"I'm sorry."

"Yeah. So am I. I miss him."

"How about your parents? Are they in Minnesota too?"

"My parents died in a car accident when I was twelve. My brother, Stan, and I were raised by our aunt."

"I can't imagine how hard that must have been, losing both parents at that age. When my father died I thought my world was over. And I was eighteen."

"We survive. Somehow. I turned to art. Stan turned to drugs."

Eliana suddenly stood, walked over to him and adjusted the light. She moved calmly, with a natural grace that was pleasant for Ross to watch. But it was more than that. There was something honest about her movements, something indefinable that made him trust her — that made him feel as if he could tell her anything. In fact he just had told her something. She was only the second person he had ever told about Stan. She smoothed the shirt above his shoulder then sat down again.

"Is that spotlight too hot?"

"A little."

"You're sweating. Don't sweat."

"I'm sorry."

She started drawing again. As she traced the

outer lines of his face, she thought again what nice features he had. She felt a little guilty in the pleasure she experienced in drawing him, as if she had run her hand across his face. "Have you ever been married?"

He hesitated. "No."

"Near misses?"

"I was engaged once. Four years ago."

"What happened?"

Again he hesitated. "It didn't work out."

Eliana wondered what that meant, but from his demeanor she decided that it was best left alone for now.

"Your hand looks kind of awkward like that. Let's try something different. Put your one hand on your knee, like this. Move the book over." She demonstrated, Ross obeyed. "That's good. Now turn your other hand this way a little, so your palm's up."

He paused momentarily then slowly turned his hand. For the first time she noticed the thick scar that ran diagonally across his wrist. She flinched when she saw it but said nothing. Ross's gaze did not leave her, and she tried to act as if she hadn't seen it, which, as the silence grew, became only all the more obvious.

"It was a hard time," Ross said.

"I'm sorry."

They were both quiet for a moment then Ross spoke. "So what was the last portrait you did?"

"I haven't done any for a while. My last was a portrait of an elderly Italian man I took a picture of in a piazza. He was just sitting there reading a newspaper. My mother-in-law liked it, so I gave it to her."

"What's it like having an Italian mother-in-law?"

"You don't want to get me started on that."

"Are they as close to their sons as they say?"

"Butter on toast isn't that close. She has a key to our apartment, which kind of says it all. I once came home and found her ironing Maurizio's underwear. She tore into me for neglecting her son and grandson."

"That's awful. How do you deal with that?"

"At first I just did my best to ignore it. But she had a stroke about three years ago and she doesn't leave Siena anymore. Maurizio has another sister who lives with her and takes care of her."

"I noticed that there's a lot of coming and going around here."

"The villa is pretty open. Our home is what the Italians call a *porto di mare* — a harbor. Everyone just walks in: Anna, Manuela, Vittorio, Luca. In fact you're about the only one who knocks."

"Does that bother you? Not having any privacy?"

"Not really. I have three uncles in America and they never knocked before walking into the house." She grinned in remembrance. "We've had a few embarrassing moments. Once I came walking out of the shower to get some underwear and one of my uncles was sitting there reading the paper. I don't know who was more embarrassed. He was so shocked he started stuttering. But that's just Vernal. Even our neighbors don't knock when they come in."

She stood up again, went to him and ran her fingers back through his hair, messing it up a little on the top. "There, it looks a little fuller. The heat flattens everything."

Ross liked the feel of her fingers through his hair.

"So when you're done what are you going to do with the painting?"

"Give it to you. Maybe. Then again I might just decide to keep it."

He looked over to the other portraits. "To add to the stack."

"No, I'll frame this one."

She stopped talking as she sketched. After another twenty minutes she set her pencil down.

"I think that's enough for one night."

"May I move?"

"Not yet. Let me take some pictures." She brought out a disposable camera and snapped a few shots. "That's so I can work on this while you're not around. You can move now. Let me get the lights."

Ross exhaled, yawned. He stretched, raising his arms above his head. "Modeling is tougher than it looks."

Eliana turned on the lights. "In a college art class we were sketching a nude model when he passed out. Not enough circulation, our instructor said."

"Should I be worried?"

"It's okay, I know CPR."

She put away her brushes then she followed him down the stairs.

"I hope that wasn't too boring."

"Not at all." Then he said, "It's nice being with you."

Eliana was suddenly quiet. "You too," she said softly. They stopped at the door.

"So when is the next sitting?"

"Is Saturday good for you?"

"Anytime Saturday is good."

"Good. Then we'll just play it by ear."

For a moment they just looked at each other. Both of them were unsure of how to punctuate the evening. Finally Eliana said, "How about if we just hug?"

"That would be good."

She leaned forward and hugged him. "*Buona notte,* Ross."

"*Buona notte.*"

As he left her, her thoughts lingered pleasantly on their conversation. Then she thought again about the scar on his wrist. After an evening together she was left with more questions than answers. What had happened to this man?

CHAPTER 14

"La vita e un sogno."
Life is a dream.
— Italian Proverb

"I had a dream last night that has filled me with fore-boding, like a harbinger to unknown events in which I must somehow play a part."
— Ross Story's diary

For a moment, in the blurred twilight between slumber and consciousness, Ross thought his dream real. Then his senses came to him and he groaned and rolled over off his pillow. He reached to the floor and dragged his fingers across the cool tile until he found his alarm clock and lifted it to view. It was only three a.m. He rolled to his back and thought of the dream as he fell back asleep.

He had dreamt that there was a woman standing next to his bed. The Vestal Virgin from Eliana's portrait. She was young, but ancient, clothed in a pale linen tunic partially concealed by the dark scarlet robe that draped from one shoulder. In one hand she held an oil lamp, without flame. In the other hand she held a loaf of bread.

Though he couldn't see her face, he knew she was looking at him. It was as if a cloud masked her. He didn't know how long she had stood there before he asked her who she was. Only then did he see her eyes — dark and fearful and sad. Then she stepped back into the shadows and vanished.

As he lay back in bed he thought about Eliana's painting. There was a reason for every painting.

Ross woke four hours later. There were no tours for him, so he went on a run, then showered and dressed, and drove off to the ancient city of San Gimignano, riding his scooter through the winding back roads of Chianti, past Greve, west at Castellina in Chianti, to Poggibonsi and into San Gimignano — the ancient city some guidebooks called the "medieval Manhattan," due to its abundance of bell towers. Though only thirteen of them remained, still a fair number for any town, at one time there were more than seventy bell towers in the city.

Ross quickly fell in love with the town. It was smaller than Siena, less commercial, quieter. Do tourists know that a city changes to meet them, Ross wondered, to fulfill their expectations? The very act of tourism seemed to defeat itself. As he wandered through the cobblestone streets, he stopped where a crowd of tourists stood in line, awaiting access to an exhibition. He stopped to see where they were going. Il Museo degli Strumenti di Tortura (The Museum of Torture Devices): a collection of instruments of torture, mostly remnants from the Inquisition, when men and women were tortured in the name of God. Ross turned away. After the last three years of his life he didn't need reminders of man's inhumanity to man. He certainly wasn't going to pay to see it on display.

He ate lunch at a sidewalk pizzeria, where he had a pleasant conversation with an elderly Italian woman from the town who wanted to know why he spoke such good Italian for an American, then invited him over to meet the family, which he carefully declined as he had an appointment back at home.

On his way from town he passed a hotel. He stopped and stared at it: Albergo dei Gigli (Hotel of the Lilies). He must have passed it on the way in, but hadn't noticed it then. Why did it seem so familiar to him? The longer he looked at it the more convinced he became that he had seen it before.

He walked up to its glass doorway and stepped inside. The lobby was small, marble-floored. A red and gold rug led to a dark walnut registration counter, the wall behind it emboldened with a bright brass lily — the symbol of Florence.

Suddenly it occurred to him why it was familiar. This was one of the hotels he had seen in a travel guide four years ago. It was one of the hotels that *she* had chosen for their honeymoon.

The man behind the counter spoke. "May I help you, sir?"

Ross looked at him, momentarily speechless. "No. I'm in the wrong place."

His heart raced. He walked out of the hotel and stood in the street, directionless as if suddenly lost. Two worlds had unexpectedly collided. It wasn't supposed to be this way. This hotel was to be a pleasant memory pasted in a photo album, not a reminder of all he had lost. He held his hand over his face until his thoughts calmed then walked back to his scooter.

It was past six when he arrived at Rendola. Alessio was in the corner of the courtyard kicking a soccer ball against the wall, its dull thud echoing in the square. Ross stopped to watch, his hands in his pockets.

"Looks like you're pretty good."

Alessio coughed. "I'm not."

"You're not?"

"The other kids call me *lumaca*. I can't run very fast. Sometimes I run out of breath."

Ross frowned, watched him kick the ball. *Lumaca*, he repeated to himself. He'd have to look it up. "May I see the ball?"

He kicked it to Ross.

Ross picked it up and spun it in his hands like a basketball. "Do you ever watch American football?"

He shook his head.

"Do you know how they play football?"

He shook his head again.

"It's like soccer except you carry the ball. And people try to throw you down to stop you from crossing the goal. Sometimes the coach decides to kick the ball into a little goal instead. When I

172

was little I was smaller than the other kids. I tried hard, but everyone just ran over me like I wasn't there. So the coach never let me play. I just sat on the side and watched everyone else play. Then I had an idea. I decided it didn't matter how big I was if I was a goal kicker. I practiced kicking the ball every day until I was the best kicker on the team. I won our biggest game of the year by kicking the ball through the goal."

"Wow."

"Just because you're not the fastest runner doesn't mean you can't be a good soccer player. Maybe you're just playing the wrong position. You look to me like the kind of guy who should play the most important position on the field. You look like a goalie."

"Really?"

"Most important job in the game. If the goalie doesn't stop the ball, it doesn't matter how good all the other players are, right?" It sounded right. "You know how to play goalie, don't you?"

"I stop the ball."

"Exactly. Where's your goal?"

"That rock. And the flower pot."

"Do you want to try?"

Alessio nodded.

"All right. You stand there and I'll kick the ball to you." Ross set the ball on the ground. "I'll take it easy for a while, but only at first." With his toe he nudged the ball toward the goal. Alessio fell on it.

"That was good. Let's try again."

Alessio threw the ball back to Ross. Ross kicked the ball slightly harder. Again Alessio stopped it.

"You are a soccer ball magnet."

Alessio grinned.

Eliana heard their talking and looked out from an open window. Then she walked outside to watch. She stood in the entryway, her arms crossed at her chest.

"All right, here it comes again. Remember, watch the ball, not me."

Alessio's gaze was focused. The ball bounced off of him, out of reach.

"Good block."

"Thanks."

Ross kicked it again and again, increasing some in speed, but just enough to guarantee Alessio's success. Alessio blocked all of them but one.

"Man, where I come from they have a name for guys like you. You're the bomb. You better let me get some through here or I'm quitting."

Alessio giggled with delight. He would raise each stopped ball triumphantly above his head and do a short victory dance while Ross pretended to get mad. "That does it," Ross said. "No more mister nice guy!"

Suddenly Alessio noticed his mother watching. "Look, Mom! I'm good."

"I can see that."

Ross glanced over at her and she smiled at him. Then he walked up to Alessio. He put his arm around him, looked over his shoulder at

Eliana and said in a whisper, "Listen, Alessio, man to man. You're making me look really bad here in front of your mother. Let me make just one goal, okay?"

Alessio considered his proposition. "All right. But just one."

"Thanks." Ross walked back with the ball under his arm. He set it on the ground and squared off in front of it. He eyed Alessio fiercely then gave him an obvious wink as a reminder. Then he kicked the ball right to him. Alessio fell on it, laughing loudly. Ross threw his hands in the air. "That's it. Enough humiliation for one day. I quit."

Alessio laughed. "I won!"

Eliana laughed too. "Good, because it's time for dinner. Come on, Alessio." She looked at Ross fondly. "Why don't you join us, loser?"

"So you can rub it in? I think not."

"Oh, don't be a sore loser. It's fried chicken."

"*Per favore*, Mr. Story."

"All right. But I want a rematch."

The three of them walked into the house, Alessio bouncing the ball on the ground until Eliana finally made him put it up in his room.

Eliana grabbed an extra place setting for Ross, then they sat down together at the dining room table. Alessio snatched a piece of chicken, followed by Ross.

"Mr. Ferrini, what are you forgetting?"

"Prayer?"

"Yes."

175

Ross surrendered his piece of chicken. "I forgot too. Sorry."

She winked at him. "Don't do it again. Alessio, would you say grace, please?"

He took Ross's hand, as well as Eliana's. "Okay."

After the prayer Eliana asked, "Ross, would you like some wine?"

"Please."

She uncorked a bottle of their house wine and poured him a glass, then one for Alessio and herself as well. "I hope you like our cantina's wine. It would be seditious to serve anything else."

"I do. It's different. What kind of grapes are these?"

"Mostly Sangiovese. This is blended with a little Merlot. It gives it that dark, fruity taste."

"You sound like you know what you're talking about."

"I know my wine."

The three of them ate until the chicken was nearly gone. Eliana offered Ross the last piece of chicken.

"Do you like it?"

"I love it. It's not something you can get at the local pizzeria."

"I like cooking American dishes now and then."

Alessio asked, "Can we play again tomorrow?"

"Mr. Story doesn't have time to play soccer," Eliana said.

"Mr. Story does have time," Ross said. "In

fact I demand a rematch."

"What's a rematch?"

"Another chance for me to win."

Alessio smiled. "You can't win. I'm the *bomb*."

"Yes, you are the bomb. I'm going to have to practice."

"Okay, all bombs to the bath," Eliana said. "And wipe your hands on the napkin, not your shirt."

"Can I take a shower?"

"Whatever. Call me when you're done."

"Goodbye, Mr. Story."

"Good night, Alessio."

Alessio ran up the stairs. Eliana followed him up with her gaze then looked back at Ross.

"Thank you for doing that."

"For doing what?"

"Playing with my son. It means a lot to him. He doesn't have a lot of friends out here and doesn't get to play much."

"It was my pleasure. He said the other kids tease him sometimes. What's a *lumaca?*"

Eliana frowned. "Did someone call him that?"

"Yes."

She shook her head. "It's a snail, no, it's a . . . ," she had a momentary lapse of English, "it's a slug."

"Children can be pretty mean."

"What makes it harder for Alessio is that the Italian children say Americans can't play soccer. Come to think of it so does his father. He forgets that Alessio is listening."

177

"Do the children think of him as an American? He has an Italian last name, he speaks perfect Italian."

"They still do. They know I'm American." She stood up, collecting the plates from the table.

"If it makes him feel any better, tell him that Italians can't play basketball."

"Unfortunately neither can he," she said from the kitchen. "Would you like some coffee?"

"No, *grazie.*"

She came back into the room. "I finished the backdrop of the portrait this morning. Do you want to fit in a session?"

"Sure."

"I need to get Alessio to bed first."

"I'll meet you in your studio in, what, half an hour?"

"Great. Just let yourself in."

When Ross returned, Eliana was already upstairs in her studio waiting for him. An Andrea Bocelli CD played softly in the background. The lighting was already set, the spotlight focused on the empty chair, the room lights dimmed. The smell of oil paints wafted through the room. Eliana was touching up a few spots in the background and she looked up as he entered. "Hi."

"Hi." He stepped inside. "Is Alessio asleep?"

"I hope so. He was still talking about your soccer match when I put him in bed."

"He's a good little kid." Ross sat down in his chair, positioning himself the best he could remember. "Is this close?"

"Come forward a little. There. Now turn a little to the right."

"I was wondering, is it dangerous for Alessio to participate in sports with his asthma?"

"There's always a risk. Sports can provoke asthma, especially sports with a lot of running."

"Like soccer."

"Like soccer. That doesn't mean he can't do it. There's been Olympic gold medalists who have asthma. You just need to know your limits. Maurizio thinks I baby him. Maybe he's right. It's a fine line between teaching him independence and keeping him safe. I just hope I'm not ruining him."

"He's hardly ruined. He's a bright, cheerful little boy. What more do you want?"

She smiled. "I guess nothing."

Ross looked around the room. "So Machiavelli really lived here."

"Lived and died here. In fact most of his works were written here."

"That's amazing. I was reading about him the other day. Most of his stuff is pretty heavy. What I didn't know is that he wrote some comedies."

"I didn't know that either."

"One was called *Belphegor*. It's about a devil who takes the form of a man and comes to earth in order to try marriage. After a little while he finds himself so wretched that he gladly returns to hell."

"Maybe it's his ghost that haunts this place."

"Cosa?" What?

"Nothing."

"So what are you working on today?"

"Shades. I always paint my pictures in black and white before I add color."

"Black and white."

"I prefer black and white. A lot of artists use burnt umber."

She looked over her brushes, carefully selected one, then rolled it in the paint. Then she looked at Ross, her eyes direct and unblinking, studying his face, the subtle curvature of his cheeks, his strong nose. She studied his features and as much admired them as she thought to commit them to the canvas. The colors would come later — it was the shades and proportions and distances she was concerned with now. It was nearly ten minutes before she spoke again, her voice coming calm and unexpected like a hypnotist's. "So you're really never going back to America?"

"Never."

She cocked her head. "Surely you miss something there."

"I miss a lot of things."

"Like what?"

"My brother," he answered immediately.

"Then what?"

He thought for a moment. "Then, I would have to say Swedish pancakes."

"Swedish pancakes?"

"You know the thin kind with those berries on top, dusted with powdered sugar."

"I know what they are, I just expected something more . . . meaningful. And more American."

"Since when aren't Swedish pancakes meaningful?"

Her eyebrows rose playfully.

"There are other things. I miss real maple syrup, the kind from Vermont. Decent corn on the cob. Ice in drinks. Lots of ice. Mexican food. Binaca. Doritos. Being able to eat out at two in the morning. Good plumbing. And Minnesota Vikings football."

Eliana liked his answer. It reminded her of home. "Anything else?"

"I miss hearing the Rolling Stones on the radio. 7-Elevens. Cars without the driver's side mirror ripped off. Hot chocolate with three inches of whipped cream. Streets wide enough to turn around on and people driving like they don't have a death wish. Dick Clark on New Year's Eve."

"Now you're making me really homesick."

"So what do you miss?"

"My mother. And my horses."

"You have horses?"

She sighed happily. "Two of them. A sweet, old Appaloosa named Apples. Also a part-Arabian named Sheba."

"Apples and Sheba." Ross smiled. "I've only ridden a horse twice. It just wasn't part of my city boy upbringing."

"Oh, and a clothes dryer," she suddenly added. "I miss having a dryer." She opened a tube of black paint and squirted another small circle on her palette. "What do you like most about Italy?"

"Another list. Cenci during the Carnival and porchetta sandwiches."

"It's always food with you, isn't it?"

"Hold on, there's more. I like the way the Italians respect the ancient. I love that no one cares when all the scooters move to the front of the intersection. That people don't walk around looking for someone to sue. I love Smart Cars. I love the whole idea that every town has a bell tower and a piazza. I love that you can park anywhere your car can fit. That people dress up for everything. And that they drink espressos that could clean an engine. I like how the women look sexy riding scooters. How the whole city just shuts down for holidays. I love the whole idea of Venice. The feel of a train station. Frutella candy." He glanced at her. "Okay, I'm back to food. It's your turn."

She thought for a moment. "I love the people and their sense of family. I love all the beautiful cathedrals. I love that Italians work to live instead of the other way around — at least most Italians. And the time I love most of all is the *Vendemmia*. The harvest."

"You help pick the grapes?"

"Well, not really. I usually take Alessio out for

the first day of picking when everyone's still fresh and excited. But there's something spiritual about the harvest. I don't know if I can describe it, there's a smell to the earth, when you're tramping through the grapes — you just have to experience it." She smiled. "And you will. We're starting the harvest next Wednesday morning. If you can come, we'd love to have you."

"I'll plan on it."

She lifted her brush again and began painting. "So what's the most unforgettable thing you've seen since you came here?"

He thought for a minute. "That's a hard question. Maybe St. Peter's Basilica and the Sistine Chapel." Suddenly his face brightened. "No, I know what it is. The Church of the Immaculate Conception."

"I've never heard of it. Where is it?"

"In Rome. It's just a few blocks from the Borghese Gardens. Near the American Embassy."

She peeked around the canvas. "Is it beautiful?"

"I thought it would be. There's kind of a nondescript staircase that leads up to it from the sidewalk. So I walked up thinking there might be some murals or tapestries inside. Instead there are rooms decorated with human bones and skeletons. On one wall I counted more than two hundred skulls. Different bones were set in plaster in mosaics. The chandeliers were made out of clavicles and pelvic bones and they hung from the ceiling by human spines."

"Are you making this up?"

"I'm not that macabre. And in the last room there were skeletons dressed in monk robes and a sign on the floor. It read, 'As you are we once were. As we are you someday will be.' "

"This is morbid. I don't like talking about this."

"There's a moral to this. As I walked out, I thought, *They're right, you know. It's all going to end. How can you justify wasting a single day of unhappiness? Not chasing what you really want in life.* That's all that divides us and those bones, time and this ethereal thing, life."

Eliana was suddenly somber. "So what if the things you want are in conflict with each other?"

"You either change what you want, or you find the back door."

"The back door?"

"There's always a back door. Sometimes you have to look for a while. But it's there."

Eliana looked at her portrait. "I'm not getting much done tonight."

"I talk too much. May I stretch?"

"Yes."

Ross raised his hands above his head. "What are you doing in the morning?"

She set down her brush and began putting away her paints. "Washing and ironing. And you?"

"I was thinking of going to Arezzo for the day. It's the jousting of the Saracen. You've probably seen it a dozen times already."

She shook her head. "I haven't. It's one of those things you intend to see but never get around to. Alessio asks every year if we can go. I guess he forgot this year."

"If you want, we could go together. I hate going to places alone with big crowds. It makes me feel like a ghost."

"What time does it start?"

"The jousting starts around four or five, but there are festivities all day long. I was planning to leave around noon."

"I need to call Maurizio first to see if it's all right, or if he's coming home. Can I let you know in the morning?"

"He's welcome to come along."

She smiled but said nothing. "I'll let you know."

She stood up, then they descended the stairs together. At the doorway she kissed his cheek. "That's for being so good to my son."

As simple as the kiss was, it warmed him. "It's not hard. I'll wait to hear from you," he said, his voice light with hope. "I'm getting up at sunrise to run so don't worry about calling too early."

"All right. Good night, Ross."

"Good night, Eliana."

Maurizio was lying in bed when his cell phone rang. He reached over and lifted it from the hotel nightstand. *"Pronto."*

"Hi, Maurizio? It's me."

He hesitated a moment. "Eliana? What's wrong?"

"Nothing's wrong. How are things?"

"*Come al sòlito.*" *Always the same.*

"Where are you?"

"Leeds."

"I'm sorry, I can't ever keep up with you." There was a silent pause. "The last time we talked you said you might be home tomorrow."

"No, I'm sorry, I need to be in Venice tomorrow. I won't be back until Wednesday."

"It's okay. I was just thinking of taking Alessio to Arezzo for the festival tomorrow."

"I'm sure he'll like that."

"Ross Story invited us to go with him."

"Who?"

"Mr. Story. Our new tenant."

"Oh, yes. Well, I will not be back until Wednesday, maybe even Thursday."

"Then I guess we'll go."

"Great. Have a good time. *Buona notte.*"

"*Buona notte.*"

Maurizio hung up the phone and rolled again to his back.

"*Chi era?*" *Who was that?* The woman stepped from the bathroom. Her copper-red hair was wet and she was wrapped in a bath towel.

"My wife."

A thin smile lifted her cheeks. "*Sei birichino.*" *You are a bad boy.*

Maurizio motioned her over and she came back to the bed.

186

CHAPTER 15

"Non si può dettar leggi al cuore."
One cannot make laws to rule the heart.
— Italian Proverb

"I spent the day with Eliana in Arezzo. Even amidst all the pomp and pageantry it was difficult keeping my eyes from her. I hope that I was not too obvious."
— Ross Story's diary

Ross's phone rang about eight. He was waiting for Eliana's call. *"Pronto."*

"Ross, this is Eliana."

"Ciao, bella."

"Ciao. Did I wake you?"

"No, I've already been out running."

"If the invitation is still open we'd like to go with you today."

"Great, I was hoping you would."

"I was thinking I could make a picnic supper."

"You don't need to go to that much trouble."

"It's no trouble. There's a lovely picnic site just past Incisa."

"What can I bring?"

"Just yourself. When do you think we should leave?"

"Around noon."

"We'll come over. *Ciao."*

"Ciao."

Eliana and Alessio knocked on Ross's door shortly before noon. Eliana held a large wicker picnic basket in front of her with both hands. It was a bright day and Eliana wore sleek, Italian sunglasses and a crimson tank top with matching shorts, vibrant against her bronze skin. She wore sandals that laced up past her ankles. She had clearly inherited the fashion sense of the Italians. She always looked different whenever he saw her. She was like a work of art; each time he saw something new in her — each time he saw the same painting in a different way, a perspective that belonged only to him.

"Hi, Alessio."

"Hi, Mr. Story."

Alessio wore denim shorts that fell past his knees and a gray T-shirt with the word *CIAO* in large black letters across the front. He also wore a small backpack, though his most notable accessory was the large grin on his face.

"Can we bring the soccer ball?"

Ross smiled at Eliana. "Of course," he said, stepping forward to help her. "Here, let me take that." He lifted the basket from her.

"Thank you. It's a little heavy."

They walked outside the courtyard, then Eliana opened the car's trunk for Ross. He set the basket inside and she handed him her car keys. Ross opened her door while Alessio threw his backpack onto the backseat of the car and followed it in. As soon as they were on the freeway, Alessio began drawing pictures.

Ross glanced up at him in the rearview mirror. "Are you going to be an artist like your mom?" Ross asked.

"Yep," he said without looking up.

Eliana smiled.

Forty-five minutes later they exited the freeway and headed east toward Arezzo, passing several small hamlets along the way. It was clear they were headed in the right direction, as colorful flags from the different competing quarters hung from the buildings and street corners of the cities they passed.

The weather was beautiful, tranquil blue skies with a few wisps of clouds, and the city was crowded for the event. Arezzo is an ancient city of stone, cold and dour, built as if its primary hope was to keep people out. A modern writer called the city nothing less than a dignified prison.

The closest parking they could find was a half mile from the square, and so Ross put Alessio on his shoulders and they followed the crowds into the city, which had been closed off to all but police cars and foot traffic. The narrow cobble roads, flanked on both sides by stone and stucco buildings, inclined steadily, feeding into the larger roads like tributaries of a river, all leading to and away from the main square — Piazza Grande.

The sounds of drums and trumpets could be heard around them, though in the echo of the stone corridors it was difficult to tell whether they were coming or going. The roads were lined with vendors selling wares brought especially for the day: roast pork or tripe sandwiches, wine and beer, miniature replicas of the Saracen, and scarves and flags representing the individual teams of the competing quarters.

The crowds were equally composed of natives and tourists, along with police and a sampling of those dressed in colorful Renaissance costume of the sixteenth century, when the tournament began.

The tournament has followed the same routine for more than three centuries. It begins with the herald's proclamation of the event in each corner of the city. This is followed by the parading of the competing teams from parish to parish for the priests' blessings of their weapons, before meeting in the main square for the culminating event: the jousting competition between the knights.

They arrived in time to see the last of the herald's proclamations. They stopped at a pizzeria for lunch then wandered around the center of the city, carried along in the flow of the masses, taking in the revelry. They came upon one of the teams as they arrived at a parish church for the blessing of their weapons. They followed the troop on to the cathedral square, where their weapons received the final blessing of the day by the bishop.

As the cathedral bells rang, the crowds moved steadily toward the Piazza Grande. When Ross,

Eliana and Alessio arrived, the square was already crowded nearly to capacity, as were all the surrounding buildings. People leaned from windows or gathered on balconies, and flags hung from nearly every window. Flowers, vibrant costumes and large bouquets of balloons were set in bright antithesis to the dull stone of the square.

Running diagonally across the stone square was a thick strip of dirt that had been brought in for the event. The strip was about six yards wide and led to the Saracen — the focal point and namesake of the tournament. The Saracen was a wooden figurine of a bearded Saracen soldier, the ancient enemy of Arezzo.

Eliana spotted a vacant spot on a stone ledge next to the bleachers and they sat down. A half hour later the first of the knights arrived, carrying their lances aloft. They were followed by the foot soldiers, dressed in armor, carrying shields and spears or crossbows. A page, a young boy about Alessio's age, came next on foot. He was wearing a beautiful purple velvet costume and a hat with feather quills. Then the herald they had seen earlier arrived, on horseback, led by his servant. He stopped in the center of the square and held out a large scroll that he read from, proclaiming the opening of the tournament. He was followed by the *bandieres,* the flag bearers. The flag show lasted the longest of the exhibitions. Flags flew across the square, spun, leapt and flashed like fire, amid the spectacular acrobatics of the bearers. During the performance Alessio pointed heavenward. "Look," he said. Hundreds of birds were circling immediately above the square, spectators to the proceedings.

The square, already loud with the crowd's applause and shouts, was suddenly shaken by the blare of trumpets, then the thunder of drums. The band marched into the square, the corps fully dressed in costumes as colorful as a royal flush. The trumpets were more than four feet in length, and tied to each of the silver, fluted instruments was a flag. The music suddenly stopped and the master and vice master of the field arrived, escorted in on horseback. They spoke briefly to the crowd about the history of the event, then raised their scepters, the sign for the tournament to commence.

When they were done, four men, each in different costume and carrying a lance, stood before the Saracen dummy. They each tested their lance against the Saracen's shield.

"Who are they?" Eliana asked.

"They're the captains of the teams. They're checking the Saracen to make sure that it spins freely." Ross could tell from her expression that she didn't understand. "The Saracen is mounted to a pivot. When the knights hit the shield of the Saracen with their lances, the Saracen spins around. Part of their objective is to not get hit by the Saracen's mace as it swings around."

"So that's what he's holding in his other hand."

Ross nodded. "In ancient days the balls used to have sharp spikes so you could actually see if the knight got hit. Now they're just made of leather and judges do the scoring. Much less exciting."

"Cool," said Alessio.

Eliana shook her head. "You men."

Before the tournament began, the knights lined up flank to flank, the horses and knights wearing matching ceremonial costumes, the effulgent colors of their quarters' flags. The horses were adorned in blankets and head masks that matched their riders' outfits. The knights wore uniforms with satin capes and tall, elaborate helmets — some mounted with figurines of saints or animals. Their lances were striped like large candy canes and held aloft like flagpoles — the flag of their quarter attached to the tip.

"Who do you think is going to win?" Ross asked Alessio.

Alessio pointed toward one of the knights. "Him."

"The blue guy?"

"Yeah."

"I think the red and green man will win," said Eliana.

"Why?"

"Women's intuition."

"Really?"

"That and because his costume is the prettiest. It's kind of Christmasey."

"Christmasey? Is that English?"

She playfully hit him. "Who do you think will win then?"

"I'm with Alessio. I think the blue guy."

"Why him?"

"Because he looks *crudele*."

"And cruel people win?"

"In wrestling matches and horse jousting tournaments cruel usually wins."

"Ten thousand lire says Christmasey does better than *crudele*."

He shook her hand. "You're on."

The first horse trotted to the end of the dirt trail as the crowd hushed in anticipation. The rider carefully eyed the Saracen, balancing his lance in his hand and beneath his arm while his horse strained at the bit, moving impatiently beneath him.

Then the knight leaned forward and shouted and the horse galloped toward the Saracen, the animal's legs and head flailing wildly. The knight absorbed his mount's motion with his legs while the rest of his body remained perfectly still, his eyes and lance focused on the target mounted to the Saracen's shield. When the lance struck, the crowd erupted. The Saracen spun around, his mace narrowly missing the knight.

Alessio clapped wildly. "Did you see it! Did you see it!"

Ross smiled at his excitement and ran his hand through Alessio's hair. "Pretty cool, huh?"

"Yeah!"

"Beautiful, aren't they?" Eliana said.

"That's right, you have horses," Ross answered.

"I was talking about the knights."

Ross laughed. "You women and your knights."

She smiled. Then, without word, her hand moved gently into his, as if she were unaware of its action. He looked down at her hand, then closed his hand around hers. A minute later, when she took back her hand to clap for the next knight, his hand felt remarkably empty and cold, as if suddenly deprived of circulation. The sense of her hand still lingered, as though it had left an imprint in his.

One by one the knights charged the Saracen. The crowd grew in noise and excitement, the sound rising, hanging in the air like the dust from the horses' hooves. Each run seemed faster and more furious than the previous. When all the knights had run, Porta Crucifera was proclaimed the winner and the bleachers emptied into the square to celebrate the winning knights.

Eliana and Ross took Alessio by the hands, and the three of them wound through the crowd back to the car. They drove back toward Rendola, exited the freeway near Incisa, and drove up through San Donato in Collina, to Eliana's picnic site. As the sun fell toward the horizon, they were alone at the top of a wooded hill overlooking the Valdarno Valley.

There were several tables, and they chose one that was made from a massive stone grinding wheel once used to crush olives for oil. There were wooden benches around it. Ross spread a blanket out over the stone table, and Eliana sat down and began making sandwiches while Ross and Alessio went off together into the nearby forest to gather firewood. They returned with a small bundle of branches that they stacked near a crude fire pit. The sun was setting as Ross sat down next to Eliana at the table.

"How did you find this place?"

"Anna brought me here a few years ago. It's pretty, isn't it?"

He nodded. "It reminds me of a place I used to camp with my family as a kid."

Eliana smiled at the thought. It was the first time he had spoken of his childhood, and it pleased her. "With your parents?"

"My parents and stepparents."

"How were your stepparents?" She glanced over at him. "You don't mind me asking?"

"No. They were okay." He paused. "That sounds ungrateful. It wasn't the best situation. It was hard for them. It's hard enough raising your own family, let alone having someone else's on top of that."

"They already had children?"

"Four."

"Oh my. Were you treated differently than the others?"

"Yes," he said hesitantly. "It's not that they meant to make us feel like an imposition; they just didn't hide it very well. We felt like guests who had overstayed our welcome. To make matters worse my brother was pretty difficult. He was always rebelling against them. He ran away every fcw months. One time, when he was sixteen, he just never came back. He ended up living with friends."

"Do you keep in touch with them now?"

"I did until —" He stopped abruptly.

She glanced up. "Until what?"

"Nothing." He stepped toward her, his mind fishing for another conversation. "What kind of sandwiches are you making?"

Eliana looked at him. She wondered if subconsciously he wanted to tell her more. Her instinct told her to wait for him — that he would tell her everything when he was ready. Or maybe it was a matter of when she was ready.

She smiled. "A peanut butter sandwich for Alessio. For us there is salami and my not-so-famous PLT."

"PLT?"

She held a sandwich aloft. "Pancetta, lettuce and tomato. It's like a BLT only saltier."

Ross grinned. "I'll start the fire. Do you need anything else from the car?"

"There's a grape pie still in the basket."

"Grape pie?"

"You haven't lived until you've had my grape pie. Actually it's an American recipe, but living in Chianti, on a vineyard, I couldn't help but try it."

"Is it good?"

"Oh, yeah. Trust me."

Ross brought the grape pie from the car then called for Alessio, who was kicking his soccer ball around the tables.

"Hey, Alessio, want to help me make a fire?"

"Can I?" He glanced toward his mother, who had indoctrinated him with the evils of matches and fires since he was old enough to know what they were.

"You can help," she said. "But be careful."

"I will."

Ross showed Alessio how to start a fire by building a tepee with small twigs and filling it with wood chips.

He looked at Alessio seriously. "Remember, don't try this at home," he said. He glanced at Eliana for approval. She smiled at him.

"Okay, sir."

After finishing supper, they sat around the fire eating grape pie, talking and then laughing as Alessio reenacted the jousting tournament. They stayed at the picnic site until the night was cool and pitch-black around them, the dying fire glowing orange and white, with occasional sparks rising in the air like fireflies. The sound of frogs and insects grew loud.

Alessio had trouble keeping his eyes open and leaned sleepily against Eliana. Still Eliana procrastinated. It had been a good day. She didn't want it to end. For the first time in years she felt like part of a family — the way she always thought it should feel. Finally Ross kicked out the fire and carried Alessio to the car, while Eliana piled everything else into the picnic basket. Alessio stretched out across the backseat.

He was asleep by the time they arrived at the villa. Ross carried him upstairs to his bed while Eliana pulled down the sheets. She tucked him in, kissed his forehead, and then Ross and Eliana descended the stairs together. As Ross walked to the front door, Eliana said, "Not so fast. You still owe me."

"For?"

"Don't tell me you've already forgotten our bet. My knight won."

"Oh, right. The one you chose because it was pretty. No, Christmasey." He reached for his wallet. "Ten thousand lire."

"Christmasey beats *crudele*. Remember that. And let's make that dollars, not lire."

"That will only take me about six months to earn," he said. Then he added, "Thanks for coming with me. It's been a good day."

"It has been a good day. Thank you for inviting us. We're surrounded by this amazing culture and we never go out and do anything anymore."

She looked at him, her eyes shining. "I'm glad you came to Rendola, Ross."

Ross just looked into her face. He smiled, and for a moment neither of them knew what to say, though this time it wasn't awkward. Then Ross asked, "Another session tomorrow?"

"I can't tomorrow. Anna gets back from the sea."

"Anna. I'd almost forgotten about her."

"Then Wednesday we begin the grape harvest. Would you like to join Alessio and me? We only go out for a couple hours."

"I'd love to. What time does it start?"

"Eight o'clock. a.m."

He made a mental note. "Eight o'clock Wednesday. I'll be there."

"Good. Good night, Ross." She leaned forward and kissed his cheek. This time he put his arms around her and held her against him, her body warm and soft against his. The gesture surprised Eliana, but she didn't move away.

"Good night, Eliana."

Her voice was lower, almost a whisper, "Good night, Ross."

Back in his apartment, he wrote in his journal then lay in bed and looked at the ceiling, recounting the day. All the noise and excitement and pageantry seemed to pale against Eliana. He couldn't remember the last time he had felt so good. Then he suddenly could. It was the last time he had fallen in love.

CHAPTER 16

"Chi vuol nascòndere l'amore sempre lo manifesto."
When one tries to hide love,
one gives the best evidence of its existence.
— Italian Proverb

Anna returned to Rendola with all the subtlety of a summer thunderstorm. She held her horn down for fifty meters as her red, vintage Renault climbed the drive to the villa. Eliana heard her and called for Alessio.

"Come on, Alessio, Aunt Anna's back!"

Alessio screamed and raced to the front door. "Slow down, sport!" They arrived outside the villa just as Anna climbed out of her car.

"Ciao, ragazzi!" she shouted, "I'm back."

"Welcome home!" Eliana shouted. They hugged and kissed cheeks. And Anna crouched and kissed Alessio. "You grew!"

"Really?" Alessio asked, touching the top of his head.

"Sì. Now come see what Aunt Anna has brought you." Anna took a large plastic sack from the backseat of the car and handed it to Alessio.

"For me?"

"Just for you."

He lifted out a plastic dump truck.

"Wow. *Grazie.*"

The women each pulled a bag from the car and started back to the villa.

"So how was everything?" Eliana asked.

"Marvelous. Absolutely marvelous. The sea has never been bluer, the weather never kinder."

Eliana smiled at Anna's dramatics. "So Claudia wasn't unbearable after all."

"Claudia who? I met the most beautiful man."

"A man?"

"*Sì, sì,*" she said, twisting her wrist to imply there was more to be said when young ears weren't around.

They set Anna's bags down just inside her house. "Come on over, Anna. We haven't eaten dinner yet; we were waiting for you."

"Oh, good, I'm hungry as a wolf."

The table was already set for three. Eliana reheated their meal, and they sat down to a dish of gnocchi with ragù sauce and toasted crostini spread with a pâté made from white beans. They talked for nearly two hours before Eliana sent Alessio upstairs to bed.

"I want to stay and listen some more," he said.

"No," said Anna. "We have woman talk. It will burn the ears of small boys. Now go up. We'll play tomorrow."

"Okay," he said grudgingly.

"Good night, son. Give Aunt Anna and me a kiss."

"Yes, come, my Alessio." She kissed him.

"Now, don't forget to brush your teeth."

"I won't."

When he had disappeared at the top of the stairs, Eliana asked, "So, does Romeo have a name?"

"Andrea. Andrea Deluca." She spoke the name as if she were unwrapping a present, paying special attention to roll the r. "We danced, we drank wine, we strolled along the beach under the moon — it was so romantic."

Eliana laughed at her excitement. "I'm so pleased for you."

"You should be. I forgot how wonderfully intoxicating it is to be in love."

Though she said nothing, Eliana understood. "Where was Claudia during all this?"

"At the house sulking. Claudia won't be speaking to me for a century, but that's just one of the many benefits."

"So where did you meet?"

"Claudia, bless the boar, and I had a little tiff, so I went out alone for a walk. He followed me six blocks before he asked if I would have coffee with him."

Eliana smiled. "Where does he live?"

"In Genoa. He was staying at a beach house with his cousin."

"Will you see him again soon?"

"Yes. He's coming for the *Festa della Vendemmia*."

"Oh, good."

"Che fico, che uomo!" What a fig, what a man!

Eliana smiled at this as she stacked their plates on top of each other, then gathered up the silverware from the table. "So what's he like?"

"*Carino,* short and plump. A little Botticelli. And he's a magician in the kitchen. He can cook like my grandmother." Then she said, "Did I tell you he has the most marvelous lips I've ever tasted?"

"No, you didn't."

Eliana took the plates into the kitchen. Anna collected the glasses and followed her in.

"So what happened while I was gone?"

"Alessio had a bad attack. We had to rush him to emergency."

"*Mamma mia.* I'm sorry." She shook her head. "Anything else?"

"Nothing. Maurizio was only here for two days. Same old life."

Anna looked vexed. "I don't believe you. Something happened."

"What do you mean?"

"You've changed."

"In what way?"

"You seem breezy."

"I'm just glad you're back."

"Did you meet someone?" Anna scrutinized Eliana's face.

"Anna."

"It's the American, no?"

"Anna."

"That is not a denial. I knew it. What is he like?" When Eliana hesitated, Anna exclaimed, "I was right. Out with it."

She rolled her eyes. "Okay, he's nice. He's very sweet."

"*Dolcezza,* you say! This is news. How did you meet him? Did you take him a housewarming gift like I suggested?"

"If I had done it like you suggested, I would have been wearing a lace negligee. When Alessio had his attack, he drove us to the hospital."

Her face widened with the expression of a teenage girl asking a secret. "And . . . ?"

"And what?"

"You and the American. How . . ."

"Anna, stop this. I'm married."

"Does he know you're married?"

"Yes. Of course he does. He's already met Maurizio."

Anna looked disappointed. "Well, he's certainly good for you. You're not the same girl I left, that's for sure."

"Still just Eliana." Eliana changed the subject. "Would you like some wine?"

"Who needs wine when you're drunk on love? I better go home; he's going to call tonight. Thank you for dinner." She kissed her. "Let's have coffee tomorrow."

"*Certo.* I'm glad you're back, Anna."

"Me too. It's good to be home."

Eliana finished clearing the table then went upstairs to her painting. From her studio window she looked out across the courtyard. Ross's kitchen light was still on. She wondered what he was doing inside. Anna's light was on too and it made her glad. She was happy that Anna was finally back.

She was dying to tell Anna about Ross — not that she needed to. Anna always saw through her. Anna was right; Eliana had changed. She felt different.

Whether he intended to or not, Ross made her feel new and beautiful again, as well as other things — a whole curious palette of bright and exotic feelings.

She turned on her music and began working on his portrait. Even the portrait was evidence of change. She had never before felt so connected to a painting.

She remembered, back when she was in college, a painting instructor had once confessed to her that he got a tremendous rush in working with live models. He felt as if, in painting them, he owned a portion of them, in the way some aboriginal tribes believe a photograph captures a soul. Maybe that's what she felt now, that in painting him she might in some way own him, in a way her conscious mind would not allow.

Artists and authors often fall in love with their subjects, though the attraction she felt had started even before she touched brush to canvas. It started that first night they met.

Ross Story was a different kind of man from Maurizio, and she didn't know if it was the influence of culture or personality, or perhaps the sum of both. The truth was that she didn't know men that well. She had no brother, and her father, though loving, had always been a little distant. She hadn't dated all that much. She had

had a few boyfriends in high school. Cowboys. In a small town and a small school, with a graduating class of thirty-six, the pickings were meager and one tended to be branded as so-and-so's girl, and the brand inevitably stuck longer than the relationship. She often laughed when she thought of the modern mystique of the cowboy — usually proffered in bodice-ripper romance novels — talk of free range and wild horses, soft-spoken Marlboro men with hard bodies and steely eyes. *Marry one,* she thought. She wanted more from her life than getting up at four to milk the cows and feed the chickens.

College was a different world. Going from Vernal to the University of Utah was like dropping from a fishbowl into a lake. But it was a blur, and just as she began to warm to the change, her father died. His absence left an empty space in her life which, consciously or not, she almost immediately felt the need to fill.

She wished that she had taken courtship more seriously. Or at least been more intelligent about it. Did anyone really spend enough time deciding whom to marry? It seemed to Eliana that most people just chose someone who looked good to them at the time, without really checking the label for its contents. The relational equivalent of fast food. The Italians said it best: romance and wisdom aren't often seen in the same company.

She had spent years deciding which college to attend, weighing the costs and benefits, and not a hundredth of that time or energy deciding something of infinitely more importance — whom she should spend the rest of her life with. And that was her intent. In the Webb home in Vernal, Utah, marriage was for keeps.

She hadn't known that there were men like Ross Story. Men who valued what she thought. Men who were emotionally available. Men who didn't have just one thing on their mind — two if you counted sports. Not that she disparaged sexual attraction. She didn't. It was pleasurable and delicious in its own way — just not at the exclusion of everything else.

Though he never spoke of it, she knew that Ross was attracted to her. It's not hard for a woman to tell. She knew by the way he smiled in her presence, by the inaudible cues when she moved in certain ways, when she brushed up against him, accidentally or sometimes not. She caught him staring at her a few times, though he turned away as if embarrassed. It was intoxicating to feel desirable again — especially to a man she found so desirable.

Sometimes, as she painted him, she found herself just staring, gathering the hues and light on his body and then unable to translate them to the canvas — as if she were trying to speak a language she didn't understand. He was gorgeous. Gorgeous and thoughtful and interesting. Why wasn't he married? Why had he come so close to marriage only to have it derailed? Something had happened. Something profound enough to keep him from talking about it. And though she wanted to know what it was, a part of her didn't. His mysterious past held its own pleasure for her, as she came to know him slowly, in the same way she painted him. One stroke at a time.

CHAPTER 17

"Anna, Eliana's sister-in-law, is back from holiday. We had the most interesting dialogue in the garden, though I likely contributed less than a dozen words to the whole of it. How often the most serious of discussions begin with the lightness of simple pleasantries . . ."
— Ross Story's diary

Ross spent the next few days mostly downtown, either at the Uffizi or nearby, keeping his distance from Rendola while Anna settled back in. He didn't know what effect her return would have on his relationship with Eliana. She was, after all, Maurizio's sister.

He came home from work late Tuesday afternoon, made himself a sandwich and, as twilight fell, went outside to the garden to relax with a new novel he had bought that morning. He didn't see Anna sitting outside on the garden bench as he came around a tall hedge of laurel.

"Buona sera, Signor Story."

Ross turned around. "Oh. *Salve,* Anna. Welcome home."

"Grazie. How are things?"

"Good."

"With the apartment?"

"All is good."

She patted the empty space on the bench next

210

to her. "Here, sit with me."

Ross accepted her invitation. He leaned back on the bench, his arms across the back of it. For a moment the two of them just looked out over the vineyards.

"Looks like storm clouds in the west," Anna said. "Rain by morning. Pretty though."

"*Sì.*"

"How could anyone look at that and doubt there's a God?" she said. "God's an artist, I think. The world is His canvas. Our most clever, our Leonardos and our Michelangelos, make only copies of what He already did." A wind blew across the land, over them, as if in confirmation.

"So how was your vacation, Anna?"

"It was wonderful. Seems the older I get the more drawn I feel to the sea."

"It seems that way to me too," Ross said.

"Still, after a week or so I can't wait to get back home. *Casa, dolce casa,*" she said. *Home, sweet home.*

Ross just smiled.

"I must say I'm surprised by how much things have changed in my absence."

"In what way?"

"Eliana, mostly. I don't remember the last time I saw her so happy."

"It's probably just because you're back. She's missed you."

"Not as much as usual, perhaps," she said cryptically. Ross suddenly felt a little uncomfortable.

"And then there's little Alessio. He was showing me the soccer trading cards you gave him. He's pretty taken with you. You're all he's talked about since I got back. I'm happy for him; it's good for him to have a man interested in him." She turned to face Ross. "But then I could probably say the same for Eliana, couldn't I?"

Ross looked at the ground. She was playing with him. "Where are you going with this?"

She smiled slightly. "*That* was *my* next question."

Ross looked over, studied her face. As direct as her accusation was, there was no hint of condemnation in her eyes.

"I know what you're thinking, me being Maurizio's sister. Don't worry, I'm not going to tell anybody. Especially my brother. I may be his sister, but I don't like him. I think he is a fool. He doesn't deserve Eliana, and when I think of how starved Alessio is for his father's approval and attention, it makes me want to cry. So if you are bringing a little happiness to my two favorite people in this world, then God bless you."

Ross still didn't speak and there was quiet again. Anna suddenly clasped her thick hands together, as if in prayer. "I think you're a good man, Signor Story. I have a sixth sense for things like that. But my allegiance is to Eliana and Alessio. Eliana's as innocent as an angel. She loves the Lord and she loves Alessio more than herself. And now she's in love with you." Ross showed no reaction, though he wondered how

Anna knew Eliana's feelings.

"Oh, don't pretend you didn't notice, she is."

"She told you that?"

"She didn't need to." She paused, swatted at a fly that had landed on her hair. "Listen to me. The road you two are on might seem like a simple joy walk now, but make no mistake, it is perilous. And you're further down it than either of you realize. If you're not serious about the journey, I suggest you get off the path, because you are setting Eliana up for a fall I don't think she can handle."

Ross only rubbed his hands together in thought.

"You know, this whole affair ought to be black and white. What God has brought together let no man tear asunder — not even handsome Ross Story. But as God is my witness I don't know what's the right thing to do. Because I can't believe it's right that a heart as good as Eliana's needs to live without love for the rest of her life. And unless Maurizio undergoes a conversion akin to the apostle Paul's on the road to Damascus, that's exactly what's in store for her." She looked away in thought. Her eyes were moist now; her voice turned solemn. "Frankly, I have no desire to spend the next decade watching her wither away. So I have no idea what's right and what's wrong here. I'm just praying that you have some idea of where you're going and what to do when you get there."

She looked again to the fields. Again there was

silence, then her expression suddenly lightened. "I think Michelangelo was right; God didn't create us just to abandon us. No one creates without leaving a portion of themselves in it. It's not possible." She smiled. "But what do I know? You're the art expert. *Buona notte, Signor Story.*" She stood up and walked from the garden. Ross watched her go then looked back out over the vineyards. He sat there, lost in thought, until the green of the garden faded to black.

CHAPTER 18

"Il vino e il latte dei vecchi."
Wine is old men's milk.
— Italian Proverb

The old men were always the first to arrive at the
vineyard. It was part of an inalterable cycle of
sowing and reaping. The vines stretched out their
new green tendrils to the maternal trellis, the
seeds appeared in small clusters, and the grapes
grew and ripened. Then the old men would come,
as if drawn by the smell of the grapes, like the bees
and birds. They'd come wobbling up on their
rusted bicycles a half hour before the harvest was
scheduled, some an hour sooner. They had already had their coffees, or if it were a cold
morning, their grappinos, and they would stand
around with the other old men, swapping stories
of past harvests, or laying out plastic harvest baskets in preparation, and waiting for the call to
work.

The young workers, mostly students, strag-
gled in right at eight o'clock or five minutes past,
harried and tired, having woken only minutes
before. The old men would grumble about the
young people and their tardiness, but it was with
forgiveness and done more to call attention to
their own work ethic than out of actual annoy-
ance.

There is a palpable excitement on the first day of the *Vendemmia,* like men standing around the waiting room of a maternity ward. Every generation felt it, was charged by its electricity. They slapped each other on the back, laughed and kissed each other. Everyone was happy.

The harvest baskets waited next to the trellises, and the tractors were fired up and brought in line to the end of the rows, pulling large metal trailers that would be filled and refilled, bringing in a kilo of fruit with each haul — more than a ton of grapes — four times a day. Each tractor drove down a wide row lined with trellises while two teams of four workers, two teams to each side of the tractor, moved down the row with it, cutting the thick, woody stems, separating the grapes from the vines with metal shears, dropping the fruit into plastic baskets.

When Ross arrived, Eliana was already there with Alessio. She was wearing denim jeans, rolled up at her ankles, sneakers and a form-fitting white T-shirt. It was the most American he had ever seen her. She couldn't have looked more beautiful. Alessio saw him first.

"Mr. Story! Over here!"

Eliana quickly looked over. She smiled at him sweetly.

"*Ciao,* Ross," she said. When he was near her, she kissed his cheeks. "I'm so glad you came."

"I'm glad to be here."

She handed Ross a pair of shears. "These are for you. Do you want gloves? It's pretty sticky business; the nectar gets everywhere."

Ross looked at the old men and their calloused bare hands. "No. I'll be fine." To Alessio he said, "Are you ready?"

"Yeah. I hope there's not a lot of bees this time."

"No one said anything about bees."

"Lots of bees," Eliana said. "We're not the only ones attracted to the ripe grapes. No one told you about the birds and the bees?"

"Not recently."

"We plant hedges of blackberry bushes around the perimeter of the vineyard because the blackberries ripen before the grapes and attract the birds and bees to them instead of the vines. Of course that doesn't stop the boars."

"Boars?"

"A pack of wild boars can decimate a vineyard."

"Have you ever seen a wild boar?"

"No. Just their tracks. They're nocturnal. One night, I think it was my second year here, I was lying in bed when I suddenly heard this terrible snorting and grunting. You wouldn't believe how loud it was. It sounded like they were right outside my door. I was terrified. Maurizio was gone and I had no idea what to do. The next day there were hoof prints all over the vineyard. Big ones and baby ones, a whole pack. They ate almost a full acre of grapes."

"So how do you stop them?"

"We put electric wires on the trellises. The

boars touch that wire with their wet snouts and they lose their taste for grapes. Some of the large vineyards use sound cannons, but Luca says that they don't work that well. At first the poor beasts are terrified out of their wits, but pigs are smart. They figure out pretty quickly that the sound doesn't hurt them, so they just go on eating."

Ross just looked at her as she spoke, listening less to what she was saying than to how she was saying it. She was showing off her knowledge of winemaking and he liked that she wanted to impress him.

"So where's Anna?"

"Anna never comes to the harvest. She says she sweats too much."

"And Maurizio?"

"He's the *capo*. It's beneath him."

"And not the *capo*'s wife?"

She shrugged. "I'm American. I don't know better."

Just then a call went out from the foreman, and the pickers all moved toward the first section of vines to be harvested.

Ross, Eliana and Alessio took their place on a row that was about a hundred meters long, sloping gently down into a valley. The vines were full, drooping with the weight of the grapes, blushed, dark and plump against the green vines.

"So how does this work?"

"It's easy." Eliana took a bunch of grapes in her hand. "Hold the bunch out like this, snip the vine with your shears," she cut the stem, "and drop them in the basket. When the basket's full, we shout *Pieno* and the tractor driver brings us a new basket and dumps this one in his trailer."

"Simple enough. Even for a city boy."

"Oh, if you come across a bad bunch of grapes, just leave them on the vine."

Ross looked down at the vine. "How do I know if they're bad?"

"Call their wives."

He looked up.

"Sorry. Just watch for mold. You can ask me. Or if you're not sure, just leave it; someone will come along behind us to check and they'll take it if it's still good. You won't have to worry much about mold; we haven't had much rain lately."

Just then an old man, barely five feet tall, with thinning silver hair and dark eyebrows, walked up on the other side of the trellis. He was wearing boots and denim pants with a long-sleeved shirt. He was missing three of his front teeth, which was apparent because he was smiling widely, happy to be working alongside the *capo*'s beautiful wife and son.

He greeted Eliana. *"Buon giorno, bella signora."*

"Buon giorno, Massimo."

Ross liked the old Italian men. They had no pretense, no inhibition. He envied their freedom.

Eliana introduced Massimo to Ross, though the old man had little interest in him and stooped instead to run his sausage-like fingers through Alessio's hair. A child was a novelty among the workers, and they were all happy to see Alessio in the fields.

"Massimo is great," Eliana said. "He's been here forever. Long before I came. We don't even know where he lives; he just shows up here the first day of harvest, ready to go. All the old guys who work black are that way."

"Work black?"

"Working *nero*. It means we pay them under the table. They have to work that way, otherwise they'd lose their pensions. These old men are our most valuable workers. They know the land here better than their own bodies.

"I don't think the grapes would grow without them. I know they'd never get picked without them. They keep the younger workers moving. If you get just young people together, they talk too much and pick too slowly. The old guys don't let them. They keep the pace. So we put one of them with every two or three of the young ones."

"How long does the whole harvest take?"

"About two weeks. Ten days to two weeks. We have seventeen hectares. Just a little over forty acres."

"Aren't there machines that pick the grapes?"

"There are, but for a premium wine, grapes should be handpicked. The machines tend to suck up things you don't really want in wine."

"Such as?"

"Mildewed grapes, green grapes, bees, spiders, lizards."

"You mean my table wine has lizard in it?"

"It could. It's not a big deal." She pulled her hair back behind her ears. "It adds to the aroma."

"*Cominciamo,*" Massimo said, lifting his shears to the vine.

"All right, let's go, gentlemen," Eliana said.

The group began cutting the grapes. Eliana was quicker than Ross, her slender fingers more experienced and nimble. For a while Ross tried just pulling the bunches from the vine, but he found that the stems were stronger than he'd expected and it actually slowed the work. He felt foolish for having challenged the wisdom of the ages. Before the end of the first two trellises, his hands were stained dark purple with juice. It was clear to Ross that Eliana was there only for Alessio's sake, laughing and playing with him, shooing away bees and eating the grapes. They stayed close together, working steadily throughout the morning as the laughter and talk of the workers slowed with the heat and fatigue of the day. Around noon some of the workers began gathering empty baskets and walking back toward the cantina.

Eliana glanced down at her watch. "It's lunchtime."

Ross took their basket over to the trailer, dumped it, then brought it back, setting it down next to the unfinished trellis.

Eliana wiped the sweat from her face with her forearm. "I think I'm done for the day. We usually just work for an hour, but Alessio was having such a good time we just kept on going."

"You're a good little worker, Alessio," Ross said. "You held your own against these college kids."

"Thanks."

Eliana bumped up against Ross as they walked. "You seem to be enjoying yourself."

"It feels great being out here. There's something cathartic about working the land. It's something we white-collar guys miss." He looked over at her. "I was thinking, you could probably get tourists to pay to come over here and pick grapes. 'For a limited time and your entire bank account, you too can experience the real Chianti.' "

Eliana laughed. "You sound like Tom Sawyer. Does the ad man in you ever die?"

"Never."

"Well, I'd never sign up. We had raspberry bushes back in Vernal. Raspberries and peas. I hated it when we had to pick."

They stopped near the cantina. "Manuela's making lunch for us back at the villa. We still have a little time; would you like a quick tour of the winery?"

"Yes."

"How about you, Alessio? Do you want to go through the winery or back home?"

"Back home."

"Okay. Tell Manuela we'll be there in fifteen minutes."

"Okay. Bye, Mr. Story."

"See ya, pal."

Alessio darted off across the field.

"Don't forget to wash your hands!" Eliana shouted after him. She groaned. "If he gets those hands on the furniture . . ." She watched him until he disappeared near the villa. Then she turned her attention back to Ross.

"Is there a place we can wash?"

"Sorry, right over there." She led him to where a brass spigot emerged from the stucco wall of the cantina, running into a stone basin, chipped and worn around its brim. Around the base of the basin wild capers grew. They washed their hands, then Ross washed his face in the cool water.

The small strips of grass around the cantina were crowded with workers who had retrieved their lunches and staked their territories. Again the line between generations was clear. There were the old men with their tablecloths and little bottles of wine and meat and cheese and bread, packed by their old wives. And then there were the young workers who lay down wherever they could find shade, with their sandwiches and chips and bottles of soda or beer. A cloud of smoke rose from the cantina as the workers all lit their cigarettes.

Eliana led Ross around the building to the back. There were men there, the tractor drivers and Luca, who wore a baseball cap and carried a clipboard. Luca looked up at them as they approached.

"Buon giorno, signorina," Luca said.

"Buon giorno, signori," she replied.

Then Luca glanced at Ross. Ross nodded, but Luca only turned away, continuing his conversation with the tractor drivers.

"This is where wine starts," Eliana said to Ross, as they approached a large metal bin brimming with grapes. "This is the collector. This is where the tractors dump the grapes we harvest, then the grapes are pushed by a giant corkscrew into the stemmer-crusher . . . that thing," she said, pointing to a machine next to the bin, "which takes off the stems and crushes the grapes."

"So the days of stomping grapes by feet are history."

"Actually we stomped some wine by feet last year. Alessio and I have pictures of our purple feet to prove it. It was a marketing gimmick Maurizio wanted to try. You were in advertising, you understand that. People like the idea of drinking something someone actually stepped on."

Ross grinned. "Especially when you make it sound so appealing."

Eliana stepped away from the vat. "Okay, then after the stemmer, the grapes, with their skin and seeds, are sucked up these tubes into the fermentation vats. This way."

Eliana led him into the cantina. The air was sweet and rich with the smell of new grapes. There were eight large stainless steel tanks, standing vertically in a row.

"Why do they take the skin?"

"Because the skin is part of the wine. Actually it's the skin that gives red wine its color. The grapes stay in these vats from six days to two weeks. During that time the color leaches into the wine."

"Do you have to do anything to the wine while it's in here?"

"A few things. We add yeast cultures to aid the fermentation. The skin of the grapes has its own yeast and it will ferment without ours, but this way we have more control and get a better ferment. And we can monitor the heat. The fermentation causes the heat to rise. If it rises too much, it will kill the fermentation. The wine also needs to be rotated because the grapes naturally separate. The seeds sink to the bottom and the skin rises to the top and forms a cap. If the cap gets too hard, it can trap carbon dioxide in the vat that can suffocate the yeast and also stop the fermentation process. It's happened to us a few times. It's not good."

"Like I said before, you know your wine."

"I should. I'm the *capo*'s wife."

Just then Luca walked into the cantina. "*Signorina* Ferrini, may I help you with something?"

"No, thank you, Luca. I'm just showing Ross how we make wine."

He glanced around the room then went back outside.

Eliana stepped closer to Ross. "Okay, after the vats we pump the wine down to the cellar, where we store it in barrels. Want to see?"

"Certo."

She led him down a concrete stairway into the large, brick-ceilinged cellar. The air was cool and musty. Large oak barrels lined the walls and were stacked in the middle of the floor as well. Each barrel was stenciled with a number.

"These barrels are called *barriques*. We let the wine age down here for a year, then we bottle it and sell it." She stopped next to a barrel and examined it. "Let's try some of this."

At the end of the room was a wooden counter. She retrieved from it a wineglass and a large glass tube resembling a turkey baster. She worked the plastic plug from the barrel then inserted the tube. "They call this a 'thief,' " she said, smiling, "because it steals wine from barrels."

The glass tube turned burgundy as it filled. She took the thief from the barrel and released its liquid into the glass. She lifted the glass to the light, examined the wine's color, smelled it, then sipped it.

"Mmm, that's really good. Try this." She handed Ross the glass.

He tasted it. "That is good."

"I don't know what it is. I'll have to ask Luca. That was a good harvest. I'll have him get some bottles of it for you."

"Thanks." He took another drink. "So, you're pretty powerful around here."

"Oh, yeah, I say jump, and all these men ask how high."

"Well, I'm sure you were used to that even before you were the *capo*'s wife."

She just smiled, then took the glass from him, her hand touching his in the exchange. She took another drink then handed back the glass.

"Do you love Maurizio?" Ross asked.

The question struck her so abruptly that she laughed. "Now, there's a question to ask a girl after a glass of wine. Where did that come from?"

"I'm sorry, it's a bad habit of mine. I just say what comes to my mind."

"I've noticed." She put down the glass. "Truthfully?" She sighed. "Truthfully I do better with questions about wine." Her voice softened. "I don't really know. I mean, if I didn't love him, why would I hurt so much when he cheats on me?"

Ross thought it a strange barometer. "Maurizio cheats on you?"

She looked down. "Earlier this year I caught him. Not actually with someone; I probably would have killed him if I had. I found the girl's earrings in his coat pocket. He first tried to lie about it. He said that he had bought them for me. But the used lipstick I found with them kind of ruined his excuse." Her eyes filled with sadness. "I knew he'd been cheating for a long time.

227

It was just the first time I called him on it."

"What did he say?"

"Nothing at first. Then he said that's just the way things are and it's me who has the problem, not him."

Ross looked at her, weighing her words. "So what did you say to him?"

"I told him that I was leaving. He said that I could, of course, but that I couldn't take Alessio with me — as if leaving Alessio behind was an option."

Ross frowned. "Could he really stop you from taking him?"

"From Italy, yes. I can't take Alessio out of the country without Maurizio's permission."

"What if you just went home and didn't come back?"

"Believe me, I've thought of it. But it's not that simple. Without Maurizio's permission, I couldn't stay out of the country for more than two weeks. If I stayed a day longer, Maurizio could call the police, and the FBI would be notified, and I would be charged with kidnapping. It's something the international community actually cooperates on. I would have to bring Alessio back, and they would take away his passport until he was eighteen. I might even go to jail. At the least I would lose custody of Alessio. I suppose I could live a life on the run like some women have, but that's no life for Alessio. And with his asthma it would be dangerous."

"Could you take Maurizio to court?"

"I could. But I would lose."

"Why is that?"

"For one, because Maurizio's family is *ben introdotta* — well connected. They are rich and his father was a *conte*. A count."

"Then doesn't that make Maurizio a count?"

She nodded. Ross looked at her for a moment. "And you a countess?"

"Yes."

Ross was taken aback by the casualness of her response. "What does that mean?"

She carefully thought about her reply. "Not much, really. Though it was definitely part of the whole fantasy. Every now and then someone will kiss my hand. But Italy's a republic and nobility is just a title. Still, there is power to be had and Maurizio knows how to use it."

"I can't believe the system really works that way."

"You have no idea. Italy is all about who you know. It's always been this way. But even if Maurizio didn't have connections, I would probably lose in court."

"Why?"

"Because I would have to prove that I could give Alessio a better life in America."

"Couldn't you?"

"Not as a single parent. I got pregnant before I finished school and then we moved here and I've been home ever since. I have no skills, no profession, other than my art. I can't even type. Then there's Alessio's asthma. You know how expensive hospitals are in America. I'm in the emergency room at least every other month. Plus there are his medications and doctor visits." She stopped, exasperated at the thought of it. "I could never do it, even if the courts allowed it."

"You've thought this all through."

"A million times."

Ross ran his hand across the barrel's smooth surface. "If he's never around, why does he care if you go?"

"It's just different here. Here, breaking up a family, whatever the reason, is seen as worse than having an affair. Besides, why would Maurizio want to? The status quo works for him. He gets a wife and mother at home and the freedom and excitement of the road."

"And the fact that he cheats doesn't bother him?"

"To him cheating is irrelevant. Have you heard the word *scappatella?*"

"No."

"It means a little love affair. Some believe that an occasional *scappatella* is good for a marriage. That it keeps it fresh."

"So fidelity in marriage isn't important to Maurizio."

"No, it doesn't matter if *he* cheats. If *I* were to cheat, that would be something very different."

"A double standard."

"Big double standard." Then she added, "Maybe I'm just old-fashioned, but I believe there are some things a man and a woman should only share with each other."

"So how do you get by?"

She finished her wine then set down the glass. "I raise a little boy. And I paint."

"And you do both of them very well."

"Thank you," she said softly. She checked her watch. "We better go. I'm sure Manuela has a feast prepared." As they walked toward the stairs, Ross slipped his arm around her and she leaned her head against his shoulder. She said, "If you're not busy this afternoon, we could get further on the painting."

"I'm all yours."

She smiled at the thought of that possibility.

"So how many sessions do we have left anyway?" Ross asked.

"I don't know, five or six." She looked over at him. "Are you getting tired of them?"

"No."

"Good. But no more serious talk tonight. Or we'll never get done."

Then the two of them walked together back to the villa.

CHAPTER 19

"Il rumore d'un bacio non e cosi forte come quello del cannone, ma la sua eco dura molti piu lungo."
The sound of a kiss is not as strong as that of a cannon,
but its echo endures much longer.
— Italian Proverb

"I suppose I had my first real Italian lessons today."
— Ross Story's diary

Manuela was gone for the day and Alessio was asleep in his bedroom. The windows of the studio were open, though not as much as they would have been just a week earlier. The air was now laced with a coolness — a harbinger of fall's approach. Ross was in his chair. She had been painting for more than an hour and their conversation had been light. Ross was feeling more like a bowl of fruit than usual.

Suddenly he said, "Dorian Gray."

She looked over from around the easel.

"What?"

"*The Picture of Dorian Gray* by Oscar Wilde. Did you ever read it?"

"A long time ago. When I was in high school. Why?"

"I just suddenly remembered it, sitting here having my portrait painted."

"Hmm," she said thoughtfully. After a prolonged moment she said, "Doesn't he end up killing the artist who painted his portrait?"

"I think you're right."

Pause.

"We can talk about something else."

"Are you tired from this morning?"

"I'm a little sore."

"I'm surprised, the way you're always exercising."

"Grape harvesting takes different muscles, I guess. Trying to keep up with those old men just about did me in."

"I told you. And you should have used gloves. Now your hands are purple."

"Sorry." He stretched then apologized for moving. "Would you tell me the truth if I asked you something?"

She groaned. "I don't know how much more honesty I can stand today."

"This won't hurt you. Only me."

"If it's only you," she said facetiously.

"How is my Italian? Really."

She was relieved at the question. "*Bene*. It's good. You have a remarkable vocabulary."

"I can remember words. It's the pronunciation I don't think is very good. I still have a little trouble rolling my Rs the way Italians do."

"Most English speakers do. I couldn't roll my Rs at all my first year here. Then I met an American woman with flawless Italian. I told her that I couldn't roll my Rs and she said, *Honey, speaking Italian is like kissing. It's not so much what you do*

233

with your tongue as how you hold your mouth. Then she taught me this trick. Before I knew it I could say, *arrrrrrrrrrrrrivederci.*"

"Now you're showing off."

"Want to learn how?"

"Certo."

She put down her brush and came out from behind her easel to sit down next to Ross. "Okay, repeat after me. Bitter. Batter. Butter."

"Bitter. Batter. Butter."

"Now smile when you say it and hold the first vowel, like this," she said, sticking her lips out in exaggeration. "Beeeter, baaater, booooter."

"Do I have to look dumb like that when I say it?"

"Yep, just like that. Now you try it."

"Beeeter, baaater, booooter."

"Good. Now your mouth is in the right position to roll the R. In fact it's almost automatic."

"Beeeterrr, baaaterrr, boooooterrr."

"Stick your lips out more on the r."

"Beeeterrrr, baaaterrrr, boooooterrrr."

"No, you need to stick them out more. Like you're kissing."

"Beeeterrrr, baaaterrrr, boooooterrrr."

"Like this." She put her hand on Ross's face and squeezed his cheeks together until his lips were pursed. "Now try it."

"Beeeter, baaater, booooter."

She released her hand. "Come on, Ross, don't you know how to kiss?"

"Let me try." At this Ross leaned forward and

kissed her. She froze and closed her eyes as the warmth of his mouth melted into hers. He slowly drew back from her and her eyes were locked on his, in surprise and awe. She felt a little breathless.

His voice was low. "I'm a little rusty. Was that all right?"

She swallowed. "Not bad."

There was a light rap on the open door.

They both looked over. Luca, the winery manager, stood in the doorway. He looked back and forth between the two of them. "Excuse me, *Signora* Ferrini, I saw your light on. I didn't want to wake Alessio."

Eliana was suddenly pale. "What do you need, Luca?"

"I brought the menu for the *Vendemmia* feast for your approval."

"Of course. Just set it right there. I'll look over it in the morning."

"Very good." He set the paper on a shelf and looked at Ross again. "Sorry to disturb you. Good night." He walked off.

When the door shut, Eliana groaned, briefly covering her eyes with her hand. "I didn't see him standing there. Do you think he saw that?"

"I don't know. I'm sorry."

She looked down for a moment. "It's okay. It didn't mean anything."

"It didn't?"

She looked at him in silence. She didn't know what else to say.

Ross stood. "I better go."

Eliana followed him down to the foyer. At the doorway she put her arms around him and pressed herself into him. He held her. Their partings had lost their awkwardness, but now they seemed more difficult each time.

"Same time tomorrow?" Ross asked.

She looked down. "I'm sorry. I'm so flustered. What day is tomorrow?"

"Thursday."

"No, I need to get ready for the *Vendemmia* feast. You're still coming, aren't you?"

"I was planning on it."

"Good." She leaned forward and kissed him on the cheek. "Sleep well."

"Good night. I'll see you Sunday."

She shut the door behind him and leaned against it, thinking about a life with just him.

CHAPTER 20

"D'amor non s'intende che prudenza ad amore."
One who tries to unite prudence and love knows nothing about love.
— Italian Proverb

"I had never supposed a woman could be so lovely."
— Ross Story's diary

The caterers from the restaurant Osteria di Rendola arrived Sunday at one o'clock. They pulled their three-wheeled Ape truck up to the side of the building, threw open its doors and began carrying large platters of food to the kitchen on the top floor of the winery. The *Vendemmia* feast was a thing of beauty. The antipasta included mushroom and mint focaccia bread, pheasant salad with grape reduction sauce, fig and walnut bread with Tuscan ham, chicken liver–Vin Santo pâté crostini and wild bitter greens omelette. There were two kinds of soups: tomato and bread, and corn meal and chestnut. For the first plate there was cannelini bean and ricotta lasagna, flavored with rosemary, and from the grill porcini mushroom caps with grape leaves, roasted pork ribs with wild garlic and black pepper and Sangiovese wine-marinated Chianina steak. There were four kinds of dessert: grape focaccia, chestnut flour crepes with chocolate mousse, and chilled Sangiovese grape and peach soup.

The guests, the vineyard and winery workers, began arriving three hours after the caterers. They came by automobile, bicycle and scooter but mostly by foot, dressed in their Sunday best; the older men wearing hats with the musty dark wool suit coats that they had worn for decades, their women plodding silently beside them. Once at the winery, they tediously climbed the steps to the top floor, where the *salone* was prepared for the feast. There they divorced themselves from each other's company, the old men gathering in a pack at one end of the hall while the women gathered in the kitchen, where they found ways to busy themselves, helping the caterer stir sauces or spread pâté across crostini.

The young men came dressed in leather jackets or sports coats and collared shirts unbuttoned to their abdomens, with young ladies on their arms and imperious smiles and cigarettes on their lips. The young people congregated in their own section of the hall.

There were five long banquet tables brimming with food and large demijohns of wine, Merlot and Sangiovese, from the previous harvest.

Ross had taken a small group through the Uffizi that morning and arrived at the winery a full hour after the festivities had gotten underway. He climbed the stairs and walked into the room alone, wearing slacks and a sports coat with a black T-shirt underneath. There was music playing in the hall, a band of elderly men with an accordion, a recorder and a guitar, playing cheerful Tuscan folk songs. Laughter and conversation filled the room.

Anna was the first to notice Ross's entrance, and she walked to the doorway, escorted by a portly gentleman, moon-faced with a curt tuft of hair on his chin. Anna greeted Ross affectionately, kissing both of his cheeks.

"Good evening, Mr. Story. How are you today? So glad you could come." They were the only three lines of English that she remembered verbatim from Eliana's lessons, and she had recited the lines so formally that Ross had to fight the impulse to laugh.

"*Ciao*, Anna. You said that very well. You have very good English."

She flushed. "No, my English is poor."

"Looks like the festivities are in full swing."

She looked at him blankly, not understanding what he said. Ross switched to Italian. "Thank you for inviting me. Is this your friend?"

The man reached out his hand. "I'm Andrea."

"*Piacere*, Andrea. I'm Ross."

"*Piacere mio.*" *My pleasure.* "And I don't speak a word of English."

Just then Maurizio walked up to Ross, wearing a loose-fitting beige Armani suit. Eliana was at his side, holding his hand, her eyes softly following him. She was made up for the occasion. Her cheeks were lightly rouged, accenting the deep crimson of her lips. She wore a sheer dress, orchid in color, that fell to her knees, with an open top that was slit down the middle to her waist. The two halves of the blouse were brought together with string, laced up, yet still open, exposing the pale, smooth skin of her breasts. He guessed Maurizio had bought the dress for her, dressing her up for show. If so, he had done a good job of it. She had never looked more beautiful, and it made Ross ache inside.

Maurizio raised both his hands to shoulder height, as if in surprise. "Mr. Story, you made it after all."

"Yes. I had to work this morning. Thank you for the invitation."

"This is your first *Vendemmia?*"

"Yes. Well, I don't recall going to any in Minneapolis." He looked over at Eliana, who was silently gazing at him. He tipped his head. "Mrs. Ferrini."

"Hello, *Signore* Story. I'm glad you could come."

"Thank you." There was a momentary pause — a tension between them that Eliana hoped Maurizio would not notice.

"Where's Alessio?" Ross asked.

Maurizio spoke. "He's out playing with the other children."

Ross rubbed his hands. "Well then, I'm new at this; where shall I sit?"

"Wherever you like. We're at the table up near the front, but I'm afraid it's full already."

"There are plenty of other tables."

Eliana looked away from him, and the tension was growing unbearable for Ross. "You have a lot of people to greet. Thanks again for the invitation."

"You're welcome," Maurizio said. "Enjoy yourself. Drink lots of wine. There is much wine."

Maurizio stepped away, pulling Eliana with him. She glanced back at Ross, her face revealing nothing but her eyes shining with longing.

Ross went to the buffet table. He loaded up a platter, took a glass of wine, then sat down at a table with an older couple and two young, caramel-skinned girls in their mid-teens who were already eating. The girls were awkward around him at first, as he was both handsome and foreign; their dark eyes darted from each other to him.

One of the girls said to the other, "He's *carino*. Was he one of the workers?"

"My brother said he came for the first day. He's Eliana Ferrini's friend."

"Where is he from? England?"

"No, he looks American. Don't you think he looks a little like Mel Gibson?"

"Mel Gibson isn't American."

"What if he spoke Italian? Wouldn't that be embarrassing?"

"*Certo, certo.*" They both giggled at this.

Ross let them talk about him for several more minutes before he greeted them in near-perfect Italian. The girls both blushed, but Ross only

241

laughed and they soon overcame their embarrassment. They began asking him questions about American music, American girls and whether or not he had ever met Tom Cruise or Mel Gibson.

Though he resisted looking at Eliana, it was difficult and he failed occasionally, glancing at her as she played the proper role of the *capo*'s wife. She shared her table with Maurizio, Alessio, Manuela and her husband, Vittorio, Anna and Andrea, Luca and his wife Concetta, who was busy talking with Alessio. Alessio was also dressed up for the occasion, wearing a clip-on tie and a little sports coat. As he looked at them, Ross felt like an exile.

Eliana suddenly looked over at him as if she knew his thoughts; their eyes met briefly and she smiled then turned away.

Before Ross finished his plate, some of the men began moving the buffet tables to an adjoining room, and the musical trio moved among the tables, enticing the guests to dance. The older couples pirouetted to the liscio, an Italian waltz, while the younger generation mimicked them with their own, more physical version.

After every few songs the band would take a break and turn on a CD of Latino music. Then the older generation would retire or try to follow the younger dancers. During a Latino song one of the young women at his table took Ross's hand. *"Vorrebbe ballare?"*

He answered, "I don't really know how to dance."

"See Giacomo?" She pointed to an elderly man not five feet tall, with a face as wrinkled as olive bark. He was joyfully dancing by himself, his arms out as if around a phantom partner, oblivious to the cessation of the music. Ross smiled at the sight of him.

"He's eighty-nine," she said. "If Giacomo can dance, so can you."

"Ci provo." I'll try.

Ross danced four times, twice with each of the young women, as they were now trying to outdo each other. After the dances he sat back down to catch his breath as the accordion music started up again and the older couples retook the dance floor. Suddenly Eliana was standing next to his table. "Is everyone having a good time?"

Everyone at the table responded enthusiastically. One man raised a glass of wine to her.

She looked at Ross. "Are you having fun, Mr. Story?"

"Sì. Molto." Much.

She leaned into Ross and whispered to him, "Meet me at the bottom of the vineyard road behind the cantina in ten minutes. I want to show you something."

She walked back to her table. Ross watched her, and then, after a few minutes, Eliana said something to Manuela and casually walked toward the ladies' room. After a short while Ross excused himself from the table and walked toward the opposite door. Across the room Luca watched him leave.

Ross walked down the stairs to the outside, then followed the back gravel road to a small dirt patch the workers used to park their cars, surrounded by a cluster of olive trees and bouquets of yellow broom. Eliana was there, leaning against the vertical post of a log fence, watching him descend toward her. A twilight breeze caused a few errant strands of her hair to dance around her face. When he was within a few feet of her, she motioned to him. "This way."

They walked together to where the dirt road split, one side rising, the other side gently sloping down to a small ravine near the irrigation lake and the vineyard. Eliana, wearing high heels, took careful steps over the rocks and dirt. Ross took her hand and she interlaced her fingers with his. He remembered how wonderful her hand had felt the first time he had held it, in Arezzo.

They walked a moment in silence over the spongy earth, she slightly ahead of him, pulling him toward something.

"Where are we going?"

"You'll see."

Twilight was falling fast. The music from the feast grew faint in the distance, replaced by the sound of their breathing and their feet over the rich black soil.

"It's true what you said about the earth. The soil does smell different."

"When I was pregnant with Alessio, my skin took on so many changes. It felt different. It even smelled different. I think it's the same when the earth gives birth."

Ross nodded again and agreed silently. They walked a little farther. She stopped where a low stone wall blocked their path. She brushed the wall a little with her hand, then put her back to it and pushed herself up onto it. Ross joined her. Their feet hanging a few inches above the ground, they both sat there looking out over the valley they had just traversed.

"Are you nervous, being here with me?" Ross asked.

"A little." She pushed her hair back from her face. "It will be okay for a while." She reached over and took his hand again, looked at it, ran her finger down his palm. "You have beautiful hands."

"You think so?"

"I've thought so since I first met you. They're artists' hands."

Ross still looked critically at his own hands.

"That was a compliment. Say 'thank you.' "

"Thank you."

"You're welcome."

The wind danced across the valley, stripped of her fruit and ready to wither and be reborn. It was quiet. Ross broke the silence. "So what did you want to show me?"

"That." She pointed toward the distant valley. The sun was falling and the day's last light spread out over the land, turning everything before them to gold.

Ross said softly, *"Che meraviglia."*

"Sì," she replied in a voice just stronger than a whisper. "I think this is where the first settlers must have been when they named this valley Rendola. It looks like where heaven might meet the earth. I come here alone sometimes. Whenever I need peace. I sit here and watch the sun set. Sometimes I pray." Her words trailed off in silence.

Ross closed his eyes. The air was crisp, and there was no sound but the scattered evening song of birds.

"I've always wanted to share this with someone. Some things are too lovely not to be shared."

Ross sat quietly thinking about her words, then he turned to her. "Like you."

She turned and looked into his eyes. Then, as if filling a vacuum between them, they came together and kissed, deeply and without restraint. When they finally parted, she was breathless, her lips slightly open, her eyes unable to leave him.

Ross looked into her eyes with deep intensity. "I love you, Eliana. With all my heart, I love you."

She closed her eyes as if to feel his words, like a warm breeze brushing over her. Then she leaned forward again and they kissed, softly at first, then with growing passion. They wrapped their arms around each other, grasping, clenching, entangling themselves. It was as if she was drinking from his mouth, from his soft lips,

246

quenching a thirst that had built up for years. He slid from the wall, still in her embrace, but now standing in front of her and kissing her face. She tipped her head back so that he could kiss her neck, and her arms went around his head, pulling him into herself. Then suddenly she stiffened.

Ross looked up, breathing heavily. She looked troubled. "What?"

"Did you hear something?"

"No."

"Wait." She untangled herself from him and they were still. The valley was quiet except for the wind and their breathing. Ross leaned back from her. He saw her eyes light with comprehension.

"It's Manuela. Wait here."

Eliana slid from the wall. She took off her shoes, then carrying them in one hand and lifting her dress with the other, she ran back toward the winery. A minute later he heard Manuela's voice echoing in the valley.

"Eliana! Eliana!"

Eliana was down the hill and up again as Ross watched her. Manuela suddenly appeared on the opposite hilltop. She ran toward Eliana, stopping at the ridge Eliana and Ross had just descended. Eliana shouted as she ran, *"Che c'e, Manuela?"*

"Alessio's having an attack."

In the pink glow of the fading twilight Ross could see the crowd emerge from the winery, congregated around Alessio. He could see everyone but Eliana, who had vanished in the midst of the crowd. He saw the crowd part as Luca's miniature Fiat pulled up, and then he caught a brief glance of Eliana as she climbed into the back of the car with Alessio in her arms, and his helplessness made Ross feel sick to his stomach. He could see Maurizio and his wild gestures. He watched Luca's car lurch forward and drive away.

The group milled about for a while, then a few couples left for home, though most just went back inside. Maurizio was the last to go. He glanced around the vineyard, like an elk suddenly stopped to smell for danger, then he turned and walked back inside. Ross sat on the ground next to the wall until the sky turned dark. And when all was dark around him, dark and cold, he walked back to his apartment alone.

CHAPTER 21

"Caro è quel miele che bisogna leccar sulle spine."
Dearly bought is the honey licked from a thorn.
— Italian Proverb

Eliana didn't come home the next day and Ross worried about her. Tuesday he led three groups and didn't return from Florence until after dark. When he opened his door, he found a folded square of paper lying on the tile floor of his foyer.

Dear Ross,

Alessio and I got back from the hospital early this afternoon. If you have time tonight I'll be up late painting. Maurizio is out for the evening so just come on in.

Con affetto,
Eliana

He put the note in his pocket. From his doorway he could see the light from Eliana's studio. He crossed the courtyard and let himself into her home.

Eliana looked up as he entered her studio. "Hi."

"Hi. Got your note."

She looked tired, he thought. And there was

an unfamiliar look in her eyes. He noticed that his unfinished portrait leaned up against the wall and she was working on something new. He sat down in his chair, though he knew her request had nothing to do with his portrait.

"Did everything go well at the hospital?"

"Yes," she said softly, then added sarcastically, "Just another race for life."

Her hand pushed the pencil against the canvas. He noticed her eyes were suddenly moist.

"Eliana?"

She didn't reply.

"Eliana?"

She exhaled. "I'm fine, Ross."

"No, no, you're not."

She sighed, put her pencil down. She ran her hand through her hair. "No, I'm a mess." There was a long pause. "We need to talk."

"About . . . ?"

"About *it*. You know, the elephant in the room."

"The elephant?"

"The one that we trip over, squeeze around and try to pretend isn't there."

Ross didn't answer her right away, wondering where she was. "Why don't I go first?"

She looked down at the floor for a moment, then her eyes leveled on him. Her face showed her weariness.

"I left America not knowing if I could ever love again. But I can. To me it's a miracle. You're a miracle. I think you are the most beautiful, kind and loving woman I have ever met. You're all I think about."

She closed her eyes.

"You have become my meridian, Eliana. I measure my time by when I'm with you or when I was last with you or when I will be with you again. I love you more than anyone or anything in this world. And I want you. That I am sure of."

He looked at her carefully, hoping his words would evoke some response. Her eyes did not open immediately, and when they did they were only more wet. She tried to respond, but was overcome by emotion. Then she tried and failed a second time. Only in looking away from him could she speak. "But I'm married, Ross."

Her words hung in the air.

"Eliana, this isn't news."

She raised her hand to her eyes. "I can't do this anymore. I can't lie in bed every night thinking about you, wishing you were with me. It's wrong. I try to tell myself that it's not, but I'm lying. I made a promise to love and honor and obey Maurizio for better or for worse."

Ross's throat felt dry. "Maurizio doesn't deserve you."

"It's not about Maurizio," she said forcefully, then, in a weaker voice, "and it's not about you."

"Then who is it about?"

"It's about God. It's about promises I've made. I'm such a hypocrite. A couple weeks ago

I told you how Maurizio cheats on me and how awful it is, then the next thing I know I'm kissing you." She looked at him with love in her eyes. "Ross, you make me feel beautiful and alive, and so loved, but then there's this guilt that paints gray over everything. I try to pretend it isn't there, I try to rationalize my behavior, but the truth is I am tired of feeling guilty and bad all the time. I feel like I'm spending all my energy rationalizing my actions. I keep telling myself this is the last time I'll do this, the last time I'll hold your hand, or want you . . . then I see you and it all goes out the window. I can't stop myself from being with you . . ."

Neither spoke for several minutes. Ross looked up. His forehead was wrinkled; his voice came low and deliberate. "Are you saying that you want me to leave?"

"Ross, this has nothing to do with what I want. What I want is to be with you. I'm just afraid of where this is leading."

"And where is that?"

"You know where. We both do. When we kissed, I knew I had gotten in too deep. I kept telling myself that I could walk this line. That I could keep my marriage vows but still find love. But that line gets thinner and hazier every day. I'm afraid that I would do anything you ask."

"I would never ask anything of you that would hurt you."

"Really? And how about Alessio?"

Ross gazed at her silently. "Do you think that

what we did had something to do with Alessio's attack?"

She turned away from him. Ross suddenly understood. "You do. You think God was punishing you."

"Maybe He was."

"Maybe He wasn't. What kind of God is that?" Ross's voice turned bitter. "Don't kiss another man or I'll kill the boy. That's not a God, that's a thug."

"It's not for kissing you."

"Then what was it for?"

"For falling in love with you. For loving you more than my husband. For all the thoughts I have of you that won't go away."

Ross lowered his head into his hands to think. "You make me sound like a sickness."

His voice turned softer, his head rose. "I didn't come to Italy to steal another man's wife. It's against everything I believe in, Eliana. If Maurizio was a good husband, if he was even trying to be, I would have already been out of here. I would have left in the night and I would ache every time I thought of you for the rest of my life, but I would do it for you and Alessio and your family." He looked intensely into her eyes. "You deserve to be loved, Eliana. Everyone deserves love. Everyone *needs* love. And what I've learned of this world is that those who need it the most are usually those who feel the least worthy of it. And so they bend and stretch to please and miss the entire point that conditional love isn't

253

love at all. Conditional love is a means of manipulation and control." His voice was direct. "At some point you need to choose love for yourself."

Eliana closed her eyes. "And God?"

Ross stood. He walked to her. "If your God only loves you conditionally, then He isn't much of a God."

She covered her eyes, though tears still escaped beneath her hands, rolling down her cheeks to her chin. She began to tremble. "It was so close at the hospital. The steroids didn't work. You know how when you're so afraid you'll promise God anything?"

Ross's brow furrowed. "What did you promise?"

She began to cry harder.

"Eliana, what did you promise?"

"I promised that I wouldn't break up this family."

Ross lowered his head and groaned. "Oh, Eliana." Then he looked at her, his eyes moist. "You can't break something that's already broken. Your marriage contract was broken the first time Maurizio cheated on you. Ethics 101, one party violates the contract, the contract is null and void." His voice suddenly lost its force. "Please don't make me go."

For several minutes neither said anything. Then Eliana took his hand. "I need some time alone to think. I can't be with you for a while."

Ross felt a tremendous fear rise within him

and with it the familiar walls he had relied on for so many years. He was retreating, he knew it, and though he feared it, he feared it not nearly as much as the possibility of losing her. He rubbed his hand across his face. "How long do you want me to go away for?"

"Maybe a week." Her voice was apologetic.

He took a deep breath then slowly exhaled. "I'll be waiting for your verdict." He walked to the door.

Seeing him this way filled her with pain. "Where will you go?"

He shrugged. "I'll know when I get there. I'm good at going nowhere." Then he looked at her; his eyes were honest and clear. "I love you, Eliana. Nothing will ever change that."

Then he walked out of the room. She heard him descend the stairs, heard her front door shut. The door echoed as if the home was empty: as empty as her heart. She looked at the unfinished portrait on the floor. She went to it; she touched his face. It had been a long time since anyone had told her that he loved her. It might never come again. Is this really what life exacted of her? To live without love. It seemed too great a price for any woman. A life without love seemed not only pointless, it seemed more than she could bear.

CHAPTER 22

"Gatto scottato dall'acque calda, ha paura della fredda."
The scalded cat fears cold water.
— Italian Proverb

"Oftentimes, too often, the most vital of life's decisions are not made by deliberation, but rather by momentum. This is a mistake. It is like waiting to reach the ground before deciding when to open your parachute."
— Ross Story's diary

The sun had hours earlier fallen into the Tyrrehnian Sea and was displaced by a rising moon as the train squealed into the Pisa station, waking Ross from his thoughts. It was an odd, painful predicament to be in — to be hurting over the prospect of losing someone who was never his. Anna's question of the other day still dangled before him. *Where are you going with this?* Eliana had somehow changed everything. He had been a fool to get close to someone he could never have.

Ross called Francesca from the train and apologetically told her that he would be gone for a while.

She sensed his anxiety and replied kindly, "Don't concern yourself, my friend. Everything will be okay here. Just hurry back."

Ross thanked her. As he hung up he wondered if he'd ever see her again.

Ross really didn't know where he was going, as his only thought had been to leave Florence. At the train station he had noticed that there was a direct train traveling from Pisa to Switzerland. He had wanted to see the Chagall stained-glass windows of the Fraumunster Church in Zurich, and though it was as good a destination as any, he changed his mind. The idea of leaving Italy made him feel dark inside. It had been hard enough leaving Rendola.

He walked to a nearby café, where he watched soccer and drank cappuccinos and grappas with the old men until closing time. Only then, when the prospect of sleeping in the street seemed a reality, did he ask for suggestions on a good place to spend the night. The old men at the café told Ross of a small hotel and bar that was inexpensive and known for good food. Ross paid his bill then went off to find the hotel.

Hotel Fedora was only a few blocks from the train station, in the direction of Pisa's famed leaning tower. Ross walked into the hotel and laid his pack on the tile floor near the front door. It was quiet inside, dim and dingy. The room was lit by electric wall sconces, and the paint on the wall behind them was peeling in places. A thirty-something woman sat at a check-in counter watching television. She glanced up at his entrance. The woman was voluptuous; dressed in all-black, form-fitting clothing. Her blouse was tight with a plunging neckline. Her raven-black hair was thick and curled, as untamed as a bramble. She had a naturally blushed look to her face, which made her cheeks glow as if she were inebriated. She had large eyes, dark and pretty and kind. She reminded Ross of a young Susan Sarandon translated into Italian.

"Hello, sir," she said with a thick accent.

"Hello."

"Would you need a room?"

"Yes, please."

"For how, uh," she paused to think, "very days?"

"I'm not certain. Two, three days. Maybe longer."

"Three days?"

"Yes. Do you have a room available for that long?"

"Yes, I have. It is fifty thousands lire for day. That is . . . one hundreds and fifty thousands lire."

Ross pulled two one-hundred-thousand lire bills from his wallet. He set the money on the counter. She took the bills then counted back his change in English, setting the bills on the counter.

"Twenty, forty, sixty."

"You gave me too much."

Her brow furrowed. She didn't understand.

"You gave me too much money back."

"It is not too much money. It is reasonable rate."

"You gave me too much change," Ross said in Italian. "You only owed me fifty thousand."

"*Mamma mia,* you speak Italian," she said in relief, raising a hand to her breast. "Why didn't you speak Italian to begin with?"

"You were doing fine in English," he said.

"No, my English is awful." She looked at her register. "I did give you too much." She took back the bills then handed Ross a fifty-thousand lire note. She reached behind her for a key. "Thank you for being honest. The owner is such a miser he probably would have fired me."

"It's nothing."

She handed him a key. "Our best room is on the second floor. It is bigger than the others and quieter. It's being used tonight, but if you come down after checkout time I will give it to you for the rest of the week at no extra charge."

"*Grazie.*"

"Tonight you have room three, zero, seven. I am Valentina if you need *anything,*" she said, flirtatiously twisting the last word.

"*Grazie,* Valentina."

"*Grazie* to you. See you later."

Ross went to his room. He tried the television but found that it didn't work. So instead he wrote in his journal then lay in bed. All he could think about was Eliana.

The days passed slowly for Ross, but he extended his stay for the full week. He slept in later each day, stayed up each night, his mind too

filled with thoughts to sleep. When he did leave
the hotel, he went to great efforts to avoid the
crowds that flocked to Pisa. He traveled only by
foot, walking more than ten miles a day. In his
wanderings he took in a few sites, the smaller at-
tractions that the tour buses pass over, the
Tower of Hunger and the Church of St. Stefano
dei Cavalieri, with its beautiful inlaid ceilings
representing the deeds of the knights. He didn't
shave; he ate only one meal a day and that was
taken at the hotel's restaurant.

The one person he did talk to was Valentina,
who was not only the hotel's counter help but
cook and barmaid as well. She mostly just flirted
with him. And though he felt some obligation to
flirt back, his heart wasn't in it. His heart ached.
Still, the longer he was away from Rendola, the
farther away it seemed to him. The more he
doubted that Eliana would let him back.

It was thirty minutes past midnight, Friday.
Ross was on the lobby's couch watching a
retelevised soccer game when Valentina called to
him from the bar. "I'm closing up, Ross. Would
you like a cappuccino?"

"No, *grazie*."

She finished wiping down the coffee machine,
threw the cloth into the sink and took off her
apron. A few moments later she came around
the bar. She sat down on the arm of the couch a
few feet from Ross. She looked at the screen.
"Who is winning?"

"Roma."

"Sempre." *Always.* "They won this morning too."

Ross grinned. "That's the game I'm watching, it's just retelevised. You just spoiled the ending."

"Sorry," she said without meaning it. She slid off the arm onto the couch itself. "Would you like something to eat? You are getting too skinny."

"No, thank you."

"You don't eat enough."

"I eat enough."

"May I ask you something?"

"Of course."

"Are you lonely?"

"Yes."

"Anch'io," she said wistfully. *Me too.* She watched the game for a while. Then she asked, "Would you like to come home with me tonight?"

Ross looked into her face. "Yes. But I better not."

She frowned. "What are you doing here? In Pisa?"

"I came to think."

"You came to the wrong place. No one thinks in Pisa. You are thinking about a girl?"

"How did you know?"

"What else do men think of?"

"Fair enough."

"Maybe I can help you. Tell me about your problem."

Ross considered her request. "I fell in love with a beautiful woman in Florence."

"Ah, yes, that's good. But she doesn't love you?"

"No, I think she does."

"Better still. Then what's the problem?"

"She's married."

Valentina's face twisted. "That package comes with too much pain. Especially when there are so many other options." She cocked her head just in case Ross missed that she was speaking of herself.

Ross smiled at her. "There's something special about this one."

"I suspect her husband thinks so too."

"I'm not sure that he does."

"What is he like?"

"Gone, mostly. He's home less than a week out of the month."

She nodded. "Recipe for disaster. One part neglect, two parts attraction. Is she unhappy?"

"Abbastanza." Enough.

"I don't understand married people. They neglect their partner's most basic needs then wonder why they go somewhere else to have them met, blaming everyone but themselves. It is the stupidity of the ages."

"True."

"Can you give this woman what she needs?"

"I would cherish her."

"Then she would be a fortunate woman. So what is holding you back? Besides her husband."

262

"I don't know. Fear of the unknown. I haven't had the best luck with love."

"*Capisco.*" *I understand.*

Just then the hotel's front door opened and an older couple walked in. Valentina met them at the counter and registered them for a room. When she came back, Ross was immersed in the game. For a while she watched as well. Then she said, "The thing about soccer is that whenever someone takes a shot they don't really know if it's going to score or not. But they miss every shot they don't take."

Ross's eyebrows rose.

"If you're not going to try because you're not sure of the outcome, then you might as well not even play."

"That's the wisest thing I've heard since I came to Italy."

"Someday they are going to bury me next to Marcus Aurelius. There's more to me than meets the eye." She rested her chin on her hands. "And there's a lot to meet the eye, isn't there?"

He smiled. "So tell me, why is such a beautiful woman, who knows so much about love, alone tonight?"

"I'm one of those who learns the hard way. I have the scars to prove it." She suddenly stood up. Sighed. "I'm going home now. Last call."

He took her hand, kissed it. "Sorry."

"Me too. We'd have fun. *Buona notte,* Ross."

"Good night, Valentina. Thank you."

"It's nothing." She stopped at the door. "Oh . . . and if the shot doesn't go in, I'm sure that I'll still be here." She winked. *"Ciao."*

The door shut behind her, leaving him alone in the lobby. *It was pure Italian,* Ross thought: *beauty and truth where you least expect it.* He knew what he wanted. Each day away from her had confirmed it to his heart. His only question was, would her heart concur?

CHAPTER 23

"D'amor ne regno non v'è contento,
che tel tormento no, sia minor."
Love is not content to merely reign,
but it must torment. Nothing else satisfies.
— Metastasio

"So what's the matter with you?" Anna asked. Eliana was preparing dinner as Anna sat on a nearby stool watching her.

"Nothing's the matter."

"You walk around like a ghost. Where's the American?"

"Why do you call him that, you know his name."

"I like the sound of it," she said. "Where is he? I haven't seen him for a while."

"He's gone."

"So you're acting differently because he is gone." Then she raised her finger. "No, actually you are not different, you are the way you used to be."

"You say that like it's a bad thing."

"It is. Where did he go?"

Eliana looked back at her. "I sent him away."

Anna looked surprised. "For good?"

"No. Just until I figure things out."

"And what have you figured out?"

Eliana sighed. "Only that I miss him. I miss

265

him terribly." She turned off the stove and came around the counter. "I've never met a man like him before. He hasn't asked a thing of me, yet he gives me a whole new world. I feel love and hope again. Even Alessio is happier." She sat down. She frowned. "You should have seen him when I asked him to go. It broke my heart."

"So what are you going to do?"

"I honestly don't have any idea. I wish he would tell me what to do. I'd do it. I don't think I could deny him anything."

"Well, one of you better figure something out." She went to the refrigerator for a drink. "Is Maurizio home?"

"Yes."

Anna made a face. Eliana went back to her cooking. "As soon as I finish making dinner, I'm taking Alessio out shopping for school clothes."

"*Mamma mia,* is it time for school again already?"

"*Sì.* Next week."

"Have you forgotten I'm leaving this evening to see Andrea?"

"I'm sorry. I forgot. How long will you be gone this time?"

"I don't know, a week or two. Until I get tired of him." She smiled. "Why don't I go shopping with you and afterwards you can drop me off at the train station? My train doesn't leave until the nineteenth hour."

Eliana smiled. "I'm so pleased that you have someone."

Anna walked to the door. "I'll finish packing. And I hope to say the same about you someday."

CHAPTER 24

"Piccola scintilla può bruciare una villa."
A little spark kindles a great fire.
— Italian Proverb

Maurizio sat alone in his den, his legs crossed at his ankles, newspaper in his hands, *La Nazione.* The lights were off and the drapes were drawn, leaving the room lit by what light illuminated the silk curtains. The smoke of a cigarette rose from a glass ashtray within arm's reach. Eliana walked in on him.

"I'm going now."

"Where?" he asked without taking his eyes from the paper.

"I'm taking Alessio into Florence for school clothes."

"Va bene."

"Do you need anything?"

"No." He lowered the paper. "Thank you. What time will you be home?"

"I'll be back around dinnertime. I have dinner all made; I just need to heat it up when I get back."

"Okay. Shut my door on the way out."

"Ciao."

He went back to his paper. Fifteen minutes later Luca knocked on Maurizio's door, then pushed it open. *"Ciao,* Maurizio."

Maurizio looked up.

"*Ciao*, Luca. What's going on?"

"I have the report from the lab." He stepped into the den and handed the papers to Maurizio. Maurizio studied them, then looked up. "We did well. Almost twenty-five percent premium. Five percent better than last year."

"Our total volume is nearly one hundred and thirty tons. That is five tons more than the last harvest."

"I'll drink to that." He handed back the papers. "Anything else?"

"I just heard from Steinco. The new bottling machine will be delivered tomorrow."

"Very good. What time?"

"In the morning."

"Call me when they arrive with it. I'll come down and meet them with you."

Luca walked away but lingered near the door. His brow furrowed. "Maurizio, I have a concern."

"*Cosa?*"

"You trust me to look over your things while you are gone."

"I trust you implicitly."

He swayed nervously from foot to foot. "This American, he is family of Eliana's?"

"No, he's only a tenant. Why?"

"Perhaps she just misses her country."

"What are you saying?"

"He is often with her."

Maurizio tensed. "How often?"

"Maurizio, Eliana is a friend. I don't mean to make something of nothing."

"Just tell me what you know."

"The night of the *Vendemmia,* when Alessio had the asthma attack . . ."

"Yes, when Eliana was gone . . ." His face reddened. "She was with him?"

"Yes."

Maurizio was quiet, his mind sorting through the evening. "What else do you know?"

Luca was breathing heavy. He was now wondering if he had done the right thing. "Last week I walked in on them . . ."

The blood drained from Maurizio's face. "In bed?"

"No, no. Eliana was painting him."

"She's painting his picture?"

". . . and they were kissing."

Maurizio looked straight ahead, emotionless, but his thoughts grew both angry and panicked.

"Thank you, Luca. You are a loyal friend."

"I hope so, Maurizio. To you and Eliana."

He walked away, leaving Maurizio alone with his jealousy. Maurizio's imagination raged, producing a vivid cinema of his wife and her lover's liaisons — their touching, kissing and lovemaking, their whispered plotting of betrayal — and his imaginings became his reality. He had to know everything about their affair.

He climbed the stairs to Eliana's studio and saw the portrait for himself, and it validated every thought he had. He considered putting his foot through the picture but restrained himself: there were answers to be had first.

He went to their bedroom and foraged through Eliana's drawers for letters, jewelry, new lingerie — any clues of their relationship. He found nothing but a necklace that he vaguely remembered giving to her himself. He went to her computer and pulled up her email, but found it password protected. He tried for nearly an hour guessing at what she might have used as a password, but without success.

Then his rage turned toward his enemy. He wanted to know more about Ross Story. Still on the Internet, he went to the Minneapolis phone book and found nothing. Then he went to the Minneapolis public records and input Ross's name. To his surprise not one entry, but hundreds, came up. He read a dozen or more of the entries, read them until he understood, and then he printed some of them. The more he read, the more his sense of power grew. He had discovered what Eliana had failed to — he knew why Ross Story had left America and what role his fiancée had played in his leaving. He alone knew why Ross Story had come to Italy.

CHAPTER 25

"Meglio il marito senz'amore, che con gelosia."
Better a husband without love than with jealousy.
— Italian Proverb

"Sorry I'm late," Eliana said, walking into the house, her arms full of boxes. "I had to see Anna off at the train station and the traffic downtown was *brutto*."

Maurizio looked over at her from the living room couch, his expression cold and hard.

"I'll get dinner right on, honey. Alessio, go get into your pajamas."

Avoiding Maurizio's glare, she set the packages down near her laundry room then retrieved the rest of the packages from the car. Then she went to the kitchen and heated everything up. She guessed that Maurizio was angry at her because he had to wait for his supper. It was a pet peeve of his that particularly annoyed Eliana since he never gave a second thought to being late for dinner himself.

Within fifteen minutes Eliana called everyone to dinner. She brought out a steaming dish of tortellini with basil and cooked ham, a second plate of chicken cacciatore, and an arugula salad with pears and pine nuts. Alessio came down first, then Maurizio. Peculiarly he brought his briefcase to the table.

They ate mostly in silence. Maurizio would not look at her, his anger simmering beneath a thin veneer of control.

The tension at the table was thick and nobody spoke until Maurizio asked Alessio gruffly, *"Come la scuola?" How is school?*

Alessio looked at his father blankly. "I don't have school."

"School doesn't start for another two weeks," Eliana said.

Maurizio said nothing but went back to eating.

Alessio asked, "May I be excused?"

"Yes," Maurizio said.

"It's time for bed," Eliana said. "And don't forget to brush your teeth."

"Can I read in bed?"

"Yes you *may*. For a little while."

Alessio left the table, leaving the two of them alone. After a few minutes Eliana tried to make peace. "I'm sorry I was late with dinner. I didn't mean to be. I thought I would be back earlier."

"Where were you?"

"I told you. I was shopping for school clothes with Alessio. And I had to drop Anna off at the station."

His gaze darkened. "Really?"

"What does that mean?"

Maurizio pushed back a little in his chair. "You were right, I know too little about how you spend your time. Or with *whom*." There was a bend in his last sentence that disturbed her. "Tell me about that portrait you are working on. The one of the man."

"You went in my studio?"

"The man in your picture looks just like our tenant, the American." Maurizio's eyes narrowed. "Have you been seeing him?"

Eliana didn't answer. She knew Maurizio. This was his way, asking questions he already knew the answer to, coaxing you into a trap until you had sealed off all your escape routes.

"Or I should say *former* tenant. I'll be kicking him out when he returns."

Eliana just stared at him. Her throat was dry.

"Do you want to know why?"

"No."

"Because you already know why, don't you?" He pushed back in his chair.

"Well, you should be glad he's gone, *amore*. I did a little research. Ross Story is a murderer."

Eliana looked at him blankly.

"You don't believe me. *E vero, amore.*" *It's true, love.* "He killed his own fiancée." He reached down, extracting papers from his briefcase. He set them on the table in front of her. She looked down at them. There were six sheets in all, newspaper articles printed off the Internet. She lifted the first article to read.

MINNESOTA AD MAN MURDERS FIANCÉE.

Below the headline was a picture of Ross. His hair was shorter then, he was younger, fresher in face, but it was definitely him.

274

Advertising executive Ross Story of Wayzata was arrested Friday evening for the murder of his fiancée, Ms. Alyssa Boyd of St. Paul.

Ms. Boyd was found bleeding and in shock, by joggers, in Como Park less than an hour after neighbors had complained to apartment management of a domestic disturbance involving her and Story. Story was seen chasing Ms. Boyd out of her apartment into the park. Ms. Boyd was rushed to Regions Hospital but was pronounced dead on arrival.

Story is a founding partner of Twede Story Advertising, one of Minneapolis's largest advertising firms. The couple was to be married three days later. Boyd, a resident of St. Paul, was 21 years of age and graduated last summer from the University of Minnesota.

Eliana looked at the other articles, reading the headlines and photo captions, and scanning the stories in disbelief.

MINNEAPOLIS ADVERTISING EXECUTIVE CHARGED IN FIANCÉE'S MURDER.

JURY CONVICTS ADMAN OF FIANCÉE'S MURDER.

FAMILY FILES CIVIL SUIT AGAINST DAUGHTER'S MURDERER.

The headline on an article from a Minneapolis advertising publication read: END OF STORY — THE FALL OF RISING AD STAR ROSS STORY. The photograph showed Ross in happier days, clad in a tuxedo, accepting an advertising award.

275

Eliana read the articles as numbness spread through her. As much as her heart had already suffered, it was as if a sledgehammer had come down to finish it off.

Maurizio watched as she read. When she finished she looked up at him, speechless.

"You should choose your boyfriends a little more carefully. Especially those you trust with our son. If you as much as talk to him again, I will see to it that you pay."

For a moment Eliana was in too much shock to speak.

"Where is the American now?" he asked.

"I don't know."

His eyes narrowed in distrust.

"Honestly, I don't know."

"When is he coming back?"

"I don't know."

He leaned toward her, his face only six inches from hers. "When he returns you will not see him. You will not speak to him. Do you understand?"

She was trembling. "Yes."

He pulled down on the skin below one eye. "I will be watching." He stood. "Everyone at Rendola will be watching." He walked from the room. When he was gone, Eliana looked again at the newspaper articles. She wanted them to change. It couldn't be him. The Ross Story she knew wasn't capable of this. She looked at the pictures until they made her ill and she could not look at them anymore. She slowly cleared the table. Then she went into the bathroom and threw up. She kneeled in front of the toilet holding her head. It was too much at one time. How could he not have told her?

CHAPTER 26

"Non mettere il tuo cucchiaio nell'altrui zuppa."
Don't put your spoon in another man's soup.
— Italian Proverb

Maurizio was alone in the courtyard when Ross entered. It was late at night and the sound of his scooter had alerted Maurizio to his return. Maurizio was leaning against the wall next to his apartment's doorwell, the smoke from his cigarette rising, curling in the air above him. Ross waved to him.

"*Ciao,* Maurizio."

Maurizio only glared at him as he lifted his cigarette again. From his hateful expression Ross deduced that he knew about Eliana and him. He wondered if Eliana, under the pressure of her own guilt, had confessed to him her feelings. The hypocrisy of it angered him. It would be like confessing a speeding ticket to a formula race car driver.

"Did you enjoy the *Vendemmia* feast, Mr. Story?"

Ross stopped. "Yes."

He blew a stream of smoke in Ross's direction. "I didn't get a chance to say goodbye to you the other night. You just slipped away, didn't you?" His eyes and voice suddenly took on the full weight of his anger. "Just like my wife."

Ross stood emotionless. Maurizio's face turned to a scowl.

"I know who you are, Story. I know why you left the U.S." He took a drag from his cigarette and his expression turned darker. "You have been spending much time with my wife. *Troppo, troppo tempo.*" He looked at his cigarette, rolled it casually in his fingers. "You want her perhaps. Yes, you do want her. I have been watching you for some time." He took another short puff on his cigarette then threw the butt on the ground near the others. "You are no longer welcome here. You will leave now. If you try to make trouble I will make more trouble. You are staying illegal in Italy. You have only a tourist visa that is already expired. You have no *permesso di soggiorno* to be in Florence. I have powerful friends in the *questura*. If you ever come around here again, I will see that you are thrown out of Italy, if not back in prison."

Ross just stared at him.

"You are not the first, you know."

Ross flinched.

"Oh, you thought you were special? Eliana does this every year or so. She gets bored and finds some new man. How do you call it, wanderlust? An itch."

"You're a liar."

He smiled, a slim, cruel smile. "Every man thinks his love is incapable of lying to him. It is the foolishness of our gender."

"No, you're a liar. Eliana's not like you. She

actually has a soul."

"Then her soul will burn in hell, no?"

"There's been no adultery."

"Now who is lying?" Maurizio's expression turned still angrier. "You do not know how bad I can make things for Eliana. I can take my son from her, you know. If she sees you again, I will. I will throw her out and take my son. Then you will see how happy she is to be with you. Then you will see how important you really are to her."

Ross was filled with rage but constrained himself. He had no doubt that Maurizio would exact any revenge on Eliana.

"You will leave Rendola and never come back. Or else you both will pay dearly. *Capito?*"

Ross had maintained eye contact with him the whole time, but now he looked down, his face tight with duress. "I need to get my things."

Maurizio eyed him suspiciously then walked over to the apartment, took a key from his front trouser pocket and unlocked the door. He stepped back from it as Ross passed. "You have one hour. Then I call the police."

Forty-five minutes later Ross came out carrying only his backpack across his shoulder. Maurizio was still outside smoking. There was a glint of triumph in his eyes.

"There's a pasta maker and a toaster on the counter. Eliana can have them."

"The servant will throw them away. But I'll be sure to give Eliana your regards."

"I'm sure you will."

Ross walked slowly to his scooter. He stopped at the great doors of the courtyard and looked around once more. It would be his last look at Rendola, he knew it. He looked up at Eliana's studio. He couldn't be sure, it was dark, but he thought he saw her looking down at him. He wanted to take her, to ride off into the sunset with her. But things had changed. He balanced his pack on the back of his scooter and headed for Florence.

CHAPTER 27

"Dopo il dolce vien l'amaro."
After the sweet comes the bitter.
— Italian Proverb

It was more than two weeks from her departure that Anna returned from Genoa. Even though it was noon, Eliana was still in bed when Anna rang her doorbell. She would have let herself in, but the door was locked and dead-bolted. Eliana only opened the door enough to see out, and Anna let out a small gasp when she saw her. She had lost six pounds since her confrontation with Maurizio, and on her small frame it looked like more.

"*Mamma mia,* Eliana, what has happened to you?"

At the sight of her friend Eliana began to tear up, and Anna stepped inside, putting her arms around her. "*Mamma mia,* are you ill? You have lost fifty pounds. And look at your house." Anna shook her head. "What has happened, Eliana?"

"Maurizio found out about me and Ross."

"Oh, Blessed Mother, no. Here, sit down." They went over to the couch. Anna sat down first, then pulled Eliana close. "Tell me everything."

"When we came back from shopping, after we dropped you off, Maurizio was waiting for me.

Somehow he knew all about Ross and me. He kicked Ross out of his apartment. He's forbidden me to see or speak to him."

Anna stroked her hair. "I'm so sorry. I'm so sorry."

"But there's more, Anna. It's horrible."

"What could possibly be more horrible?"

She started sobbing. When she stopped crying long enough to speak, she said, "I need to show you." Eliana went to the cupboard drawer and brought out the articles.

Anna looked at the pictures then said, "I can't read them. They're in English."

"I'm sorry." One by one Eliana translated the articles for her. When she finished, Anna looked more confused than concerned. "I don't believe he is capable of this. Do you?"

"But it's all right there."

"*Sì*. But how long ago was this?"

"I don't know, about three years?"

"And in the United States you only go to prison three years for murder?"

Eliana had been so devastated by the news that she hadn't considered this obvious discrepancy.

"Believe me, Eliana, there is more to this. I know people. It's a gift from God — I can read them like books. What does your heart tell you about Ross?"

"My heart tells me that he wouldn't hurt anyone."

Anna nodded.

"And that I don't want to be without him."
She started crying again. "But what if . . ."

Anna pulled her in again and held her. "No *if*,
Eliana. No *if*."

CHAPTER 28

"Ammante non sia chi coraggio non ha."
Who will be a lover must be courageous.

— Italian Proverb

Ross waited to hear from Eliana for three days before he tried to contact her, careful only to call her on her cell phone. At first her phone wasn't turned on. Then, after several days, it simply wasn't answered. Nor were the multiple messages he left, each growing more emphatic. It was a whole week before he risked calling her house, but she didn't answer there either.

He was unwilling to accept that she could so fully desert him, and it was a full week before he began to struggle with the reality that her silence might be, in fact, her verdict. After two weeks, three weeks if he counted the time in Pisa, he believed it was, and he took it hard.

He considered risking a visit to Rendola but decided against it. The property had eyes other than Maurizio's — the workers in the vineyard and winery, Luca and the gardener Vittorio. As hard as it was to accept, he knew that if she wanted to see him she would see him. And after three weeks he had lost hope. Heartbroken, he did what came natural to him. He returned to his art.

Francesca welcomed Ross back with kisses on

285

both of his cheeks. The Vestal exhibit had arrived in his absence and she took him through the displays, introducing the pieces with her usual flamboyance. To her surprise Ross seemed disinterested. In actuality it depressed him. He could not look at the exhibit without thinking of Eliana, her painting of the virgin and the night in her studio when she told him about the fallen Vestals. Even though his pain was still fresh, it already seemed like a long time ago.

Ross's first tour group was a baker's dozen of newspaper journalists from Brisbane, Australia. They completed the usual tour of the gallery and then gathered on the first floor before a marble statue of a Vestal as sallow-faced as the Medici Venus.

"*Le Vestali*, or *The Vestals*, is a new exhibit and on loan to the Uffizi for only a short time," Ross explained. "Vesta, the goddess of hearth and home, was an important deity to the ancient Romans. I was told that you've already toured the Roman ruins, so you might remember seeing the temple of Vesta near the Forum. The keepers of the temple were called the Vestals. They lived near the temple, in a building that is thought by some to be the predecessor of today's convents.

"The Vestal Virgins were very powerful women. They were not just the guardians of the temple, but the guardians of Rome's homes and families as well. These women were chosen as Vestals while still young, between the ages of six and ten, and upon her selection the Vestal made three sacred vows. The first was complete allegiance to the goddess Vesta, as her priestess and handmaiden. The second was to keep the sacred fire of her temple burning. The last promise she made was to take upon herself a vow of chastity."

Suddenly a woman from the crowd asked, "What happened if she broke the last promise?"

Ross looked to find who had asked the question. The woman was standing just outside the perimeter of his group, in the shadow of the arched doorway. Her gaze was fixed tightly on him. It took him a moment to realize it was Eliana. They shared eye contact, then Ross turned back to his group.

"If the final vow was broken, punishment was severe. The Vestal would be bound in linen burial clothes, then placed in a small chamber, where she was buried alive."

There were audible gasps from the group.

Eliana still stared at him. "Was it worth it?"

A few of the journalists laughed at her question and nearly all turned to see her. Only Ross knew that she was serious.

"I guess only the Vestals could say. But apparently eighteen of them thought so. That's how many of them were buried alive."

There was a moment of silence then Ross looked away from her, back at his group. "If there are no further questions, go ahead and look through the exhibit. I will meet you in front of the large, circular portrait in the next room in ten minutes."

Ross waited until the group had mostly dissipated before he approached Eliana. She waited alone in the doorway, eyeing him timidly.

"Hi," she said softly.

His voice was guarded. "Hi."

"You probably never thought you'd see me again." Her eyes betrayed her uneasiness. "Or maybe you just hoped you wouldn't."

Ross's thoughts ranged too wide for a concise answer, so he just remained silent.

"I wanted to bring you something. I had to leave it out front. It's the portrait." She spoke nervously. She forced a smile. "I didn't think the guards would take well to me walking around the gallery with an oil painting in my bag. It took longer than I thought it would. And Maurizio's been home a lot more lately. So I couldn't work on it as much as I'd like."

Ross's mind reeled with questions, but he held back. He wanted to ask her why she hadn't returned his calls. And why she had come back, when he was finally starting to accept her absence. "I . . ." He stopped himself. "Just thank you."

The silence stretched into awkwardness and Eliana smiled to keep from crying. She had never seen him this way before.

"I was wondering if," she looked down, gathered her courage, "well, if maybe we could talk."

"I've been trying to talk with you for weeks."

She looked down, ashamed. "I know. I'm sorry." She suddenly felt foolish for coming to him. She had abandoned him. What kind of a reception had she expected? She exhaled and again forced a smile. "Well, you have people waiting. I just wanted you to have the painting. I left it at the front desk, where they rent the headphones."

"How's Alessio?"

Her lower lip began to tremble. "He's been okay. He asks about you all the time. Yesterday he asked if you could come to dinner. He misses you." She paused, looked into his face. "So do I." Her eyes began to moisten. "I'm sorry, Ross. I've . . ." She stopped herself, no longer daring to look into his eyes. She put her hands in her pockets, brought out her leather gloves and put them on as she waited for his response or rebuke, hoping for one of them, hoping for anything but his silence. Still Ross said nothing. She looked up again. "I'm sorry I hurt you. You deserve better." She leaned forward and kissed him on the cheek. "Goodbye." Then she turned and slowly walked away. She was past the door onto the landing when Ross called after her, "Eliana. Wait."

She turned around and he saw that her cheeks were already wet with tears.

"I'll be finished in about a half hour. We can meet in the café on the second floor."

She wiped her eyes with the back of her hand. Too emotional to speak, she nodded in agreement and walked off to wait. Ross watched her go, then went off to finish his tour.

CHAPTER 29

"Sdegno d'amante poco dura."
The anger of lovers lasts a short time.
— Italian Proverb

Ross found Eliana sitting at a small round table near the back of the café, nervously twisting a napkin into rope, a cup of coffee in front of her. She seemed to him fragile and beautiful, like a porcelain figurine.

She saw him enter and followed him with her wet eyes until he stood by her and pulled out a chair to sit across from her. They were both unsure where to begin. Ross took a deep breath. "Maybe I should just tell you what I'm thinking."

She nodded.

"You broke my heart," he said. "You broke my heart and then you deserted me without an explanation. I think I could have handled anything, except not knowing if I would ever see you again." He closed his eyes, trying to stop the emotion that was beginning to surface. "Not knowing if you still cared about me."

She touched the corner of one of her eyes to wipe at a tear.

"And then, just when I'm starting to get used to the idea that you are really gone, you return. If you're trying to torture me, you're pretty damn good at it."

"I didn't mean to hurt you."

"What did you mean to do?"

"I don't know," she blurted. A couple at a nearby table glanced over at her. She repeated, softer, "I don't know."

"I must have called you twenty times."

"I couldn't talk to you. Maurizio is home all the time now."

"In three weeks time you haven't had five minutes to talk to me?"

"The thing is . . . ," she answered, again attracting the attention of those around her. She stopped, took a deep breath, then continued in a softer voice, "The thing is, it's not five minutes. I talk to you for a minute and I would have felt it for a week." She looked into his eyes and her voice rose unchecked. "Do you really believe that I haven't thought of you every minute since you left? You're all I think about. Do you know how much it hurts every time you call? I'm a mess for the rest of the day. All twenty-three times. Yes, I counted them. I held my phone and cried and wanted to hear your voice so badly that I shook. I cry myself to sleep every night and all I want is to be held by you."

Ross looked down, covering his eyes with his hand. When he looked back up, his voice was soft. "Why didn't you just pick up the phone?"

"I was confused and afraid. Maurizio was threatening me. Somehow he found out about us. He told me that you were a murderer. I thought he was crazy, but he shoved these in front of me." She reached into her coat and brought out the newspaper articles. She set them on the table in front of Ross. "Is it true?"

At first he didn't respond, then he pushed the papers back toward her. "Why do you ask? You have it in black and white."

"Is it true?" she repeated, looking into his eyes.

"What do you think?"

"I'll believe whatever you tell me."

Ross hadn't expected this. As he looked into her eyes, his anger dissipated. It had been a long time since he'd been given the benefit of the doubt by anyone.

"No, I didn't murder her. But I killed her."

Ross had looked down as he said it, and when he looked back up, he expected there to be fear or shock in her eyes. There was only empathy.

"Alyssa was my fiancée. I loved her more than anyone or anything in this world. I loved her even as much as I love you. We were going to get married." He ran his hand across the table. "The world was mine. I had just won the largest advertising account in Minneapolis. I had the girl of my dreams. I guess no happiness goes unpunished. Four days before our wedding my brother calls. He tells me that he saw Alyssa eating dinner with her ex-boyfriend. He said they were holding hands and kissing." Ross slowly shook his head in remembrance. "Rational man that I am, I go crazy. I went to her apartment and confronted her. At first she denied it. But I kept on her until she admitted that she had been with him. She begged me to let her explain. She said that she and her ex-fiancé had parted without finality and that she wasn't sure whether she still had feelings for him or not. She wanted to give all of herself to me and didn't think it was fair to marry me without knowing for sure."

Ross rubbed his forehead. "She said that after they talked she realized that there were no feelings — that she wanted only me." He looked up into Eliana's eyes. "It should have been enough.

"But I was so blinded by jealousy that I didn't hear what Alyssa was really saying. She started to cry and ran out. I followed her to the park near her apartment. Then she turned and asked me to just leave her alone. I knew I was wrong, I wanted to apologize. I was so afraid of losing her I didn't know what to do. So I did as she asked and walked away."

Ross's eyes began to moisten. "It was the last thing she would ever say to me. A half hour later she was found in the park by some joggers, bleeding to death."

Eliana raised a hand to her mouth. "Dear Lord."

"I drove around Minneapolis for almost three hours. Finally I just decided to go home. By the time I got back, the police were waiting for me. I was charged with her murder."

"But why?"

"We were pretty loud. There were at least a dozen people who heard our fight, and some of them saw me follow her into the park. I had no alibi. When the joggers asked Alyssa who had done this, all she could say was my name. She died with my name on her lips. I was given fifteen to life for criminal homicide.

"My brother blamed himself for what had happened. He had been clean for nearly three years. He was holding the first steady job of his life. After I was convicted, he just disappeared.

"I was carrying the pain of Alyssa's loss, the guilt and the loneliness, and then prison. I realized my first day in prison that I wasn't going to make it. That's when I did this." He slightly rotated his wrist to expose the scar. Eliana began to tear up. "A guard discovered me before I bled to death. Ironically, my attempted suicide is what saved my life.

"The prison counselor recommended that, for my own safety, I be put in prison industries. I was a big shot in the Minnesota advertising scene. I had won a lot of awards, both regional and national. The man in charge of prison industries knew of my work. I started an advertising agency in the prison. We started making money. The system takes care of itself. I was put in honor block, given my own cell and special privileges.

"Some men turn to God in prison, I suppose I did too, but through a form I could understand — art. It was the same thing that got me through my parents' death. I began filling my cell with pictures. Most of the inmates had pictures of women ripped from porn magazines. My nudes were seven-hundred-year-old statues and plump women in oil paintings."

"And the Uffizi?"

"It started with a wrinkled *National Geographic* article showing the works of Botticelli. I would stare at his pictures and the prison walls just melted away. You can't be confined where there's art. It became my hobby. I started collecting pictures of the Uffizi's masterpieces and filled my cell with them, until I had constructed the entire Uffizi in my cell.

"Up to that point I had just been waiting for the right time to take my life. I changed. I decided that I would live and that they would steal as few years from my life as possible. I started lifting weights, taking vitamins, anything that would prolong my life. And I promised myself that I would leave America and move to Italy the day I was released."

"So you learned Italian."

Ross smiled. "All it takes to learn a language is time. I had plenty of that. Fifteen to life." Ross exhaled. "Then one fine day, three and a half years after I was incarcerated, a guard knocks on my cell. 'Hey, Story, your attorney's here to see you.' My attorney's sitting behind the glass. I haven't heard from him in three years. I spent more than a hundred thousand dollars in legal fees and not even a Christmas card.

"He tells me that the day before the police had picked up a guy in lower St. Paul, some petty drug dealer. It was his third offense and he was scared and begging for leniency. He told the police that one of his users had killed a woman in Como Park that some businessman had taken the fall for. He said he could prove it because the guy carries the woman's driver's license around like a souvenir and had given him her engagement ring to pay off a debt. The dealer liked it, and his girlfriend was still wearing it.

"My attorney tells me that they've picked up the guy and everything checks out. The D.A.'s office is all over this and it looks like I'll be out on the streets by tomorrow afternoon. Just like that. Next day a judge signs a release. 'Clean your cell, Story, and get out.' Three years in hell and not so much as a 'Sorry, pal.' I tried to find my brother but he was gone. So I bought a one-way ticket to Rome."

Eliana stared at him, struck by the horror of his tale. It had been a long while since Ross had told the story, and it left him weary. Eliana wanted to hold him. She put her hand on his. "I'm so sorry this happened to you. I'm so sorry for ever doubting you."

Ross just sat there. "I once believed that art was the only evidence that we are more than animals. I believe differently now. I believe love is that evidence. Art is just an outward expression of love."

She brought his hand to her lips and kissed it. "I want to be alone with you."

He stood up and took her hand. They walked

to the front counter of the Uffizi, where they re-trieved Ross's portrait. It leaned against the wall, and he stared at it for a moment while Eliana awaited his verdict.

"What do you think?"

"We should hang it in here right now."

"Seriously."

"I am being serious. We could move one of Rembrandt's self-portraits into the corridor. He did eighty of them; no one would miss one."

She smiled. "Do you really like it?"

"I really do. Notwithstanding the subject, it's beautiful."

She took his arm and laid her head against his shoulder. "It's the subject that makes it beautiful to me."

Ross put his arm around her. Then he carried the portrait with him out into the Uffizi court-yard.

"How did you get here?"

"I drove. I'm parked a couple blocks away."

"Let's take the painting back to your car, then I'll take you to dinner."

She smiled. "That sounds nice."

They walked down a one-way street from Piazza della Signoria until they came to Eliana's car parked on a corner, the wheels up on the sidewalk without apology.

The restaurant was only a few minutes' walk away. It was eight o'clock, still early for dining in Tuscany, and their dinner was brought out quickly.

"You know, some of the women in that last tour group were talking about you," Eliana said.

Ross was twirling spaghetti on his fork. "Anything interesting?"

"One compared your physique to the *David*, then she said, and I quote, *I'd like to take him back to my hotel and sink my teeth into him like a Sicilian pizza.*"

"Who said that?"

"The one with an Australian accent."

"They all had Australian accents."

"The skinny one with the leather skirt, spiked heels and too-tight blouse."

"Oh, her." Ross slightly smiled. "I didn't notice her."

"Yeah, I'm sure you didn't."

"So what did you say?"

"Nothing. But I wanted to hit her with one of her spike heels."

Ross lightly chuckled, and it made Eliana happy to hear his laughter.

"So you really like my portrait?"

"It's beautiful work. I see great things for you." He grinned. "Even though I sound like a fortune cookie saying that. I admit that I'm a little disappointed that you're giving it to me."

"Why?"

"I had hoped that you might want me hanging around."

"I would hang it on my bedroom door if I could. But I don't think Maurizio would go for it."

"No, I don't suppose he would."

She took his hand. "Besides, I have the real thing."

He brought her hand to his lips and kissed it.

CHAPTER 30

"I frutti proibiti sono I piu dolci."
Forbidden fruit is sweetest.
— Italian Proverb

They ate and flirted and laughed, then ordered coffee as the restaurant grew in occupancy and noise. An hour later the restaurant's ambiance had grown too loud for them to hear each other without shouting.

"Want to go for a walk?" Ross yelled.

"Love to," she shouted back.

Ross signaled the waiter from across the room by pretending to write in his palm. Ross handed payment to the waiter. *"Tenga il resto."* Keep the change.

"Grazie, signore."

It was night when they emerged from the restaurant. Holding hands, they wound their way through the narrow city streets until they reached the Arno. Neither spoke for a while.

"I suppose I'm rather awkward at this," Eliana said.

"Awkward at what?"

"Dating." She turned to him. "That's what this is, isn't it? A date."

Ross didn't answer immediately. "A rose by any other name."

They walked east for several more blocks parallel to the river, until they came to a place where the crowds had thinned. They stopped and looked out over the river. The water ran slow and dark, like ink beneath them, reflecting the thin, quivering reflection of a half moon as clearly as if it had fallen into the river. Ross found a gradual slope and led Eliana down to the bank of the river, where a fence sequestered a private boating club. A "No Trespassing" sign spelled out in five different languages was posted on the fence, but Ross ignored all of the languages and climbed around the fence then helped Eliana.

They sat down on the soft grass, and even though the temperature had been falling with the season, the heat from their bodies was enough for them to keep each other comfortable. Ross lay his head in her lap and they sat in the quiet, the moon high above them, bright and smooth in the sky. Eliana ran her fingers up his cheeks to his hairline, where she gently massaged his temples.

"Have you ever seen a moon like that?" Ross asked.

"Only here. I've decided that the moon really belongs to Florence. The Florentines just share it with the rest of the world."

"Who's watching Alessio tonight? Anna?"

"No, Manuela. Anna's in Genoa again with Andrea. She's so in love."

"I can relate."

Eliana bent over and kissed him.

Ross sighed. "When do you need to be home?"

"It doesn't matter. I told Manuela that I'd be out late."

There was another pause.

"And Maurizio?"

"He left three days ago. He's in Switzerland."

Ross brought her hand to his lips and one by one kissed each of her fingers. Then he suddenly began laughing. "This day is turning out very differently than I expected."

"Better, I hope."

"*Much* better."

"It's not over yet," she said, her words laced with promise. "How did you find this place?"

"This is my neighborhood. I live right over there." Ross pointed across the Arno to a row of old buildings that overlooked the south bank of the river.

"Which building?"

"The second one to the left. The tall yellow one."

"I see it."

"That's my home."

"It must be lovely overlooking the Arno. What's your apartment like?"

"It's small. It's a studio with a bed and a table. The kitchen just has a hot plate."

"Do you like living there?"

"It's convenient to work," he said. "But the view's not as pretty as it was in Rendola."

"You think Rendola's nicer than the Arno and her bridges?"

"I was talking about *you*."

She squeezed him. Then she asked, "Do you think I'm a mistake?"

"No, I think you're a gift."

"Maybe I'm both. Sometimes I think most of the things I cherish in life were mistakes. We weren't trying to get pregnant when Alessio came."

"Just because you didn't plan it doesn't mean it was a mistake. There are things that come to us because they're supposed to."

"Like you," she said. "I don't know what it will cost me to be with you, Ross, but I know that I can't be without you."

"Then come with me. I promise that I'll spend the rest of my life making you glad that you did."

His words swept over her heart, and she lay back on the ground and closed her eyes. Ross rolled off her, to his side, and raised himself over her, studying her face, marveling at its perfection. "You are the most beautiful woman I have ever known," he said. He touched her eyelids, and she closed her eyes still tighter, forcing a pool of tears from them. He gently touched the inside corner of her eyes, wetting his finger with her tears, then touched his finger to her lips. She could taste the salt of her own tears. He leaned over her and their mouths touched. She wanted him with all of her being, and she knew, at that moment, that she could give up everything in her life to feel this way.

"If I leave Maurizio, will you take me?" she whispered.

"Do you need to ask?"

"For Alessio's sake, I do."

"Yes. If you and Alessio will have me." This made Ross think. "Will Maurizio fight you for custody of Alessio?"

"Custody is the last thing Maurizio would want. He's never around as it is. Custody is only an issue if I try to leave Italy. But you don't want to leave Italy, right?"

"Right."

She closed her eyes again, and again Ross drew his finger across her face, tracing the delicate lines of her cheeks and brows.

"Ross . . ."

He touched his finger to her lips again. She stopped, as if there was some virtue to his touch that could stop her thoughts or freeze her speech, and in truth there was. She smiled as she felt him draw his finger across her lips then she kissed it. He drew his finger lower, down her chin, her neck, down the front of her shirt. Bumps rose on her skin. He lifted the gold necklace that hung just above her breasts. "What's this?"

"It's a gold florin. My mother gave it to me the night before I left for Italy."

He lowered the medallion then leaned over her again, pressing his mouth against hers. The emotion Ross now felt was overwhelming, more spiritual than physical. He desired to weep as their mouths touched and his hands caressed a woman who seemed more beautiful than could exist for him.

Then his eyes began to well with tears. He tried to hide it from her, but a tear ran down his cheek and fell on her face.

Eliana pulled back from him. "Ross, what's wrong?"

He only shook his head and looked away.

She kissed his forehead, then pulled his head in to her breast. "Tell me what's wrong, love."

When Ross could speak, he looked up at her with wet eyes. "I am so afraid."

"Afraid of what?"

"Of losing you."

"You're not going to lose me."

"Eliana, everyone I have ever loved has gone away. *Everyone.* My parents, my brother, Alyssa. I can't lose you, Eliana. I can't lose you too. My heart will never survive it."

She kissed his forehead. "You'll never lose me. Never. I can't live without you. I promise. You just need to have hope this one last time."

Ross fell into her again and they held each other tightly and love rose around them like a vapor. At that moment they found what they had both been denied, fulfillment of the greatest of all human needs: the need to love and to be loved. Night stretched itself deep and black and still, and for them even the sounds of the city ceased. They were no longer in want or pain or even in Florence. They were only in love.

CHAPTER 31

"Che dolce piu che piu giocondo stato saria di quell d'un amoroso cuore."
How sweet is the rapturous state of soft passions in a heart full of love.
— Italian Proverb

Dawn comes early to Florence. It was only five o'clock, and the curtain of morning rose across the city and exposed the two of them still together on the bank of the golden Arno, Eliana lying against Ross's chest, encircled in his arms. They had talked most of the night, about the past and present, but mostly about their future.

Eliana didn't know what time it was when she had fallen asleep and she didn't know where she was when she first woke. But she smiled when she realized that she was still with Ross. It was like waking from a pleasant dream only to find it real. There could be nothing sweeter, she thought. How long had it been since she had felt this way? It seemed like forever. For as long as she could remember all she had wanted was to be held — to be held and cherished. Now she had both. It was right that they were together for the sunrise, Eliana thought. It was a dawning for both of them.

She realized then that Ross was also awake, and she tilted her head back to look at him. *He is beautiful,* Eliana thought. Night and its magic have more than once played tricks on lovers, turning their affections into illusions. But he was no illusion. If anything he was more beautiful in the light. His face was rough with new growth and his hair tousled, slightly matted, boyish-cute, she thought. One of his hands pressed above the curve of her hip, the other gently rubbed her lower back. She loved the way her body fit against his, the way their bodies twined until she no longer knew where hers stopped and his began.

He kissed her on her forehead and she moved up to press her lips against his. She would follow him anywhere, she thought. She didn't have a choice anymore. He brushed her hair back from her face, again looking into her eyes.

"Good morning." His voice was raspy.

"Good morning. When did I fall asleep?"

"A few hours ago."

"Did you sleep?"

"No. I've just been watching you." Then he said, "I love you."

She sighed happily. "I know. And I love you." She pulled herself closer to him, her cheek pressed against his warm chest.

Then Ross said, "If everything I have suffered was the price to bring you to me, then it was worth it."

His words pierced the very inner walls of her heart, draining it in a flood of emotion. She closed her eyes. He held her and let her cry. After a long while she asked, "How will we live, Ross?"

"Happily."

She ran her finger along his chest. "We *will* be happy. I'll get a job. Alessio's doctor bills can be heavy."

Ross smiled because she still didn't understand. "Money's not a problem."

"I know it's not. I don't mind working. I don't need things. As long as I have you."

"You have me." He was silent awhile then explained. "My partners wanted me out of the agency at any cost. So they bought me out. You won't have to work. You can stay home with Alessio."

It all seemed too good to be true. They kissed awhile longer then she said, "Do you have any idea what time it is?"

"No idea in the world."

"I'm afraid Manuela will worry." Eliana sighed. "I wish we didn't have to wake from dreams."

"This one's just started."

She ran her fingers across the base of his neck, causing goose bumps to rise on his skin.

"You have no idea how good that feels," Ross said.

"Hmm. I think I do." After a few more moments she sighed. "I better go." She rubbed her hands back through her hair. It was matted on one side and Ross also ran his fingers through it. He stood, took her by the hand and lifted her. "When will you tell Maurizio?"

"He doesn't come home until Friday."

"Do you want me to be with you when you tell him?"

"No."

"Will you call me right after you talk to him?"

"You can be sure of that." He took her hand and they climbed around the fence and up to the street. The streets were still quiet and they walked the four blocks to her car. They kissed at length at her car. Finally she sighed and unlocked her door. "What about your painting? Do you want to take it now?"

"No, just bring it when you move out. This way you can still have me around for a few days."

"Good idea." She smiled and they kissed again.

"I love you," she said.

He smiled. "I love you too."

Then she reached her hands behind her neck and unclasped her necklace. She held it out to him. "This is for you until you can have the rest of me."

He looked at the medallion then back at her as he slowly closed his hand around it. She started the car, then blowing him a last kiss, drove off. Ross stood in the street watching her until she turned the corner and was gone from sight. Then he looked again at the medallion. It reminded him of her words. He would have hope just one last time.

CHAPTER 32

"In premio d'amor, amor se rènde."
Love is the reward of love.

— Italian Proverb

Eliana rolled down her window and let the cool morning wind rush by her. The ecstasy of being in love was far more potent than she imagined it could be, and she felt new. It had been a long time since she had indulged in passion or even the pleasure of hope.

She imagined their life together, and, ironically, the pull of family, the belief that they — she, Alessio and Ross — could be a family was powerful too. The drive home seemed short.

She pulled her car into the long drive of Rendola. The dash clock said seven twenty-three. She wouldn't go in. Not yet. Not when she still felt like she could fly. She parked the car short of the villa, just outside the winery, and walked down to her secret place, where she and Ross had met after the *Vendemmia*. From the low wall she could see the villa silhouetted against the morning sky. It seemed more like a prison to her now.

Her mind played out a thousand summer days and cozy, winter evenings to come. To be loved again, what could be so unimaginably sweet? The crisp, new autumn wind played with her hair, and she closed her eyes and imagined it was Ross running his fingers through it. She did not want the night to leave her. She relived their conversation, savored the memory of his voice. She thought of how her hand fit in his, his gentle touch as they kissed, his hand caressing her body, his lips against her skin, even how he had responded to her painting and how it filled her with pleasure.

"I love you, Ross," she said softly. It was not just how she felt, but a promise. Last night she had loved and felt loved in depths she hadn't known possible, and it filled her with faith that there would be other such nights — a lifetime of such nights. Could it be so in real life? Were there really happily-ever-afters? Her story had the makings of a fairy tale. In fact hers was the oldest of love stories, the beautiful princess locked away in a castle rescued by a handsome knight. Change the names and a few other details and it was all there.

She had suffered the chill of indifference for too long. She felt guilt for loving a man who wasn't her husband, yet this time it was quashed by her love for Ross. That and her newfound knowledge of just how much she had been deprived of for so long. *Il bisogno non conosce legge. Need knows no law,* the Italians said. You might as well condemn a starving man for stealing a loaf of bread.

Yet this was more than the satisfying of a hunger. There seemed to be something divine about it. This man had come from thousands of miles away, from a million indignities, to save her. Surely there was divinity in this. God is love, she had always believed, and this man had brought her love. Love and dignity and self-respect.

Finally she laughed at herself. She was as giddy as a lovesick schoolgirl, warm, wrapped up in love's cozy blanket. She sighed happily at the thought as she walked back to her car.

Then, as she came around the wall of the villa, her heart froze. The only car in the gravel lot was Maurizio's Alfa Romeo.

CHAPTER 33

"Non c'è rosa senza spine."
No rose without a thorn.
— Italian Proverb

Eliana stood outside her car for a moment. How could he be home? She paused again outside the courtyard gate, fearful to open the door and set in motion the events that would come about, as if a hurricane waited inside kept at bay only by the gate's inch of wood.

Fear and guilt rose up within her, seeping up between the cracks of her conscience like groundwater.

She opened the courtyard door, fully expecting to see Maurizio standing there, cigarette in hand, waiting for her. But the courtyard was quiet. She crossed the stone pavement, and it seemed as if all sound were amplified. She was conscious of the click her heels made against the stone pavement, her own quick breaths.

Her throat was dry. She grasped the door handle but it was locked. She fumbled with her keys, tried the wrong one, then found the right one. As she inserted it, the door opened inward. Her keys fell to the ground, ringing against the stone porch as they hit. Maurizio stood in front of her, his eyes dark.

"Where have you been?" His voice was low and sharp-edged.

She didn't answer.

"Where have you been all night?"

She stooped to pick up her key ring, still avoiding his gaze. "Since when do you care where I am?"

He grabbed her by the shoulders and pushed her forcibly up against the stone threshold. She gasped.

"Guardami!" Look at me!

"Let go."

"Who have you been with?"

She turned away from his face.

"Tell me where you have been."

"I just went out."

"In the city?"

"Yes."

"With the American?"

"Leave me alone."

"My friend saw you with him, at Ristorante Alle Due Fontanelle. Do you deny it?"

She shrugged herself free from his grip. "Why do you care? You don't care about me." She started to walk from him, but he grabbed her blouse and yanked her back.

"I warned you to stay away from him."

"Like you stay away from other women? How many are there, Maurizio? Ten, twenty, or is it in the hundreds by now?"

"Shut up!" he shouted and raised his hand. She cowered slightly, lifted her hand to cover her face, but his hand never fell. His voice became more deliberate. "You want this American criminal?"

She said nothing.

"Of course you want him. Why he would want a *brutta* woman like you — that is the question. You can have him. Take your things and go."

She didn't move.

"Vai al diàvolo." Go to the devil.

He walked to the wall and flung one of her paintings from it. The frame cracked when it hit the tile of the floor. "Take all this ugliness from my house."

"Okay, I'll go. Where . . . where's Manuela?"

"Loro non sono qui," he said, and there was cruelty in his voice. *They are not here.*

"They? Where's Alessio?"

"You don't think you will take my son with you for another man. My son is not a *brutto Americano.* You go alone."

"You can't have my son."

"He is no longer your son. You have betrayed my home. Now get out."

"I'll divorce you and I'll take him."

Maurizio seemed darkly amused. "Is that what you thought? No, you will not take him. I can promise you that. You have made your decision, now get out of my house."

"I won't leave him."

"You already have. And it is not your choice now. It is mine. And my friends will see to it that it remains mine. You stupid woman, you have known me for this long and you didn't know that it has always been my decision. You should have been more *obedient*."

The word scraped across her soul like fingernails.

"You can't . . ." She did not finish her sentence. The back of Maurizio's hand broke across her face, knocking her to the ground. She lifted a hand to her face where it stung. Her nose was bleeding. Then he was on top of her. He grabbed her by her hair and lifted her head. She was too frightened to struggle. She began crying.

"Please don't hurt me."

"You puttana!" You whore!

"Please, Maurizio."

"I should beat you." He wavered, as if considering what to do, then he put his knee in her back and pushed himself up. She winced and gasped slightly, as much in fear as pain. She lay on her chest, her face to one side partially eclipsed by the floor. The blood from her nose slowly pooled in front of her, while her body convulsed with her sobs. "I didn't sleep with him," she said.

"You liar."

"I didn't, Maurizio."

"I want you out before I return."

The door slammed shut behind him, leaving all quiet except for the muffled sounds of her whimpering.

CHAPTER 34

"Chi semina vento, raccoglie tempesta."
Who sows the wind, reaps the whirlwind.
— Italian Proverb

Eliana lay on the floor crying for a long time before she struggled to the phone on the hall table. She pulled the phone off onto herself and frantically pushed Manuela's number on the handset. Her husband, Vittorio, answered.

"Vittorio, this is Eliana. Where is Manuela?"

He hesitated. "Eliana . . ."

"Does she have Alessio?"

"I'm sorry, Eliana. Maurizio has made me promise not to speak to you."

"What?"

"He made it clear."

"Vittorio, I need to know. Alessio's asthma is dangerous. If he's upset he could have an attack."

"What can I do? I'm very sorry." He hung up on her.

Now trembling, she put the phone back in its cradle. She looked down. There was blood all over the receiver. She looked at her hand; it was red.

She struggled to her feet, went to the sink and lowered her face into a stream of cool water, washing it with her hands. She felt dizzy, as if she had left her body. Suddenly she saw spots, black and white flashes. She felt the nausea of a migraine rise up in her stomach and chest. For several minutes she stood motionless, leaning against the sink. Then she went to the bathroom and vomited in the toilet. The pressure in her head continued to rise, moving up into her temples. The light of the room made her head ache, and she shielded her eyes with her hands. She went to her bedroom and drew the curtains, then curled up on top of the bed, holding a sheet over her head. She didn't move for three hours, until the phone rang. It rang nearly a dozen times before she answered it.

"Pronto."

"Eliana, it is Anna."

"Anna," she said slowly.

"What is wrong?"

"I have a horrible migraine." She suddenly began to cry.

"My poor dear. Is it that bad?"

"Anna . . ."

"Che?"

"Anna, Maurizio has taken Alessio from me."

"Finally, he's gone mad. Where has he taken him?"

"I don't know."

"What caused this?"

"It's my fault, Anna. I went to Ross. We were together all night. Maurizio was waiting for me when I came home."

"Mamma mia. Mamma mia. I will take the

next train home." She shouted away from the phone, "Andrea, get my bags from the bedroom." She came back to Eliana. *"Saro li in un batter d'occhio,"* she said. *I'll be there in a blink of an eye.*

Andrea drove Anna to Parco Principi Station, smothering her with kisses until she boarded the train, which carried her from Genoa through Pisa then into Florence's Campo di Marte. She arrived at Rendola just a few minutes past midnight. She let herself into Eliana's apartment, turned on the foyer light and called for Eliana. She saw the spattered blood on the tile floor and gasped. She hurried upstairs to Eliana's bedroom. Eliana lay on the bed. A towel was draped over her head.

"My poor baby," she said, rushing into the room. She knelt by the side of the bed and kissed her then lay close against her. "What did he do to you?"

"Anna. Will you call Manuela's house and see if Alessio's there? Vittorio wouldn't tell me."

"Of course, dear."

Anna went downstairs and called Vittorio. It was a moment before he could understand the angry woman on the other end of the phone. Again he refused to divulge Manuela's whereabouts. Anna lit into him, rattling off a string of Italian curses like strafe from a machine gun. "Don't bother to show your putrid face at Rendola again!" she screamed. "You are off the payroll. I'll burn in hell before I pay you another lira."

She slammed the phone down hard enough to crack the cradle. Then she went back upstairs to the bedroom, where she became gentle again.

"Did he say where?"

"No. The baboon."

She sat down next to Eliana on the bed and began rubbing her neck, working her hands up to her head and temples. "Alessio will be okay. Manuela will take care of him until Maurizio comes to his senses."

"What have I done, Anna?"

Anna touched her finger to her lips. "Shhh. Don't think about it. Not now, baby. Just go to sleep."

Anna lay next to her all night. The next morning she left Eliana in bed asleep, the room still dim, with its shutters closed against the morning sun. She heard someone outside and her ire rose as she prepared to meet Maurizio, but it was only Luca crossing through the courtyard. Anna made herself coffee then checked on Eliana. She was still asleep. The phone rang around eleven. Anna answered it.

"*Pronto.*"

"*Chi parla?*" *Who speaks?* a male voice asked.

"This is Anna. Who is this?"

"Excuse me, Anna, I didn't recognize your voice. This is Ross. Is Eliana there?"

"She is here, Ross, but she cannot speak. She is not well."

"What's wrong?"

She hesitated. "Ross, things have happened. Bad things."

"What kind of things?"

"Eliana should speak of these things, not me."

"Should I come to Rendola?"

"No. You must not. She will call you when she is ready."

"What can I do?"

"Nothing but pray. I'll have her call you."

She hung up. She didn't tell Eliana about the call. She needed her rest.

It was two days before Maurizio returned. Eliana had only left her bed twice during that time, once when Anna had coaxed her out for a dinner of soup and another time for a hot bath. Eliana was in bed when he came and the fighting began, Anna screaming at the top of her lungs and Maurizio uncharacteristically reciprocating, the voices combining into a tangle of Italian that became as incomprehensible as thunder. The storm grew and climbed the stairs to her darkened room. There was a scuffle outside the door then it was suddenly flung open. Maurizio stepped inside.

"I need to talk to you, Eliana."

"Get out," Anna shouted, grabbing him. "You leave her alone."

"Eliana, if you want to see Alessio ever again, get her out of here."

"Anna," she said feebly. "Maurizio and I need to talk."

"Eliana, you are too weak."

"I have to, Anna."

Anna stepped in front of Maurizio, making her five-foot frame appear as threatening as she could. "I swear on our father's grave, if you touch her again you'll regret you were born." She bit her knuckle at him, then turned and walked out.

Maurizio pushed the door shut behind her. Eliana was a dark cluster of blankets in the room's dim light. He flipped on the light switch.

"Please don't, the light hurts."

He left it on. His voice was controlled, almost cordial. "Why are you still here? I told you to go."

"Please, Maurizio. Bring Alessio back. For Alessio's sake. You don't know how sick he is."

"Not so sick that you couldn't leave him for your American."

She didn't answer. Then, seized with guilt and fear, her emotion took hold and she began to sob. Maurizio stood at the foot of the bed staring at her. When she finally stopped, she lay on her side trembling, looking up at him with dull eyes.

"Please don't make me go. I'll do anything you ask, Maurizio. Just let me have Alessio back."

He said nothing.

"I won't see him anymore. I promise."

"You said this before; why should I believe you?"

She didn't know how to answer. Maurizio

walked across the room and opened a shutter. The light broke into the room like a hammer. Eliana shielded her eyes.

"Where does your friend live?"

"Why?" she asked fearfully.

Her concern for Ross angered Maurizio. He started to walk to the door.

"Lungarno Torrigiani. There's an apartment building. It looks out over the Arno."

"What building?"

"I don't know."

He grasped the door handle.

"I'm telling you the truth, I don't know. It's the second one from Ponte Alle Grazie. It's a pale yellow color."

"What number is his room?"

"I don't know. I've never been there." Her voice trailed off into silence.

For a few moments, Maurizio just stared at her. When he spoke again his voice was only slightly stronger than a whisper. "You want another chance? I will give you another chance, Eliana, even though you do not deserve it. But be wise. I will not trust you again." He put a finger below his eye and pulled his eyelid down. "Rendola has eyes. And if he, or anyone else, ever turns your head again, you will lose Alessio for good."

Maurizio turned and walked out the door.

Anna was waiting for Maurizio in the courtyard. Maurizio glanced at her scornfully and turned away, headed for the gate. "I have nothing to say to you."

She followed him. "You swine. How dare you do this to her."

"You have misplaced loyalties, sister."

"What do you know of loyalty? The word should catch fire on your lips."

"After your husband dumped you, I really thought you'd be more understanding to my plight. I didn't see you getting sentimental over his new woman. Eliana's no different, just another adulteress."

"Il bue dice cornuto all'asino." The ox calls the donkey cattle.

He stopped at his car. "No, I'm a man."

"You're a swine."

He shook his head in disgust as he unlocked his car.

"How can you do this to Alessio?"

"I'm doing what's best for my son."

"Bugiardo! If you cared about what was best for your son, you'd have never brought him into this. You just use him to control Eliana. You don't love him at all."

He shook his head, though still smiling.

"I don't know what is more tragic, brother, that you don't love your son, or that he doesn't love you."

Maurizio flinched.

"Oh, yes. If you never came home, Alessio wouldn't think twice. Your own son doesn't give a damn about you. Someday you'll figure it out.

I pity you on that day."

Maurizio didn't know what to say. He climbed into his car and sped away from Rendola.

Anna ran back inside to check on Eliana. She found Eliana on her feet getting dressed.

"What are you doing?"

"Is he gone?"

"Yes."

"I need to go. There's something I must do."

"Eliana, you can't go out. You're not well. This is crazy."

"It is all crazy, Anna."

"Then let me drive you."

"No. I need to do this alone." She kissed her cheeks. "I will be back soon. I will need you then."

CHAPTER 35

"All is lost to me now."
— Ross Story's diary

Eliana drove slowly up the snaked, tree-lined street to Piazzale Michelangelo. As the hill peaked, the large, oxidized replica of David in the center of the piazza came into view, flanked by myriad tourists. She turned into the square and parked her car on the end of a long row of tourist buses.

The piazza was crowded, was always crowded. It was the one place where the whole view of Florence could be taken in. Visible in the distance were the three towers: Badia, Giotto's and Bargello which, next to the baptistry, flanked the Duomo. There were other domes, other towers. The Basilica of Santa Croce, Arnolfo's tower, the belfry of Palazzo Vecchio near the Uffizi, overlooking the Arno, where Eliana had fallen head and soul for Ross, as if the river had delivered life and love itself, the two intermingled. The river would forever mean something else to her. It would serve to remind her of her incompleteness. The Arno might as well cease to be, or be diverted to a more useful realm as Leonardo and Machiavelli had once schemed.

It had been days since Ross had spoken with Anna, and from that moment on he had waited helplessly for Eliana's call. When her call did come, she explained nothing to Ross though her voice frightened him. He knew something had gone very wrong.

Eliana looked around for Ross through the throngs of tourists and frowned at their number. She had thought that being amid the crowds would somehow make it easier, but now she regretted choosing this place. Now she only wanted to be alone with him. She wanted to leave this city, this world, for his arms, even if just for a few minutes.

She found him standing in the back of the *piazzale*, in the northwest corner where the great, wide railing angled back toward the main street she had ascended. And then she saw nothing else: the towers, the lights, the centuries of labor and humanity's cleverness blurred into insignificance against this one miracle. He was wearing a black body shirt. Her gold florin necklace was draped over the front of his shirt and was bright against its dark fabric.

The thought of what she had come to do sickened her.

Just then two attractive young Italian women stopped by him, spoke to him. From their body language she could see that they were flirting with Ross and she felt jealous. She wondered how it was that she felt entitled to jealousy. He wasn't hers. He never would be.

The women smiled and laughed and Eliana hated them. Ross spoke back but shook his head, raised his hands in refusal. One of them wrote something on a card and handed it to Ross then they left, laughing and chatting with one other. Ross watched them go then dropped the card over the side of the fence. He checked his watch again. He looked out over the plaza then back out over the city.

She was equally desirous to run to him and to run away from her horrible errand. Then the reality of her predicament, their predicament, flooded back into her mind and she slowly climbed out of her car, her legs and courage growing weaker as she neared him. When she was within twenty feet of him, he noticed her.

"Eliana. What happened?"

They embraced, then she buried her head into his chest as she began to cry. He wrapped his arms around her, one arm around her back, the other around her head, and held her tightly, crushing her hair between his fingers.

"Eliana?"

She could not speak but shook with her weeping. His instinct was to fix whatever was wrong — to make everything better. He put his hands on her face and gently tilted her head back until she looked into his eyes. "What happened?"

She was breathing heavily, trying to catch the breath lost from sobbing. When she spoke, her words were strained. "The night we were together. Maurizio was home. He waited for me all night."

The weight of her statement fell on Ross. "Eliana, it's okay. We'll do just as we planned. We'll go away. You and Alessio will have a new life."

At this she began to cry. Unable to speak, she held him until she could continue. "Ross, I don't know if I can say this."

Her words pressed a blade of panic into his chest. Ross stepped back from her and looked at her expectantly.

"Maurizio has taken Alessio away. I'm so frightened. He doesn't know how dangerous his asthma is. He doesn't know what to do if he has an attack. I'm afraid something will happen. It will be my fault."

"No, it won't be your fault."

"Yes, it will. I should never have left him."

Ross's voice pitched with resolve. "I'll go to Maurizio. I'll bring Alessio back."

"No, Ross. You don't understand." She was crying harder now. "Ross, I can't have you and Alessio." He could not speak, only stare into her eyes. Her voice was weak. "We lost. You have to leave, Ross. You have to promise to leave me and never come back."

Her words cascaded over him like ice water, leaving him breathless. He erupted. "And what if I won't? What if I tell you to run away with me right now and leave Maurizio and Rendola and all this behind you?"

"And Alessio?" She looked down for a moment then back at him, her eyes now gray and

329

hard as concrete. "You would never have the woman you loved."

Ross knew it was true. Eliana would never forgive herself for abandoning her child. She would hate herself. And someday she would hate him too. His mind reeled. This time there was no escape from circumstance, no back door. To take her was to lose her.

Filled with grief, Ross's eyes began to moisten. He closed his eyes tightly and turned back, grasping the piazza's steel railing, looking away from her so she wouldn't see. But she did and his pain only added to hers. She touched him but he would not turn back. "Ross, please, no."

"Didn't you promise me? Didn't you say to have hope just one last time?"

His words, her own words, stung. She lay her head against his back and sobbed. "I'm so sorry. I thought it was possible. All I wanted was to be loved. Don't hate me, Ross. Please don't hate me. I can't live with that too." She held to him. "I can't live without you."

After a few minutes he turned and held her. She felt warm in his embrace. Then his eyes locked on hers. His voice was dull with pain. "Remember, Eliana, love doesn't give second chances." He looked to the ground, swallowed. Then he said, "You better go. Alessio needs you."

Eliana just stared at him intensely. The reality that they were parting filled her with panic.

"Where will you go? Back to America?"

"America holds nothing for me." He paused and wiped back the tears from his face. "It's best that you don't know anyway."

He drew a long breath, exhaled, then kissed her cheek. "*Addìo, Amore.* I will always love you."

Then he walked away. As Eliana watched him, each step of his drew greater pain — as if she were being torn in two, which she was.

At the bottom of the stone stairway he stopped, turned slowly and looked at her. She did not speak. She just looked at him, and a thousand colors of thought blended into a single gray image. Then, with his head bowed, he turned away from her and was gone, vanished into the crowds.

As she walked back to her car, her mind dizzy with pain, a verse came to her, words gifted from some long-forgotten reading

"Love knows not its own depth until the hour of its separation."

CHAPTER 36

"Chi si pasce di speranza, muore di fame."
He who lives by hope dies by hunger.
— Italian Proverb

As a little girl in Saint Mark's Sunday school in Vernal, Utah, Eliana remembered learning about hell in catechism. As an adolescent she had studied Dante's inferno and the nine levels of torment. She had wondered about it then too, if such a place really existed and what horror it must hold. She wondered what it might be like confined for an eternity to those dark places. Now she knew. She felt, as real as fire, the pain of betraying those she loved — her son and Ross — the guilt emblazoned across her heart like a brand.

Back inside her home she went to her studio and prayed. She prayed for more than an hour, begging for forgiveness and for her son's safety. In her desperation she offered her own life in recompense for her son's, though her offer felt moot, as her life meant nothing to her now. She prayed for Maurizio, that his heart might be softened and because she had been taught to pray for her enemies. And she prayed for Ross. His portrait was against the wall, staring at her, and she could not look at it. A part of her felt that she had wronged him most of all. For in her heart taking hope from someone was among the gravest of sins. She did not know if there could be forgiveness for such.

She felt more dizzy, more confused. Nothing made sense to her. She had lost her heart; she now wondered if she might lose her mind as well. Something had to give. She was confident something would. She was moving toward something — release or destruction, she didn't know which. Neither did she care anymore.

CHAPTER 37

"Il primo amore non si scorda mai."
The first love is never forgotten.
— Italian Proverb

In the unwatched hours of early morning the phone rang. It took Eliana a moment to figure out where she was and what had woken her. She reached over for the telephone, knocking it out of its cradle as she tried to lift it.

"Pronto."

"Chi e? Sei tu, Eliana?" Who is this? Is this you, Eliana? The caller did not recognize her voice.

"Sì. Manuela?"

"Yes. It's me."

Sleep left her. "Manuela, where are you? Where's Alessio?"

Anna stirred. "Who is it?"

"I'm with Alessio. You must come to Ospedale Santa Maria."

The words chilled her. "What's happened? Is Alessio all right?"

"He is all right now. He had a serious attack."

"I'm coming now."

Eliana dropped the phone in its cradle.

Anna had slept at Eliana's side to watch over her, but now she was sitting up. "Eliana, what is it?"

"Alessio's at the hospital."

334

The dark roads were empty, and it only took them fifteen minutes to make the usual twenty-minute drive.

Manuela was standing in the front lobby of the Santa Maria Hospital, waiting. The women embraced. "I've been so worried for you," Manuela said. "I'm so sorry, Eliana. I had to go along with Maurizio. It was the only way to protect Alessio."

"I know, Manuela, I know. I'm not angry at you."

"Alessio's been so upset since Maurizio took him. He had several attacks. This one was his worst. We thought we lost him."

Eliana turned pale. "Lost him?"

"The line on the machine went flat."

"Oh, *Dio* . . ."

"He's okay now, Eliana. He's sleeping."

"Who's with him?"

"The *dottore* just left. Only Maurizio."

"Maurizio?" Eliana asked. Knowing where Alessio was, she was no longer fearful. Anna had bristled at the mention of his name but Eliana didn't want Alessio any more upset than he already was. "Not in front of Alessio, Anna."

Anna replied, "I will control myself." She thought a moment then said, "I'll wait outside the door."

The hospital was dark and the corridor echoed with their footsteps. Near the center of the second-floor corridor a single door was ajar. Eliana looked inside. The room light was off and only a table lamp illuminated the wall behind the bed. She could see Alessio's small form beneath the covers. An oxygen mask covered his face and an IV needle ran into his arm. She ran to his side. She took his hand and fell to her knees next to him. His eyes opened, and he looked at her as tears ran down her cheeks. She rubbed his hand with hers then pressed it against her wet cheek. "I didn't know where you were. I'm so sorry, Alessio, I didn't know. I would never leave you alone. I would never."

Alessio gazed at her then he glanced fearfully past her, over her shoulder.

Eliana followed his gaze. Maurizio stood in the corner of the room, in the shadows. For a moment they stared at each other. He didn't look terrible anymore. He looked small and impotent, whereas she was filled with strength — the innate ferocity of a mother guarding her young. He could no longer threaten her. He would have to kill her to take Alessio away from her again.

Manuela noticed their exchange and left the room.

Maurizio cleared his throat. "He has cried for you ever since I took him. He had an attack almost immediately. A small one. He has had several. Last night the inhaler didn't help. We brought him here." He paused, then his voice came frail and laced with emotion. "We thought he was going to die."

Eliana saw that he was trembling. Other than

the afternoon of the *Vendemmia* feast, in which he had only marginally been involved, he had been present only once during an attack, and then he had panicked while Eliana ministered to Alessio. She remembered it clearly because she was surprised at how distressed it had left him. Even then, that seizure was mild compared to most others — nothing compared to this attack. Eliana turned away from him, nuzzling back up against her son.

"He's not really my son, is he, Eliana?"

Maurizio's question enraged her. She turned back, her eyes fierce. "Of course he's your son. How dare you say that in front of —"

Maurizio held up a hand to stop her, then said calmly, "That's not what I meant." He swallowed. "He doesn't call me father." Then he said softer, "He hates me."

Eliana suddenly understood why Maurizio had called for her. Maurizio was more than frightened at the prospect of losing his son; he had come to the realization that he already had. She suddenly felt pity for him.

"Being a father takes time. He never sees you. Even when you're home, you're not really there. You're not a part of his life."

Maurizio looked down for a long time, nervously rolling an unlit cigarette in his fingers. The room was quiet except for the strained wheeze of Alessio's breathing.

"I almost killed my own son." Maurizio was silent again. The time stretched into what seemed minutes. Then he spoke without looking at her. "You may go, Eliana. You may take Alessio back to America with you."

She looked at him in disbelief. He did not look at her. *"Mi dispiace per tutto." I am sorry about everything.* "I am so sorry I hit you." His eyes were wet. She closed her eyes tightly. When she opened them again, something miraculous had happened. Eliana saw the man she had fallen in love with. She looked at him softly.

"I'm sorry for what I have done," she said. "It wasn't to hurt you. I was only lonely."

"I know."

There was a long moment of silence. "Do you want to try again?" she asked.

He looked at her and his eyes moistened. He nodded his head slowly. "No. It is who I am, Eliana. I would only hurt you again."

Despite all that she had been through, she was suddenly filled with deep sadness. She wanted to weep for both of them. He stepped forward. He touched her hair, lifting it in his hand, then he stooped and kissed her forehead. He looked at Alessio for a moment. "Be a good boy, son. Obey your mother. She is a good mother."

Alessio looked up at him, then back at Eliana, as if for an explanation.

"Bye, *amore*." Maurizio smiled, then added, *"Tesoro mio."*

Eliana remembered when he had first spoken those words to her. It was the first time he had told her that he loved her. The circle was complete. Tears welled up in her eyes, and she smiled and he smiled back. Then he walked from the room. Eliana lay her head down on the bed next to her son and cried.

CHAPTER 38

"Quando l'amore vuol fuggire e inutile inseguirlo."
When love flees it is futile to pursue it.
— Italian Proverb

As soon as Alessio was sleeping, Eliana called Ross's cell phone from one of the hospital's pay phones. He didn't answer. In all she called six times before she took Alessio back to Rendola the following afternoon. After he was settled in and watching a video, Eliana left him with Manuela and drove down to Ponte Alle Grazie, where she parked her car and ran to Ross's apartment. She found his name and apartment number on a lobby mailbox and knocked on his door. A stout, elderly woman answered.

"*Mi scusi, signora.* I am looking for Mr. Ross Story?"

The woman looked at her blankly.

"The man who lived here."

"Whoever was here has gone."

"Do you know where I can find him?"

"No, *signorina.* Why would I know that?"

"May I look through his apartment?"

"No, *signorina.* You will have to ask the landlord. But there's nothing in here."

"Where can I find the landlord?"

"*Sotto.* On the ground level, apartment seven."

Five minutes later Eliana knocked on the land-lord's door. A woman, pale-skinned, broad as a wine barrel, opened. *"Cosa vuole?"*

"I'm looking for one of your residents. *Signor* Ross Story. Room five twelve."

"Mr. Story moved out."

"Do you know where I might find him?"

She gazed at Eliana for a moment.

"No. He left yesterday. He gave me his key and left. He seemed to be in a hurry. He didn't even wait for his deposit."

"Do you have a forwarding address?"

"No, *signorina.*"

"Anything at all with an address? A check or something?"

"No, he paid in cash. He's paid up to the end of the month." She noticed the desperation in Eliana's face. "I'm sorry, *signorina.* I would help if I could. He just came and went. Sometimes men do that."

In the street Eliana hailed another cab and directed it to the Uffizi. They stopped in the court-yard and she ran out, past the crowds to the man standing guard at the entrance.

"Excuse me, *signore,* I need to speak with one of your tour guides. It's very important."

"There are many tour guides, *signorina.* You will have to make a reservation inside. Do you have a reservation number?"

"I'm looking for someone in particular. Ross Story."

The man's expression lightened. "Ross."

"You know Ross?"

"*Sì*. Only Ross doesn't work here anymore. He has left Florence."

"Did he say where he might be going?"

"No, *signora*." He parted the rope. "You ask inside. There's an office past the gift shop."

"Thank you." She went inside, found the office and knocked. Patrizia answered the door.

"May I help you?"

"*Mi scusi*. I'm looking for a man who used to work here. His name is Ross Story."

"Ross has left."

"I know. Did he leave a forwarding address?"

She shook her head. "No."

"Maybe a bank number." The woman continued shaking her head. "No, I'm sorry."

"Anything?" she asked desperately.

"I'm sorry, *signorina*."

"But you must have some record of him."

"No, Ross was an *abusivo*."

"An *abusivo*?"

"It means that he did not have a permit from the *Comune* to work here. He helped out Francesca, one of our tour guides. They had an arrangement. I think she must have his cell phone number."

Eliana frowned. "I've tried that."

"I was sad to see Ross go. I liked him. Maybe Francesca can help you. She is here; would you like me to ask?"

Eliana nodded.

Patrizia left the room. She returned a few minutes later. "If you can wait for twenty minutes, Francesca will speak with you. She is leading a tour right now."

"I'll wait. *Grazie.*"

"I was just leaving. You can wait in here if you like. Please shut the door behind you when you go."

"*Grazie.*"

The woman finished gathering her things. "*Buona fortuna.*"

Eliana breathed in deeply. There was hope. Ross had mentioned Francesca. They were close. This woman would know something about his whereabouts. Wouldn't she? She paced the quiet office until a half hour later there was a light knock and the door opened. Francesca walked in.

"I am Francesca," she said in coarse English.

Eliana spoke back in Italian. "*Buona sera.* I am Eliana Ferrini. I am looking for a friend of mine."

"*Sì.* Ross."

"Do you know where I can find him?"

"No, *signorina.* Ross left Florence yesterday."

"Did he tell you where he might be going?"

She shook her head. "Only that he was leaving Italy for good. He gave me the key to his scooter."

"That's all he said?"

"*Sì.*"

Eliana looked away. A lump rose in her throat. The woman watched her. "You're her, aren't you?"

Eliana looked up.

"You're the reason he left. He said you might come looking for him someday."

At this she bowed her head, fighting back the sadness welling up inside. Francesca watched her for a moment, then excused herself. "I am very sorry, *signorina*. For both of us." Then, as if on second thought, she touched Eliana's shoulder. "Have hope. Love sees to itself."

Eliana stopped in the ladies' room on the way out and washed her face, then she walked out to the courtyard, lonely in the burgeoning crowd, oblivious to the bustle of the *cortile*, out to the walkway overlooking the Arno. She could see below to the grass where she and Ross had lain together. Where they had spent that wonderful night entangled in each other's arms and warmth and dreams. Where they had witnessed a dawning of a new day unlike any other, and she remembered the hope that had filled her then, and it seemed impossible that he was really gone.

A brisk, autumn wind swept down the *Lungarni*, down the stone terraces toward the river, where it rippled the water in thin, white-edged plates. Winter was coming to Florence. Soon the lush countryside would be barren, the sensuality of the city and her people cloaked beneath thick coats and mufflers.

Eliana pulled her cloak tightly around herself even though her coldness was more than an autumn chill. She had suffered enough in the last week, but somehow this loss hurt most of all. For this hurt would haunt her the rest of her life. The one man she loved — the man who had taught her how to be loved — had disappeared like a drop of rain in the ocean. And the last promise she had asked him to make was to never find her again.

CHAPTER 39

"Non si conòsce il bene se non quando s'e perso."
You don't know the worth of something
until it is gone.
— Italian Proverb

Anna sat on the large roller suitcase in the center of the Florence train station, like a rock in the middle of a stream, a torrent of travelers flowing around her. Alessio played within the reach of her voice, energized by the motion of the station. Each time the train departure board changed, the letters flipping like decks of cards, he would shout and point. Eliana suddenly emerged from the bustle holding a ticket in her hand.

"The next train to Rome is in fifteen minutes. We're on track nine." She choked on the words. Fifteen minutes was not enough time to say all she felt for Anna. Anna stood and hugged her.

"*Allora.* I hate goodbyes. Don't I always say I don't say goodbye?"

"You always say that," Eliana said. She hugged her again. "Can you believe it's been almost seven years, Anna? Where did it go?"

Anna looked at Alessio and her eyes watered. "It went to him."

Eliana smiled and did not look at Anna because she did not want to cry. At least not yet.

"He was just a baby when we came."

"My little Alessio. How will I live without him? Rendola will not be the same." She lifted a handkerchief. "I hate goodbyes," she said again.

"How will we live without you?" Eliana said. "I could not have made it without you. You have been with me through all the hard times. You're my best friend. I will miss you every day."

A lump rose in Anna's throat and she changed the subject. "Did Maurizio call?"

"Last night. He wanted to say goodbye to us. He talked to Alessio for nearly a half hour."

"God works in mysterious ways."

"He does, Anna."

"Have you heard from Ross?"

Eliana shook her head.

"I'm sorry." She touched her arm. "Have hope, sister. No one can leave Rendola forever."

Eliana smiled. "And I'll be back for your wedding."

"If any of us live that long," Anna said.

Eliana waved to Alessio, who was staring at a rack of magazines. "Alessio, come now."

He sauntered up to them, and Anna crouched down and put her arms around him and kissed his head. "Don't grow up too fast. Promise?"

"I can't help it, Aunt Anna." He looked to his mother. "Can we get an ice cream cone at McDonald's?"

"No, honey. We haven't time. We'll get one in Rome."

"Sure you have time," Anna said, digging out

her change purse. "I'll be right back."

"No, Anna."

She ran off to the McDonald's in the station. Eliana sat down on the suitcase to wait. A gypsy woman walked by and stood before them holding out a paper cup. Eliana surrendered the last of her Italian coins and the woman blessed her and walked away. She glanced down at her watch.

"Oh my, there's only three minutes." She lifted her bag and took Alessio by the hand. "We need to go, Alessio."

"But Aunt Anna went to get me a cone."

"I know, sweetheart, but we can't miss our train."

She quickly validated their ticket then walked down the boarding platform, pulling Alessio by one hand and the suitcase with the other, while she kept glancing back. *Come on, Anna.* When they got to their car, Eliana stowed her suitcase on the entryway rack then helped Alessio up into the train.

"But Aunt Anna . . ."

"I know, sweetie."

Eliana waited on the step until the porter blew his whistle and Eliana was forced to step back inside while the doors shut. Suddenly Anna came running by frantically looking for them. Eliana pounded on the door's glass and Anna stopped. She walked up to the side of the train, outside the closed door, holding the ice cream cone. Tears rolled down Anna's cheeks. She blew them a kiss. Eliana kissed her fingers and waved back to her. Then the train lurched forward, and for a ways Anna walked along with it, waving and blowing kisses. Then the platform ended and the train left, taking them away from each other, filling Eliana with sadness. "You always said you'd never say goodbye, Anna. *Arrivederci,* my sister."

A moment later Alessio took her hand. "Can we sit down?"

With her free hand Eliana wiped the tears from her eyes. "Yes, sweetheart."

They found their seats, and Eliana took a picture book out of her carry-on for Alessio. When he was content, she sat back and closed her eyes. As the train rumbled away from Florence, her mind reeled through two thousand days in Italy, weaving between languages and cultures, firsts and lasts, images of Maurizio and Anna and then Villa Rendola — her maternal hills spotted with trellises. She saw Alessio growing and changing. And she knew that she too had changed, and she wondered if she could ever totally fit back into American life. She wondered if this was how a soldier felt coming back from a crusade filled with stories and thoughts no one but his comrades could ever know or understand. But through her mind's wanderings her thoughts always came back to Ross, as if he had been the punctuation of her story, and it made her want to cry. And his words haunted her. *Remember, Eliana, love doesn't give second chances.*

AFTERWORD

"Il temp è un gran medico."
Time is a great healer.
— Italian Proverb

I don't know how long I'd been sitting there, baking beneath the Tuscan sun, engrossed in Eliana's tale. At least an hour. When she finished talking, it was lunchtime and there were a few vacant lounges around us, though I didn't remember seeing anyone leave.

In the telling of her story Eliana had changed to me. Now, somehow, she had become larger than life, reminding me that the best stories aren't always in books.

"Do you believe that?" I asked. "That love doesn't give second chances."

"I did for a while."

"So what happened next?"

"I went back to Utah to get on with my life. *A fresh start.* But it was hard. I had changed so much." She laughed. "Everyone called me Ellen, and I would look around to see who they were talking to. They say you can't go home again. They're right. But it's not home that changes."

"And Alessio, how did he cope with the move?"

"It was also hard for him at first. I hadn't real-

350

ized that his grandmother was a stranger to him, and it took him a while to warm up to her. But you know how adaptable children are. We also discovered that he had fewer allergies in America, so we had less problems with his asthma."

"You found a job?"

"I started selling my paintings. It was that or leave Alessio with a baby-sitter. I was surprised at how well it went. I never had to go out and find a *real* job."

"I'd like to see your work sometime."

She smiled. "I'm always looking for clients. Do you ever get up to Park City?"

"All the time. My kids ski there."

"The Linton Gallery on Main Street has some of my landscapes."

All of my questions had been leading up to this one. "And Ross?"

"Ross," she repeated. "I thought about him every day. I thought that leaving Italy would make it easier somehow. But I was wrong." She smiled. "My broken heart followed me clear across the Atlantic and found me in Vernal, Utah. I have to admit that I was getting pretty tired of hurting. It was like being sick and wondering when you're going to get better."

"I know the feeling," I said. "But life goes on."

She smiled. "Yeah, it goes on. But never the way you expect it to. It was about six months after I returned to America that everything changed."

Doris Webb sat on a vinyl chair on the concrete front porch of her home. Her needles darted and bobbed in ritualistic motion like two cabaret dancers, indifferent to the occasional pangs of her arthritis. She was happy, and this was reflected in the yarn she had chosen for the blanket she knit: bright yellows and greens and orange.

It was a small home, with painted wood side panels, identical in architecture to the rest on the street. Like the rest, it had been built in the economic boom of postwar America when entire neighborhoods sprang up overnight in the once pastoral ridges of cow pasture.

Doris had known the home when it was young. She and Ed had bought it new, when they were just newlyweds, their entire lives open before them like a blank diary.

She had lived a life there. It was there that they had raised their one child — their daughter, Ellen. It was that same porch where Ellen had received her first kiss, the night of her junior prom, from Mike Dunlop, a cowboy Ed had never liked. He had flashed the porch light on and off until they quit, while Doris sat in front of the television set watching Johnny Carson, shaking her head and telling him to leave the young people alone.

Only four years later Ed's wake had been there, in the front room, and neighbors crossed that porch to pay their respects. He had died in the home and wanted his viewing there as well. When it was over, she and Ellen had sat and cried together on the porch until they had nothing left inside to cry out. The neighbors had cried too. And they brought hot bread and pies and potato casseroles with cornflake topping.

There had been other tears shed on that porch. She had stood on the porch and cried the day Ellen left for college, driven to Salt Lake City by her cousin who knew his way around the big city. Then she cried again when Ellen and her new baby grandson, Alessio, left for Italy to live. Then too her good neighbors came to her aid, bringing fresh-baked bread and casseroles. That's how things were done in Vernal.

The home had aluminum window canopies, once bright green but sun-faded to an olive hue. It had wrought-iron railings set in the concrete of the porch, painted white, chipped in places and rusted at the bottom. An oxidized chain-link fence surrounded the yard, with grass inter-twined and tall at its base where the lawn mower didn't reach and the weed eater had failed to bring it down. An apple tree grew in front, its boughs heavy with sour green apples, and some newly fallen fruit peeking up from the grass like bird eggs in a nest.

Yes, there had been a lot of living in that home. Someday she too would be gone. The house would be sold, to a young couple. They would come. They would tear out the harvest gold shag carpets and refinish the hardwood floors protected beneath. Walls would be painted again, this time with paints that had food names: oatmeal, vanilla or cranberry. New appliances would be bought, cappuccino makers and refrigerators with water and ice in the door. The cycle would start anew with somebody else.

But not yet. Doris's daughter was back. Her grandson was back. And she had a blanket to finish.

Doris set down her needles and waved as Eliana's car sidled up to the curb and stopped. As Eliana took the keys from the ignition, Alessio slumped down in his seat, his frown returning. "Why can't I come with you?"

"Because I said so. And stop whining. In eight blocks you've filled this car with more whine than Chianti produces in a year."

"That's dumb, Mom."

"So is your whining."

"Why do I have to stay?"

"Because I said so, Mr. Ferrini. You have school tomorrow. And mommies sometimes need time for themselves. Besides, you hate art shows. Remember last time all you wanted to do was go home? And *Nonna* —" She corrected herself. "*Grandma* would be very sad if you didn't stay with her. She's missed you."

He didn't smile. "I don't even know her very well."

"Which is precisely why you should stay."

Alessio made a face.

"Oh, stop that. You and Grandma will have a ball. I promise. By the time I get back, you won't even want to go home."

"I doubt that."

"Come on, son." She climbed out of the car. Doris shouted from the porch. "Hi, Ellen."

"Hi, Mom."

"Where's my little Alessio?"

"He's in the car." She raised her finger to her head, her hand shaped like a gun. Doris only smiled. She had been a mother once. Still was.

Eliana opened the trunk and took out a small suitcase and a backpack. Then she opened Alessio's door, giving him the eye. "You be good, or I'm not bringing you back that new Nintendo game you wanted." She dropped his backpack in his arms.

"All right." He climbed out of the car, the frown still stitched to his face.

"There's my Alessio."

"Hi, Grandma."

Doris just smiled. When she reached the porch, she greeted them both with a hug. "Come on inside, you two." They stepped in.

Eliana breathed in deeply. "It smells good."

"They had a sale on apricots at Smith's and I was making some fruit leather."

"That brings back memories."

"Alessio, I have a Nintendo game in the family room. You're going to have to set it up for me."

"Okay."

"It's right there past the kitchen."

He ran off.

"I don't want him playing Nintendo the whole time I'm gone."

Doris just smiled. "Don't worry, we've got plenty to do. So how's everything at your duplex? All moved in?"

"Yes. It's nice."

"You know, you could have just moved in here with us. Alessio would have more room out back to play."

"I know, Mom. And I appreciate it. It's just . . ."

Doris waved her hand, dismissing Eliana's need to explain. "I know, dear. I was young once too. You can't go back. Besides, having your old mother around would just cramp your style."

Eliana laughed. "What style?"

"Everyone at church has been asking about you."

Eliana picked up a thin sheet of apricot leather. It was still warm. She pulled a strip from it and ate it. "I love this stuff. So what is everyone asking about?"

"You know, the usual stuff. How are you doing . . . what are you up to . . . when are you going to get married again . . . the usual."

She groaned. "I figured."

"You know Michael Sanford's available."

"The one with six kids? He got a divorce?"

"No, his wife died of cancer last year. He's a good man, Michael. Good dad. Not a bad-looking man either."

"Six kids?" She raised her hands. *"Piano, piano."*

"Piano?"

"It means slowly, Mom."

Doris looked at Eliana thoughtfully and it made Eliana uncomfortable. Her mother could always read her, in the same way she always knew what the weather was going to do better than the weatherman, something Eliana never understood as a child and still didn't.

"You miss him, don't you?"

"For the rest of my life."

She sighed. "Oh, Ellen. I miss your father too. I sometimes find myself baking something I don't even like, just because he liked it. It's the only promise of love, I suppose."

"What promise? Torment?"

She smiled sympathetically. "Maybe."

"I sometimes wonder if it was worth it. I know, it's better to have loved and lost and all that . . . but that kind of thinking doesn't help much on cold nights. Sometimes I just ache. Why did I have to fall so hard?"

Her mother smiled. "I don't know, sweetie. But life has taught me to never regret having loved somebody. To lose love is a misfortune. But not to have loved, that is tragedy."

"Now you're sounding like an Italian."

"I'll take that as a compliment." She hugged her daughter. "It's so good having you back home, Ellen."

"It's good to be back." She sighed. "Well, I better get going. Let's go over everything." Eliana took a folded sheet from her pocket and handed it to her mother. "I've written everything down here. Alessio needs to be to school by eight-thirty. He's at Meadow Moore."

Doris nodded. "I know where that is."

"His clothes are in his bag. His inhalers are in his bag. And there's also a spare one in his backpack. You have my cell phone number and here's the gallery's number in Park City. It's the Linton Gallery. It's long distance from here so you'll have to dial a one. And, if there's an emergency —"

Her mother stopped her. "I've practiced using the inhalers. And the hospital is only two blocks away. I've already talked to Sylvia over in emergency, everything's fine. Her son has asthma too. So do Marge's son and grandson, next door. They've all agreed to help. We could practically open an asthma clinic in this neighborhood. Now, just go on and have a good time. Everything's going to be just fine."

"All right, Mom." She called out. "Alessio!"

Alessio ran into the room.

Eliana stooped down and kissed him. "I'm going now. Now, you be a good boy and do what Grandma says. I'll call you tonight."

"When will you be home?"

"Tomorrow night."

Doris put her arm around Alessio. "We'll be okay, Eliana. Alessio just needs to spend more time with his *nonna*. Now, what do you say to making some sugar cookies? I have some Halloween shapes, like bats and ghosts."

"We could do that."

"Uncle Bert is coming over a little later. I bet he'll let you drive the go-cart."

"Really? You have a go-cart?" He looked up at his mother. "Can I?"

"Yes. But only if Uncle Bert is with you."

"Don't worry, Bert's the only one who can get the darn thing started. Now, you go on, honey. We'll be just fine. I've been doing this mother thing for a long time."

"All right, Mom." She kissed her cheeks.

"I love how those Italians do that. They're such an affectionate people, aren't they?"

"They are. *Ciao*, Mom."

It thrilled her when her daughter spoke Italian to her. *"Ciao."*

The drive from Vernal to Park City was a little more than three hours, with nothing to see but scrub oak and desert terrain. Eliana didn't mind the drive. The sun-baked asphalt road stretched out before her, flat and desolate. She welcomed the opportunity to be alone with her thoughts.

It was a warm day, and she cracked her window just enough as to not drown out her car's CD player. She still listened to her Italian CDs. They were like old friends. But even they seemed different now. Foreign somehow.

Her mind wandered over the blank backdrop

of the terrain. She wondered where Ross was. England? Germany? No, she didn't see him either of those places. Spain? Maybe Spain — the dark, sun-kissed hills of Barcelona, or south in Seville. She could see him in Spain.

He'd learn the language fast. He was good with languages, and they are similar, Spanish and Italian. It would come easy for him. So would the women, she thought. This made her stomach ache a little. Would she be so easily replaced? She did not doubt him, only herself. She never saw what he was so taken by in her in the first place. Still, maybe it was different for a man. *Love is a portion of a man's life,* the Italians said, *the whole of a woman's.* The Italians had much to say on the subject. Even the word *romance* found its root in *Roman.* As much as it hurt her to think of Ross with another woman, she didn't want him to be alone. She wanted him to find a kind, beautiful woman who would care for him the way she had wanted to. One who could give him everything she couldn't. He deserved that. Her love for him demanded that.

She had gone to sleep on a thought the night before. As she walked the labyrinth of her aching heart, she realized that love and gratitude are born twins. For if she were asked what she felt for Ross, she'd say love. But what she felt most was gratitude. Gratitude for what he had brought into her life. Gratitude for the way he had loved her. Gratitude that he had made her feel whole again. In spite of what she had said to her mother, gratitude even for the pain.

Maybe she too would marry someday. As foreign as the idea seemed to her, her intuition told her that she wouldn't be alone forever. Alessio needed a father. She would make a partnership with a man and they would be friends and she might even learn to love him. Still, a part of her feared that deep inside she would always feel that she was only settling.

She ejected the CD and put in an old Eagles album. The Italian stuff made her think too much.

Four hours later Eliana arrived in Park City: the mining town turned exclusive ski resort. There was a time when land there could be bought for fifty dollars an acre. Now the old mine shacks on Main Street were being snatched up by the rich and famous for a million dollars and change. Even in the summer months, when the hills were dry and the runs bare, the town was busy with tourists.

She parked her car in the lot at the Linton Gallery then walked down the road two blocks, where she met up with her new art dealer, Marsha Ellington, at a sidewalk café.

A warm mountain flurry descended the Wasatch slopes and ruffled the fringes of the café's awning. Eliana sat sipping iced tea across from Marsha, who was meticulously spearing the olives from her pasta salad with a fork, then piling them next to a partially eaten hard roll on her bread plate.

"You heard me, I told them, no olives. How hard is that? If he hadn't taken so long to bring it out in the first place, I'd make them do it over."

"Olives are good for you," Eliana said.

"Yeah, well so is Jazzercise, but you don't see me prancing around in spandex." She speared another olive and dropped it on the plate. "There are a lot of olive trees in Italy, aren't there?"

It was like asking if there were a lot of Italians in Rome. "Yes. We had them at the villa."

"Are there two kinds of trees, black olives and green olives?"

"No. They come from the same tree. All olives are green at first. It's just a matter of how ripe they are when they're picked."

"I've wondered about that." She disdainfully speared another olive, adding it to the pile. "So how's the adjustment back to American life? Everything getting back to normal?"

"I'm not sure that I know what normal is anymore. It seems that everyone is in a hurry all the time."

"That's what we Americans do best."

She sighed. "Not this one."

"Good. Artists shouldn't be in a hurry. Are you going to stay in Vernal?"

"I don't know. It's pretty small. I guess we'll see."

"There's plenty of nice places available in Park City. I've got an ex who's a real estate agent up here. Bad husband but good agent. Give me the word and I'll tell him you're looking."

"I'm not sure if Park City is right for us."

"Well, Park City certainly loves you. You've got to be pleased with how things are going."

"I didn't know what to expect."

"Let me tell you, this kind of response for a first showing is extraordinary. I talked to Carolyn on the way up. She said there are only a couple paintings that haven't sold yet. I'm not surprised. Tuscany is so haute right now." She took a fork of lettuce and dipped it into a small cup of Italian dressing. "Taking nothing from your talent, of course."

"Toscana seems to be all the rage back here."

"I told you you'd do well. I knew it the moment I saw your first painting. I do think we should play up your countess title. It's much more exciting owning something done by nobility."

Eliana shook her head. "No."

Marsha raised one eyebrow.

"Absolutely not."

Marsha sighed, then conceded with a flourish of her free hand. "You're too humble, Ellen. You've got to learn to flaunt. It's marketing. But either way, things are going to just keep happening for you. That reminds me. I can't believe I almost forgot to tell you. Do you know Boyd McCann?"

"No."

Marsha reached into her purse and brought out a business card. She laid it on the table in front of Eliana. The card was burnt umber, with a large palm leaf in gold foil embossed with the name Boyd McCann and Associates.

"You met him last week."

"I did?"

"Yeah, he's a big Salt Lake City interior designer. Does all the Deer Valley, Walker Lane crowd. Only deals with the filthy rich, Hollywood ski bums, my kind of filth. He left me his card the other night. He wants you to do some private commissions."

"Really?"

"Oh, it gets better. Are you sure you don't remember him? He was that forty-something guy at the reception, the one with the cute butt and the Mercedes-Benz ragtop?"

Eliana remembered and grimaced slightly. "I remember him. He was the guy with fake hair, too much cologne and wandering hands."

"And too much money, I might add. Well, he's newly single. And he noticed more than your art."

Eliana grinned incredulously. "Marsha . . ."

"Don't kill the messenger, Ellen. Besides, this is a good thing. You can get a lot of work out of it."

Just then the waiter walked up and refilled Eliana's glass with ice water from a carafe. "Is everything okay, ladies?"

Marsha pointed to her bread plate. "What are these?"

He looked at the black pile of olives. "I'm

sorry, ma'am, you didn't want olives, did you? I'll get you another salad."

"Don't bother, I've already picked them all out."

The waiter held his hands out in surrender. "I'm sorry. Dessert's on me."

Eliana smiled sympathetically. "Mine's great, thank you."

The waiter smiled back at her as he took the bread plate and walked away.

"These waiters are all ski bums. This one's hit a few too many moguls, if you ask me." She turned back. "Give Boyd a call, Ellen. He thinks you're gorgeous. And he's right, you know. If I had your figure, girl . . ."

Eliana looked at the card but made no move toward it. "I don't know."

"Listen, girl, divorce happens. I've had three myself. It's not the end of the world. It's time you got back on the field and put some points on the board."

"Points, huh?" Eliana glanced down at her watch. "I better get back over to the gallery."

"Oh, go on. I'll get the check. I'm still going to have coffee. And I've got a dessert coming. I hope this guy doesn't expect a big tip."

Eliana lifted the napkin from her lap and stood. "I appreciate you watching out for me, Marsha. I'm just not ready. I'll come around someday."

Marsha's cell phone rang over the last of her words. "Just a minute," Marsha said. She dug through her handbag and pressed the receive button as she lifted her Nokia to her ear. "Hello. Oh, hi, Boyd. We were just talking about you. Ellen and I. Well, I'll let you ask her."

Eliana shook her head emphatically.

"No, you'll have to wait, Boyd, she was just running off to the ladies' room. Listen, hold on just a moment, my waiter's here. No, don't go, I need to talk to you. You can wait, honey, I'll only be a second."

She looked up at Eliana, shaking her head. "Someday doesn't always come, sweetie. I'll see you before I go. I'm coming up to the gallery to talk with Carolyn about your next show."

"Ci vediamo," Eliana said.

"Whatever that means. *Ciao.*"

Marsha lifted her cell phone. "I'm here, honey, talk to me."

Eliana slung her purse over her shoulder and walked to the curb. She waited for a passing car then crossed the street and walked the two blocks north to the gallery. The gallery was housed in a restored mining shack, narrow, rising three stories above the street. Its wood-paneled exterior was painted rust with orange-yellow trimming. A carved wooden sign that read "The Linton Gallery" hung from chains over its etched front door, blending in with the old town motif. The interior was crowded with art, Western bronzes and antiques, the rooms lit by rows of slim, black track lighting. Carolyn, the gallery's owner, was seated on a leather

366

couch in the foyer as Eliana entered.

"Well, Ellen, you better get on back to your studio and start painting. You're sold out."

"Everything sold?"

"Everything and then some. This place was a zoo a half hour ago. There were a couple gentlemen who purchased the last two of your paintings and were very interested in buying one of the portraits you brought in to exhibit."

"Which portrait is it?"

"The one of the man holding the book."

She shook her head. "It's not for sale."

"Oh, I told them. But between us, I think you should reconsider. You could always just paint another one, couldn't you?"

"Not of this one." Her brow furrowed. "You didn't promise them anything?"

"No, of course not. But they were pretty insistent. They wanted to speak with you personally."

"They're still here?"

"One of them is. The other had to leave. I told them I expected you back any minute, so I think he went back to covet the portrait some more. It would be good for you to personally thank him anyway."

"All right."

Eliana walked to the back room. There was only one person there, a man, a little older than she. He was balding and broad-shouldered, and wearing a tweed jacket, Calvin Klein jeans and snakeskin boots. He stood looking at the portrait with his hands in his pockets. His back was to the door she entered from.

"Hello, I'm Ellen."

The man turned and smiled broadly. He offered his hand. "You're the artist. I'm Stan. It's a pleasure."

"It's my pleasure."

"What a gift you have. You really have some beautiful pictures here. My partner and I bought a couple of them already. We would like to purchase this one as well, but the woman up front said it's not for sale."

"Thank you, but no, it's not."

"It's a shame. If it's about money, we're willing to talk."

"No. I'm sorry." She looked at him more closely. There was something familiar about him. "Have we met before?"

"No. This is my first time in Utah. Besides, a pretty lady like you I definitely would remember." He looked back at the painting. "Do you mind me asking what's so special about this painting?"

"It's just personal."

He nodded again, then looked back at her. "Isn't all art personal?"

"*Vero*, I mean true. It's a portrait of a friend of mine." She paused. "It's all I have left of him."

"I'm sorry to hear that. He passed on?"

"No. He's just gone."

He took a step toward the painting. He gazed at it silently then spoke without turning back. "I think the real reason you won't sell this painting is because it's not really yours."

"I beg your pardon?"

He turned back to her, pointing at the picture. "It belongs to him. You gave it to him."

For a moment she was dumbstruck. "How did you know that?"

His smile widened and he turned and faced her head-on. "Because, Eliana, he told me. He's my brother."

"Your brother . . ."

"Ross is my brother."

"Where is he?"

"Well, he said he couldn't come to you on account of a promise you made him make. The truth is I think he was just plain chicken — so he sent me to get you. But I guess he changed his mind." He looked up over her shoulder.

Eliana spun around. Ross stood behind her in the doorway. He looked at her, his face a mixture of anticipation and joy. *"Ciao, bella."*

"Ross!" She ran to him and threw her arms around him. They kissed. After a few minutes she pulled back to look at his face as tears streamed down her cheeks. "But you said there was nothing in America for you."

"That was true when I said it," he said, smiling. He gently pushed her hair back from her face. "I'm sorry it took me so long to find you. As soon as I found out you had left Italy, I came."

He looked over at his brother, who was getting teary-eyed at the reunion. "Let me introduce you. Eliana, this is my — sentimental — big brother Stan."

Eliana looked at him.

"Forgive me for having a little fun with you, but you're all Ross has talked about for the last three months. I thought I deserved a little payback."

"Thank you for looking out for Ross."

"Actually it's the other way around. But I'm glad you're back together."

She turned back to Ross, her voice softened. "But the promise . . ."

Ross nodded. "The promise." He looked into Eliana's eyes and said, "Five years ago a woman asked me to leave her and I did. I've regretted it every day since then. I wasn't going to make that mistake again. Besides you can't very well promise not to love somebody."

"But you said love didn't give second chances."

He thought about it and smiled. "Yeah, but what do I know about love? You said to have faith just one more time. You were right."

"Just hold me." Ross pulled her back into himself and she was happier than she believed possible. "Promise me you'll never leave me again."

Ross pulled her still tighter, pressing his wet cheek against hers, then whispered in her ear, "All right. But it's my last promise."

Eliana sat back in her chair as if punctuating the story's completion.

"Just another girl's story," she said.

"And living happily ever after?" I asked.

Her smile answered me. "He really is sweet. I don't know if you ever write from real experiences, but if you want it, it's yours."

I thought about her offer. "Why would you want to share your story with the whole world?"

She considered my question for a moment then replied softly, "There were days when I could have used such a story. Maybe there's another woman out there, another Eliana, trapped and wondering if life has forgotten her. Afraid to love. Afraid to hope. Afraid *of* hope. If I knew where she was, I would put my arms around her and hold her and tell her that it's okay to cry. It's okay to scream. It's even okay to pound the walls. But it's never okay to lose hope." She looked up at me. "But I don't know where she is. Maybe your book will find her."

"Forse," I said. *Perhaps.*

I looked out at the children playing in the pool. "Is Alessio here?"

"No, he's with Anna. We bring him at least once a year to see his father and all his relatives."

"Do you see much of Maurizio?"

"Actually we saw him yesterday. And we talk on the phone from time to time. I keep him updated on Alessio. He's still usually on the road, though he does try to get back if he knows we're coming. He's changed. It's funny how things go. He has more interest in Alessio now than he did before. And he's very kind to me. Anyway, he

371

has a new girlfriend. He'll probably marry her in a couple of years."

"Thank you for sharing your story."

"You're welcome."

I sat back in my chair and thought. She had given me much to think about and my mind wrapped around her story like a sculptor's hands around clay. It was about a half hour later when a man entered the pool area. He was about my height, slim, yet muscularly built, with dark, short hair. He was barefoot, wore an open shirt and swim trunks. From Eliana's expression I immediately knew who it was. She waved to him. *"Amore."*

Ross smiled as he walked toward us. *"Ciao, bella,"* he said. When he was near her, he leaned over and kissed her.

"Amore, this is Richard."

He looked at me. His eyes were piercing, yet kind. *"Piacere."*

He extended his hand to shake. As I took it, I noticed the scar on his wrist. I suppose I was looking for it.

"It's a pleasure," I said.

"Americano?"

"Sì."

"Not getting too friendly with my girl?"

"No, just keeping my eye on her for you."

"You and the rest of the men in here." He sat down on the side of Eliana's chair and put his arms around her waist, brushed her hair to one side and nuzzled her, kissing her neck. She laughed but didn't stop him. "Richard's a writer. I've been telling him our story."

He looked up at me. "The best part is that it's just beginning." He leaned over and kissed her once more, this time on the lips. "Are you about ready for lunch?"

"Yes, darling. I just need to gather my things."

"Allow me," Ross said.

"He's such a pushover," she said to me. "*Un momento,* honey." She found a pen and quickly scribbled something on a cocktail napkin, then handed it to me. "That's our telephone number. If you need help getting around Florence, just call. I know all the English-speaking doctors and dentists in the city. I even know where you can buy bagels. We'll be in Toscana until late August."

"*Grazee.*"

She grinned at my pronunciation. "And I know some good Italian language schools."

I smiled. "Thank you."

"Maybe we could all go out for dinner sometime."

"I'd like that," I said. "I'd like my wife to meet you."

"Likewise." She stood, holding hands with Ross. "Give us a call. *Ciao.*"

"*Ciao,* Eliana."

Ross saluted me. "*Arrivederci,* Richard."

"Take care," I said.

Then they left, his arm around her waist, she leaning into him, the two of them flirting like honeymooners. It was obvious that he adored her, and nothing could have made me happier. *Just another girl's story.* I smiled. Then I laughed. Then I gathered my things and went home to write.

ABOUT THE AUTHOR

Richard Paul Evans is the number one *New York Times* best-selling author of *The Christmas Box*. His best-selling novels have been translated into more than seventeen languages, and some have been adapted into award-winning television movies. He divides his time between Florence, Italy, and Utah. *The Last Promise* is his seventh novel.

Visit Richard Paul Evans's Web site for a tour of *The Last Promise* online.

See pictures of Villa Rendola, Piazzale Michelangelo, the Arno, the villa's garden and more. There are also Italian recipes from the book, including Eliana's grape pie and spaghetti carbonara.

You can also join Richard Paul Evans's e-mail list for free reading group discussion guides, book updates, inspirational thoughts and special offers.

Visit the author's Web site now at:
www.richardpaulevans.com

Please send correspondence to
Richard Paul Evans at:
PO Box 1416
Salt Lake City, UT 84110